Gravity

Gravity

a novel

---

by

L.D. Cedergreen

This is a work of fiction. All of the characters, organizations, and events portrayed in this novel are either products of the author's imagination or are used fictitiously.

Gravity

Copyright © 2014 by L. D. Cedergreen

Cover design by Robin Ludwig Design Inc. at
www.gobookcoverdesign.com

ISBN: 978-0-9893783-3-8

little cabin by the creek,

you still captivate my soul,

hold prisoner the memories untold,

reminding me of those I'll never let go. . . .

For Boyd and Elaine

Prologue

Cold, wet dirt enveloped his hands as they dug deeper into the lakeside Idaho earth, searching for the old thermos that had been buried in this exact spot years ago. *It has to be here,* he thought to himself. He knew that this idea was crazy, and he had no way of knowing if she would ever come back to this place. If she would even remember the sacred treasure that they had left behind—their "time capsule" they had called it. Even if she never thought to look for it, never found what he was leaving behind for her, he knew that in some small way he was gaining a sense of closure. A chance to tell her how he felt, a chance to say good-bye.

He felt something hard and smooth beneath his fingers, and began to dig with more urgency. Moments later he pulled a rusted steel coffee thermos from the ground and twisted the lid until it broke free. His heart beat loudly in his chest, as his mind flooded with memories.

Memories of her. His best friend, his first love, his first heartbreak. After all these years, she still haunted his soul. The one connection in his life that he compared all others to, the one connection that nothing and no one had seemed to match, leaving him alone in the end.

The contents inside the thermos looked as if they had been just placed there moments ago, rather than the twentysome years that it had been. It really was a time capsule. Pain and regret seized his heart as he held their treasure in his hands tightly, as if he were holding on to her in some way. He felt a single tear trickle down his cheek and wiped it away quickly. He refused to let himself feel regret or sadness. He had made peace with his destiny, working through his anger, accepting the hand that he had been dealt.

He returned the treasure to the thermos, adding a letter that he had written, protected inside a small plastic bag. He secured the lid and buried the thermos once again, right where they had left it years ago. Deep inside the dirt, underneath the tallest evergreen that stood behind her cabin, near the creek.

He whispered *good-bye* into the cool breeze as he held on to an image of her from years ago, an image of the beautiful brown-eyed girl who still owned his heart.

O_{ne}

I should have noticed the charcoal-gray Marc Jacobs handbag —from last season, no less—that lay conspicuously on the entryway tile as I crossed the threshold of my eighth-floor condo where Ryan and I had lived in Seattle for the past six years, or Ryan's suit jacket which he had worn to work that morning hanging carelessly from a hook of the mahogany coat rack, a family heirloom on his side. Instead, I was consumed with thoughts of how, undoubtedly, this was turning out to be the worst day ever.

Making my way directly to the kitchen, I frantically rummaged through the loose papers that were fanned out on the breakfast table, searching for the Hawkins file that I had mistakenly left behind this morning in my mad dash out the door. It would be this day of all days that the board of Hawkins Direct, the telecommunications company that I was representing, would call for an emergency meeting in the middle of the day. The one day that I had the absentmindedness to leave behind a key file in my otherwise flawless and perfectly scheduled world.

Tucking the file under my arm, I headed for the front door. Then I heard it. Muffled voices filtering in from the hallway that led to the master bedroom. My first thought was that someone was in my home—an intruder—which fueled my senses with adrenaline and an inkling of fear. But as I made my way down the hall, one foot in front of the other, scolding myself for not grabbing the magnum flashlight—my weapon of choice—from the drawer in the kitchen, I heard Ryan's deep voice.

I instantly felt a sense of relief, certain that I was not being robbed—or worse, that I was about to be attacked—but when I heard a faint giggle, an unmistakable feminine tone, my fear was quickly replaced with a sense of dread. That sick feeling that instantly begins to fester in the pit of my stomach, anticipating what I would find on the other side of the partially closed door that led to my bedroom. The room where I had shared a bed with my husband of ten plus years.

I slowly pushed open the door, my eyes taking in the bare skin of Ryan's back and the toned, tanned flesh of the small figure that lay beneath him, mostly obscured by his six-foot-four frame. I scanned every detail—from the way his short brown hair was being mussed by *her* dainty fingers to the rumpled duvet spread out underneath them as if they had been in such a hurry they hadn't bothered to draw back the bedding. The bulge of his triceps, flexed from the restraint he used to hold himself above *her* as he moved with familiar sounds of intimacy and pleasure. Sounds that I had believed were reserved only for me.

4

I had never imagined another woman eliciting such a response from him. I felt as if someone had ripped open my heart and snared every private moment that I had shared with my husband, dangling it in front of me like a carrot, mocking me. *Look what I have.* I stood motionless, trying to process the harrowing scene before me. My eyes moved from Ryan's naked body to the incredulous open-mouthed expression that he wore when he finally turned to find me standing in our bedroom doorway. It was as if—until that very moment—he had forgotten me. His wife.

Utterly shocked and instantly riddled with despair—stabbed with a pain so consuming that I couldn't breathe—I turned away and fled the scene as I heard Ryan gasp my name. I fought against the sickening sensation building in my gut, crawling up my throat as I clutched the Hawkins file against my chest and practically ran down the hallway. My need to escape outweighed all else in that moment as I buried the anguish of betrayal in order to suppress the onslaught of tears that threatened my otherwise calm demeanor.

I barreled out the front door, rode the elevator to the lobby, and sprinted straight across Blanche Avenue, dodging four lanes of traffic, all the while holding the tattered pieces of myself intact, denying myself the reaction that I deserved. I claimed a spot at a small window table in the coffee shop across the street and took a moment to catch my breath, to organize my frazzled thoughts, to plan my next move.

A short time later, the nameless woman, who I vaguely recognized from Ryan's office, appeared outside my building. I wanted to confront her, to hurt her in some way, but I couldn't move. Instead I just sat and watched her, scrutinizing the way she walked down the sidewalk, the way she ran her hand through her long, dark just-fucked hair, and the way she stared dead ahead as if she hadn't just been caught with her panties down. Unable to turn away, I took in every detail that I could observe about her from the window of the coffee shop—like the fact that she looked nothing like me.

She was an obvious D-cup from the way her chest bounced and spilled out of her white blouse with each brisk step. She was at least three inches shorter than me, which she made up for in her stiletto heels. Her coloring was darker from her hair to her olive-toned skin. My mind was a cluster of suspicion. Was she more Ryan's type even though he had always claimed to favor blondes? Did he prefer large breasts despite the years that he had led me to believe he was a strictly a "leg guy"? I was questioning everything about him —my own husband—as if I had never really known him at all.

As the woman turned the corner onto Fifth Avenue, just two blocks from the offices of Simms, Reed, and Walsh —my husband's law firm—I caught sight of Ryan as he exited our building. He stood on the sidewalk, looking completely disheveled as he glanced in one direction and then the other with his phone to his ear. I heard my phone buzz from inside my purse that lay at my feet. I was sure that it was Ryan calling me as I watched him speak into his phone, his free hand gripping his forehead between his thumb and forefinger. My heart beat loudly in my chest as I blinked away a few tears that escaped despite my strong effort of will.

I wanted to claw out his eyes, scream and pound my fists into his chest. I wanted to ask him how he could do this to me, to us? I wanted to know if he was in love with her. How many times had he had sex with her? How long had this been going on? How could he fuck her in our home, in our bed? My mind was buzzing with questions. But I knew that I wasn't ready for the answers. My heart couldn't survive another ounce of pain; it was all too much.

So I watched from my vantage point, hidden behind the tinted glass of the coffee shop window as he followed the same path of his mistress—back to the office—before I jetted across the street to our condo and hurriedly packed a suitcase.

I drove to my own office, downtown, where I spent the afternoon in the emergency meeting that had started this whole mess of a day. I couldn't concentrate despite my best intentions, and—when I was called out on this fact, seemingly obvious to Mr. Chambers, the head of the board—I claimed illness, apologizing profusely. But as I sat in my office's sleek conference room, listening to the differing opinions concerning the upcoming merger of Hawkins Direct and one of its smaller competitors, I had the overwhelming sense that I wouldn't be able to keep up this charade for much longer. I felt on the verge of a breakdown.

I paused and called in a well-qualified colleague of mine, introducing him and announcing that, in light of my illness, Clark was going to be taking over the case. I knew that this was a huge opportunity for him and that he would not turn it down. I also knew that he was perfectly capable of handling this merger.

I spent the remainder of the afternoon briefing Clark and making phone calls. All the while, I remained calm, stoic. I discussed the leave of absence that I had impulsively decided upon—claiming long-term illness—with my senior partner and left the building. It wasn't until two hours later when I reached my mother's house that the walls came crumbling down, allowing the despair to wash over me. It hurt to move, hurt to breathe, hurt to feel. My whole world had just crashed into oblivion, and I wasn't sure what came next or where this would all lead—a notion that was completely foreign to me. I was a planner, a scheduler of life's events, big or small. The only thing that I was sure of at this point was that this was, undeniably, the worst day ever.

Two

It had been exactly four days, seventeen hours and forty-three minutes since that monumental moment that had put a screeching halt on my life. The kind of moment that changed someone's life significantly. The kind of moment that divided my life into sections of time: before and after. I'd had a few of these moments already, dividing my life into quadrants like a damn pie chart. Some were obvious, like the day I graduated from law school or the day I passed the bar exam, both defining moments that began my chosen profession as a lawyer. The day that I became Mrs. Ryan Walsh—another noteworthy moment—when I promised to love Ryan in sickness and health, for richer or poorer, till death do us part.

And now I was in unchartered waters, weathering the storm of a new chapter of my life—a new segment of time—one that I had already tried to categorize, but, unaware how that moment would define the rest of my life, I was reluctant to put a label on it. *Yet.*

After a few debilitating days of ugly crying, curled up in the fetal position in my childhood bed, my mother—in a desperate attempt to offer a solution—had proposed an idea that I couldn't resist. I had finally gotten myself out of bed, loaded my car with everything I would need for the next three months, and hugged my mother good-bye.

And now as I drove north in the early morning light, I couldn't help but feel that my mother had tossed me a lifeline. She had given me something to focus on—a plan, a purpose. I gripped this lifeline with both hands and hoped like hell that my heart could hold on until I reached safety. *Or at least until I reach the cabin*, I thought. I turned up the volume on the radio allowing Coldplay to blare through the speakers at an almost unbearable decibel—my weak attempt at drowning out the tiny voice in my head reminding me that running away wasn't going to change anything. Ryan had cheated, and I had left him.

We had become *that* couple, the unfaithful husband and the pathetic wife—hurt, scorned, and hopelessly bitter. The couple that kept Ryan's law firm profitable. The couple that Ryan and I had spent many nights discussing while we cuddled under our gray flannel duvet—agreeing that we would always be honest with one another, that we would never let our relationship get to the point where one of us would cheat out of sheer misery or unhappiness. That we could prevent such a tragic cliché with our unconditional love and candidness. It seemed almost funny that two well-educated thirtysomething adults could be so naive, but, of course, I wasn't laughing.

$\mathcal{T}hree$

Ryan and I met in the midst of my junior year of college. We were both pre-law. It wasn't love at first sight by any means; in fact I think that I may have hated him at the start. Our official introduction was the night of the annual Sigma Nu Bash, Ryan's very own fraternity. His friend, James, had been aggressively hitting on my roommate and best friend, Cassie, who was completely wasted at the time. I had been trying, to no avail, to convince her to leave with me. It was my job to escort her home safely, having lost the coin toss for designated driver. Ryan had stepped in when he realized what was going on, steering James effortlessly away from Cassie and in the direction of another coed who was less intoxicated.

He helped me walk Cassie to my car, her nearly limp

body draped over the both of us. I knew exactly who he was; everyone on campus did. Ryan was charming and sexy and way too dangerous for me. He was well over six feet tall with a ridiculously perfect body. He played college baseball, and I was sure that sheer fact alone—coupled with the warmth of his brown eyes and sexy smile—made panties drop everywhere he went. Vowing to be the exception to his rule, I turned up my sarcasm and gave him the cold shoulder that I had perfected throughout my first two years of college. I thanked him for his help, truly appreciating what he had done for Cassie, but I did not accept his invitation for coffee the following day or the next.

I seemed to run into him everywhere after that and thus began our banter that bordered between harmless flirting and cold-hearted criticism as egos were deflated and feelings were hurt. I found him to be arrogant and rude, the kind of boy who could charm you and then wound you in the same breath. His perfect smile threatened my heart in a million different ways, and I refused to be one of his victims. He accused me of being stubborn and rigid, too uptight for my age. We went round for round, but still he kept coming back for more. Cassie tried to convince me that it was sexual tension. She joked that we should either "get it on or get over it"—her words exactly. I was hoping for the latter.

And then on the first day of a new semester, I found him sitting next to me in my Constitutional Criminal Procedure class, a third-year pre-req for those applying to law school, with a shit-eating grin on his face. But it was during this semester that I discovered another side to him. I saw the real guy behind the panty-dropping smile. A compassionate, intelligent, and hard-working student who cared more about his degree than the speed of his curve ball or his next female conquest. I had been wrong about him, and this new realization was both refreshing and intriguing, to say the least.

We both realized early on that we had plenty in common beginning with our paralleled majors. We became friends, our time spent together studying in the campus library or debating criminal justice issues over coffee. And then there was that moment, the moment when I realized that he was more than just my friend. He seemed to feel the shift at the same time, although he swore that he felt something for me from the first moment we met.

I remembered the rain, pouring down as if buckets of water were falling from the sky, the day that Ryan drove me to my apartment after a long study session at the library. I couldn't seem to open the passenger door of his ten-year-old sedan; the handle was stuck. Ryan leaned across the center console, reaching over to help me. His body brushed against mine, causing my heart to pound in my chest. Before he was able to open the door for me, I looked into his eyes, and it was as if I could see my whole world in their depths. His lips crashed against mine seconds later, and I was lost to him. That was it for me.

We were inseparable from that point on. Before long, everyone on campus knew that we were together, surprised that the unattainable Ryan Walsh was in a relationship. There was widespread speculation about whether or not we would last, but it wasn't long before we proved the masses wrong. By the time we both had finished law school, we were engaged.

Our wedding was just as I had always pictured it. A small church ceremony with an elegant outdoor reception. Everything was perfect, with the exception of Ryan's father walking me down the aisle rather than my own. I loved Ryan's parents as much as my own family. They were warm and kind, and, being that Ryan was an only child, they welcomed me with open arms, referring to me as the daughter that they had never had.

We honeymooned in Kauai, spending ten romantic

but lazy days lounging by our own private pool and snorkeling in the lagoon just steps away from the beach house that we had rented. I remembered looking into Ryan's warm brown eyes—not much different than my own—and feeling as if all my dreams and hopes and life adventures were staring back at me. He had owned my heart, had known me inside and out, loved every part of me—despite my faults and insecurities. He had ignited my whole being; my attraction to him physically was beyond anything that I could have imagined, but it was no match for the magnetic pull that drew me to his soul. We were so happy. So crazy in love.

We were both overachievers who logged countless hours at our respectful firms. In the beginning, I had been working hard toward corporate litigation, and Ryan had been a petty first-year associate trying to forge his way as a divorce attorney. And now, after years of hard work, Ryan had made partner, and I was well-known in the corporate world as the lawyer that businessmen would want by their side.

We had carved out a routine in our lives that we were both comfortable with, given our mutual obsession with our careers. Saturdays were usually spent working from home, together, but Sundays were reserved for just the two of us. We went out for brunch, spent the day in bed making up for lost time, or simply strolled around downtown, shopping for items to decorate our new condo. Looking back, I realized that we probably spent too many years consumed with our careers.

By the time we decided to start a family—after nearly eight years of marriage—only 50 percent of my eggs were viable, and we started down the road that inevitably ruined our marriage. I took my temperature daily, suffered through hormone shots, IVF treatments—I spent more time at the doctor's office than anywhere else, and my caseload began to dwindle. In the end, nothing worked, and our relationship became strained. I couldn't even remember the last time we had had sex just because we felt like it.

There was always a reason, a time, a procedure, but never an urge. I couldn't remember at what point we started to fall apart, when the mountainous tension began to build, and I started to pull away, fearing what would come next, or when he realized that I wasn't good enough anymore or that I couldn't give him what he wanted—a family. Of course I wanted to be a mother more than I have ever wanted anything in my life, and this maternal need had cost me my marriage. It wasn't that long ago that Ryan had asked me when having a baby had become more important to me than him. I hadn't even offered a response to his question; I didn't have an answer.

Four

With every curve of the road, my heart beat louder in my chest, reminding me of the countless times I had made this same trip as a child. The days when I sat in the back of my parents' red Pinto, smashed in between our luggage and my younger brother, Jacob, as my excitement grew with each turn, bringing us closer to the cabin where we would spend our summer. I felt that same excitement now; images from those warm and golden—almost magical—months flashing through my mind. I could faintly hear my mother's voice as she sang "The Bear Song" as a means to distract us from asking that inevitable yet annoyingly comical question that children seem to repeat every two minutes anytime they are in a moving vehicle: *Are we there yet?*

She would follow it up with a long and repetitive version of "Found a Peanut" or "99 Bottles of Beer on the Wall"—which she would change to "bottles of Coke," proclaiming to my father that a song about beer was not appropriate for children our age. My father usually rolled his eyes playfully at her and sang along with us, overemphasizing the word "Coke" just to annoy my mother. It was an annual journey that I remembered fondly; everything about it so typical, it was predictable that I felt a sudden pang of wistfulness. For *that* life, *that* girl.

I spent every summer of my childhood at Priest Lake —where my grandparents owned a small cabin tucked away behind a cluster of evergreens. The lake was just a few steps away, down the dirt lane that several other cabins were built along. Adults bonded over huckleberry daiquiris and barbecues while the children—the best of friends—played in the lake by day and told stories around campfires at night. We became strangers once again when autumn fell upon us.

My best memories could be found along this large crystal-blue lake in the northern Panhandle of Idaho. Maybe some of the only happy memories spent with my father. I hadn't been to the cabin since my teenage years, when I had landed a job as a lifeguard at the local swimming pool, officially ending our family's tradition of spending our summer months at the lake. Mom and Jacob had spent the occasional weekend at the cabin over the years, but I had stayed with friends in order to fulfill my weekend shifts at the pool until I left for college, when I hadn't bothered to come home for summer break at all, let alone travel to the lake. The cabin had been nearly abandoned for several years now. Mom had returned strictly for upkeep purposes, but, still, she could not seem to let it go. Until now.

I heard my cell phone ringing through the car stereo speakers, and I glanced down to see Ryan's name flash across the screen. He had left me an endless string of voice mails and text messages, all left unreturned. He had even called my mother several times. I had overheard her tell him firmly, "Of course she's here, and she's safe, but that's all you're getting out of me, Ryan Walsh."

True to form with any mother, my mother's use of someone's full name meant serious business, and I was sure her choice of words had not been lost on Ryan. I pictured him cowering with his tail between his legs on the other end of the phone. *Good, let him cower*, I thought. The truth was that I was afraid to speak to him. I feared where our conversation might lead. I was also angry, so, by taking control to be sure he would fail in his desperate attempts to reach me, that gave me a fractional sense of satisfaction. But that didn't stop me from obsessing over every phone call or text message, analyzing every word.

Sighing out loud, I pressed Ignore. I still couldn't speak to him. I was plagued with too many emotions. I needed time to sort out everything. That was what this trip was about, time to myself to reevaluate my life, to determine where everything had gone wrong, and to see how I got to this place where happiness was just a distant memory. I was miserable, and I feared that I had felt this way long before recent events had turned my life upside down. In fact it was difficult to recall my last moment of true utter bliss, where my face was turned into an effortless smile and my heart felt light but full.

My mind was drawing a big fat blank—it had been that long. Part of me knew that this wasn't all Ryan's fault. There were two people in this marriage, and I wondered at what point I had stopped caring about what he felt and had become caught up in my own misery, keeping him at arm's length. I knew that I was just as much to blame as he was for my unhappiness, but I was so angry with him for this choice that he had made, for the secrecy. I couldn't think beyond what I had witnessed firsthand. The betrayal cut so deep that

I wasn't sure if we could ever go back to what we had been. Or if that was even an option.

I heard a loud chime, my phone's indication of a new text message. I held up the phone in front of my face attempting to see who the text was from, although I had a pretty good idea. My heart clenched as I viewed Ryan's name on my screen. A ripple of pain shot through my chest as I tried to wash away the image of him with another woman. I feared it was stained on my heart forever, left as a reminder as to why I subconsciously pushed everything inward, relying only on myself. The disappointment was so much more manageable when I didn't expect anything from others, when I didn't depend on anyone. It was a lonely existence that I knew all too well, but lonely was better than scraping pieces of my broken heart off the pavement.

I glanced back and forth from the road to the phone, trying to read his words, though I knew there was nothing he could possibly say to change what he had done.

You can't ignore me forever, Gemma. I am so sorry. We need to talk. Please come home or call me. I love you, and I'm worried about you. I need . . . The phone slipped from my hand, landing on the floorboard near my feet. I tried to bend down to grab it without taking my gaze off the road, but the phone was out of my reach. I unlatched my seat belt, bending down farther, blindly feeling the floor mat with my hand, as my eyes followed the dotted yellow line of the road before me. I finally had my phone in my grasp and brought it to eye level, glancing down momentarily to read the remainder of Ryan's text.

I looked back at the road, but it was too late. I pumped my foot against the brake pedal in a panic, felt my foot slip from the grip, and heard myself scream in the small confines of the car's interior. The car slammed against something, forcing its forward velocity to falter. My head connected with the windshield, hard, as pain ricocheted through my skull. And, for just a moment, my world swirled around me—a slow blur of color—until there was nothing but darkness.

F_{ive}

I awoke later, my forehead resting on the steering wheel.
Completely disoriented for several seconds, I soon recalled
the deer darting out in front of the car. My head was
throbbing. I reached up to touch my brow, the source of
wetness trickling into my eye. As I pulled my hand away, I
discovered thick red blood. Grabbing the folded napkins—
which had come with my vanilla latte that morning—from
the passenger's seat, I pressed them against my forehead to
stop the bleeding. I stumbled out of the driver's door and
stood on the shoulder of the highway, staring at the large

buck now lying motionless in a pool of blood in the middle of the road.

After a quick inspection of the car, I knew that it was drivable but looked pretty beat-up in the morning sun. The deer had left its mark on the front bumper and also the hood, plus the windshield was cracked. I reached inside the car for my phone that was on the floor under my seat. I felt the need to call someone about the deer but wasn't sure who that someone might be. I was, roughly, fifteen miles from the cabin. As I stared at the screen of my phone, debating what I should do next, I noticed Ryan's text—the reason for this whole mess. *You can't ignore me forever, Gemma. I am so sorry. We need to talk. Please come home or call me. I love you and I'm worried about you. I need to see you. Please just hear me out, let me explain.* Tears stung my eyes, but I wiped them away quickly.

Settling back into the driver's seat, I fastened my seat belt securely and slowly pulled the car back onto the desolate highway, as I silently scolded myself for my stupidity. I was suddenly aware of my pounding heart and my trembling hands as I gripped the steering wheel tightly. Clearly I was more shaken from the accident than I had thought.

I took in my surroundings as I neared the Kalispell Bay turnoff, slowing my speed as I veered to the right, exiting the main highway. Dense forest bordered the road on both sides. I could just barely make out the trailhead that led to the marina by a slight break in the trees. A trail that I had explored countless times as a child. I slowed my fancy sedan and made a right turn onto the narrow dirt road, cursing each pothole which the car sunk into with a loud *thunk*. I was here.

I parked the car on the front lawn, now overgrown with weeds, and killed the engine. As I stepped out of the car, I inhaled deeply, taking in the overwhelming scent of pine that Seattle could not match. There was a chill in the air even with the sun shining brightly above me, a telltale sign that it was only May and not quite summer yet. The single-level cabin that I remembered so well seemed smaller somehow and desperately in need of a fresh coat of paint. The winters were harsh here, and the wood siding, once the color of red cedar, now looked faded, more like the silvery driftwood that littered the beach. The familiar navy blue curtains were drawn, obscuring the view of the inside through the large single-pane windows.

I found the cabin key on my key ring where I had placed it just days before and made my way up the three short steps to the porch, which extended the entire length of the cabin's face. I ran my hand along the wooden railing that framed the porch, my fingers scraping the chipped white paint. The wooden porch swing that my grandfather had built with his own two hands still hung from thick chains on the far side of the porch, where I could sit and view the lake.

The key turned in the lock, and the door swung open slowly. The cabin smelled musty from years of sitting empty. I could smell mothballs and pine, the signature scent of this old cabin, bringing fresh memories of my grandmother to mind. I took in the small open kitchen, the creamy white cabinets, the red Formica countertops. Continuing on, my gaze trailed across the large round dining table that sat in the middle of the main room, acting as a barrier between the kitchen and the living area.

I scanned the beautiful knotty pine walls surrounding the entire room until my survey landed on the large river-rock fireplace. As the main focus of the room, it gave the cabin a rustic feel. I took a deep breath, suddenly overwhelmed by the rush of emotions that assaulted me while I remembered the countless moments of my life spent within these walls. So many memories of a simpler time, a simpler life. I longed for those days now, a time before my life became so complicated.

I made my way into the one and only bathroom, just off the main room, to inspect the cut on my forehead. Rummaging through the cabinets, I found a large Band-Aid and secured it over the slightly oozing flesh.

I studied my reflection in the dust-covered mirror. I could almost see the girl who I used to be in the same warm caramel-colored eyes that stared back at me. Long blond hair fell around my heart-shaped face in loose waves; full lips framed my perfect white teeth—thanks to the braces that I wore for two years starting in junior high. I once saw myself how others described me. Pretty, beautiful, stunning even. Although now all I could see was the hollowness of my cheeks, the lines that revealed my thirty-six years, the emptiness in my eyes—vacant yet filled with longing. I turned away, unable to face myself any longer.

I walked throughout the cabin and pulled the dusty white sheets from each piece of furniture—two rounded upholstered chairs; the cream-colored sofa donning navy-and-red-striped throw pillows, completing the nautical theme that my mother had redecorated with years ago; the worn leather bench that rested in front of the fireplace—everything remained just as I had remembered. Rolling the sheets into a contained pile, I set them in the corner and ran my hand along the smooth surface of the river rocks that comprised the fireplace. It was as if time stood still here, while our lives flew by at record speed all around it. This place needed more work than I realized; everything was so outdated. If it were up to me, I wouldn't change a thing, but that would defeat my purpose for being here.

Now that both of my grandparents were gone, my mother was finally ready to let go of the cabin. But I sensed it was really because my estranged father had passed recently. She knew that no one came up here anymore. At my mother's suggestion, I had agreed to spend the summer here to update the cabin and prepare it for the competitive lake real estate market. I couldn't deny the real reason I had decided to come. The need to get away, to take a moment to catch my breath. My conscience was reminding me that I was running away from my life, but I buried my inner voice deep inside and continued from room to room, opening windows and removing sheets from the bedroom furniture, my mother's words echoing in my mind. *It'll be good for you. A little peace and quiet never hurt anyone*, and *I need someone to do this for me. It would be too hard to do myself, too hard to change anything.* In reality it hadn't taken much to convince me.

I unloaded the trunk of the car, carrying in two large suitcases and a box of cleaning supplies that I had brought from home. I opted to stay in my parents' room; yet it felt strange to consider using their bedroom. It had been the one room in the cabin that was off-limits when I was a child. But it was the largest of the three bedrooms, offering more comfort with a queen-size bed. I stripped the bedding from the old bed, adorned with a beautiful hand-carved beechwood headboard, and remade it with the clean sheets and a heavy down comforter that I had brought with me.

Working up a slight sweat, I wrapped my long hair into a tight bun—a style that I had perfected with years of having to appear professional in court—and began to clean the kitchen, wiping away the dust and cleaning the inside of the cabinets. I welcomed the distraction, something to keep my hands busy and my mind clear as the minutes ticked by unnoticed.

***

Finally satisfied, knowing the kitchen was squeaky clean, I rewarded myself with a stroll down to the lake. I walked out onto the long dock that jetted out farther than any other in the bay and sat on the end, letting my bare feet dangle into the glacier-filled lake. The cold took my breath away for a moment until my feet slowly adjusted to the frigid temperature. I had forgotten just how cold the water could be, although, as a child, it had never prevented me from jumping right in. I closed my eyes and focused on the quiet that surrounded me, a low hum from a distant ski boat the only sound in the air. The bright sun warmed my cheeks and the familiar smell of evergreens filled my nostrils as I breathed in the clean, fresh air.

As I pictured myself at a young age, standing on a piling of this very dock preparing to jump into the cold dark water several feet below from where I was perched, I could almost hear children's laughter. Along with my father's playful voice encouraging me. *Come on, Gemma. Just jump. You can do it!*

My younger brother, Jacob, and my best friend, Drew, waiting for their turn. *Come on, Gem. Jump already*, Drew would call out, his patience wearing thin. I was so scared to jump off that piling but wanted desperately to be brave like the boys. I could remember the way I had closed my eyes tight, the way my heart had pounded in my chest, as I stepped away feeling nothing but air beneath my feet. The cold water would instantly assault me, causing my heart to beat harder and faster, while I held my breath and fought for the surface. It was exhilarating and terrifying all at the same time.

Memories of Drew drifted through my mind. We were best friends before we could even talk and had grown up spending our summers at the lake as if we were joined at the hip. His family's cabin was on the shore, just two docks to the north from where I sat. He came from money, the Monroe Enterprises' kind of money. His grandfather had started the company decades ago, bringing on Drew's father after he had graduated college. Mr. Monroe had plans for Andrew and his older brother, William, to follow in his footsteps.

Drew had dreams of being an artist the last time I had seen him, showing absolutely no interest in working with his father. Mr. Monroe hadn't been thrilled with this idea. Drew's mother had died of a brain tumor when he was six, and his father had never remarried that I knew of. My mother had been close with Drew's mom, Katherine, before she became sick. It was hard on everyone, and I think that my parents always held a special place in their hearts for Andrew and William.

Mr. Monroe had sent Drew to a boarding school in Connecticut during the school year, once he was the ripe old age of ten. Luckily their father had honored Katherine's wishes to return to the lake each summer, her favorite little slice of heaven dating back to her own childhood. The lake had become Drew's oasis, the only home he knew from that point on. My family became Drew's family from Memorial Day through Labor Day each year, and it had become harder and harder to say good-bye as the years passed.

I turned my palm up in my lap and traced the small tattoo on the inside of my right wrist with my thumb. The permanent reminder of the girl who I used to be and of the best friend that I used to have. It was the infinity symbol designed by Andrew himself to mark the promise that we had made to each other before either of us knew how easily promises could be broken. I remembered the day we first made that promise like it was yesterday. We had both just turned seven. Our birthdays were in early July, just two days apart. I had found Drew by the creek behind my cabin, quietly crying into his hands. I had sat down next to him and wrapped my arms around my bended knees, contemplating what I should say. I wasn't sure how much time had passed before he finally spoke to me.

"You probably think that I'm a big baby, huh?" he had asked.

"I don't think that at all," I had said matter-of-factly.

"Really?"

"Yeah."

"Can you keep a secret?"

"Of course, Drew. That's what best friends are for."

"Best friends?"

"Yep, best friends to infinity."

"What does infinity mean?" he had asked.

"It means forever and ever."

"Best friends to infinity," he had repeated, holding out his hand to me.

"Best friends to infinity," I had reassured him, shaking his hand to seal the deal.

When he let go of my hand, he had looked out at the creek before telling me how much he missed his mommy. I didn't know how to make him feel better. I couldn't bring his mommy back. I was only seven after all. I did the next best thing; I handed him my prized pail full of my favorite rocks and let him throw them, one by one, as far as he could into the water rushing by at our feet. When I saw the smile return to his face, I had known, even then, that we could get through anything together.

I turned to take in the largest cabin along the shore, a two-story monstrosity displaying a wall of windows facing the lake, large decks protruding from both levels holding expensive outdoor furniture for lounging and dining. Yep, that was Monroe Manor, still standing in all its glamour and glory. I wasn't sure who owned it now, but it looked like someone was occupying it already for the summer.

A low growl ripped through my stomach, reminding me that I hadn't eaten for several hours. I glanced at my phone where it rested on my lap and noted the time. It was nearly dinnertime. I had to make a trip to the market before it was too late. The only establishment open after six at the lake was the kind that sold liquor into the wee hours of the morning.

Before I thought better of it, I scrolled through Ryan's text messages once again, feeling that familiar sickness stirring in my gut. I had been silent long enough. I typed out a simple message. *I'm not ready to talk about this. I need time. Please stop calling and texting me. You broke my heart, Ryan. Please just give me this one thing for now.* I reread my words three times before I hit Send. The least he could do was respect my wishes.

Moments later my phone lit up, bearing Ryan's name. I shouldn't be surprised that he would refuse to grant me just one moment of peace after what he had done. The image of him and that woman, an image that I couldn't seem to break free from, filled my mind. Relentless tears spilled down my cheeks, tears of anger. I groaned so desperately loud that I hardly recognized the sound as my own. Without thinking, I hurled my ringing phone overhead and watched it sink below the smooth surface of the water with a plop, making a pathetic little splash several feet from the dock. *Let him try to call me now*, I thought. I felt a smidge better at that moment. It wasn't much, but I'd take whatever small victory I could manage.

Six

The next morning I woke early and scrambled to the kitchen to start a pot of coffee. "Shit," I cursed under my breath as my bare feet landed on the cold tile in the kitchen. I had forgotten how low the temperature dropped here at night. I pulled on a pair of warm socks and attempted to start a fire in the stone fireplace to take the chill out of the air.

At least the ancient coffeepot still worked. Our cabin was lacking in technology, but then again, it always had. My grandfather had wanted the cabin to be a family retreat, free from all the things that cluttered our daily lives at home. He had always said, "We have the necessities, running water and electricity, and these two things mixed with love is all we need." He wouldn't allow a television or a telephone in the cabin. We had used the Sherwoods' phone next door for emergencies, and the small amount of time that we spent indoors was occupied by listening to music on the small black RCA stereo—the one coveted electronic device that Gramps allowed—or playing board games at the kitchen table.

Now that I was phoneless—reminiscent of the old days—I had resorted to calling my mom the night before from the pay phone outside the General Store, letting her know that I had arrived safely and confessing to having thrown my phone in the lake. I had felt an unexpected sense of shame from my adolescentlike behavior, but, if my mother was questioning my actions, she hadn't mentioned it. She had simply said she loved me and to call her if I needed anything.

Coffee in hand, I bundled up and settled into the porch swing, watching the rising sun cast colors across the still lake. Growing up, this had been my favorite part of the day. Sitting on this porch watching the day bloom before my very eyes, my father swinging me back and forth as he sipped his coffee, while I mimicked him with a cup of hot chocolate. The stillness of the morning only disturbed by our quiet conversation, always the same.

"What are the possibilities for today, Gemma?" he would ask. And I would list off my plans. Sometimes it was a nature walk picking handfuls of colorful wildflowers for Grams or catching frogs in the creek that ran along the back of the cabin. Sometimes it was an endless day of swimming, floating in our inflatable raft, or huckleberry picking, but one thing was for sure. Whatever I was planning for the day, it always included Andrew. We were free to roam and explore at the lake, to take control of our day. It was some of the best days of my life. I wasn't afraid to get dirty or to try new things, important traits for a little girl whose best friend was a boy. I missed that freedom and sense of adventure. My life had become overscheduled and tediously predictable, every day a repeat of the one before, always the same. *Why is that?*

I spent the majority of the day cleaning the cabin. Dusting all the surfaces, oiling the knotty-pine walls in the great room, and scrubbing the bathroom—my least favorite chore of all time. I snacked on the fresh fruit and breads that I had picked up at the market the day before, and sipped bottled water. Recent events had pretty much depleted my appetite. My already thin figure was dwindling down to skin and bone, but I couldn't stomach a full meal no matter how hard I tried. I was surviving on caffeine, a good Merlot, and light snacks. It wasn't much, but it was better than nothing.

I had found some old cassettes in the drawer of the coffee table and popped them in for a little background noise. It was too quiet here, forcing me to hear my own thoughts. I found myself singing along to the Steve Miller Band and The Cars while I worked, bringing up memories from the final summers that I had spent at the cabin. Some of them good memories, some of them moments of my life that I would rather forget.

Seven

I had been cooped up in the cabin for what seemed liked
several days—it was easy to lose all sense of time when there
was hardly cause to get out of bed. I sat on the porch swing
with an old romance novel in my lap—one that I had found
in a dresser drawer among many other forgotten items—
staring at my battered car. I couldn't put it off any longer; I
had to take it in for repairs. There was only one place at the
lake for any kind of mechanical repair for automobiles or
boats, and that was Sal's Garage. Sal was the father of one of
my good friends from my youth, Logan, and both were

geniuses when it came to their trade. I wasn't sure if their family was still around, but I had to assume the shop was.

Unlike the rest of us, Logan was a local, born and raised at the lake. For us young teenage girls, he had been a legend. He had fit the typical bad-boy mold. The one who knew where the best beach parties were, always had a liquor connection, and never dated anyone in particular—just made it a habit of working his way through the young female population that vacationed at the lake for the summer. He was absurdly good-looking, and his emotionally unavailable status gave him a certain appeal that girls couldn't seem to resist, no matter how bad his reputation was. Drew and Logan could not have been more different, but they had bonded over jet skis and dirt bikes, becoming good friends during that awkward stage between boyhood and the teenage years. I had tagged along, completing our little trio.

I slowed the car off the highway, pulling up in front of Sal's Garage. I couldn't help but notice how out of place my silver Mercedes felt among the Jeeps, pickup trucks, and SUVs. No one drove a sedan at the lake. As I stepped out of the car, I spotted a few men inside, huddled around the open hood of a classic '55 Chevy—a just-polished, sleek black model with shiny chrome wheels. An image that screamed "boys club" as I knew that I would never grasp the obsession that men seemed to have with cars.

All three of the shop's doors were open, letting in the cool breeze. Suddenly aware of my presence, one of the men walked out to greet me in a pair of dirty, faded jeans and work boots, his sleeveless white T-shirt stained with grease. When I looked into his eyes, I immediately recognized the kind large hazel eyes staring back at me. It was Logan. He still had his boyish charm, deep dimples, and longer blond hair that poked out from underneath a faded green John Deere hat. I couldn't help the grin that was plastered across my face.

38

"Can I help you, miss?" he asked, obviously not recognizing me.

"Logan?"

Hearing his name clearly caught him off guard as he stopped to take me in from head to toe. I could see that he had not changed a bit when it came to the female anatomy.

Sudden recognition reached his eyes as he smiled, flashing me those dimples that I remembered so well. "Gemma? Is that you?"

"Hi, stranger. Long time no see!"

Grinning from ear to ear, he closed the gap between us, pulling me into a bear hug. "What in the hell are you doing here? God, it's so good to see you!" he mumbled as he planted friendly kisses on my cheek, his day-old stubble rough against my skin. He stepped back, gripping my arms with his hands. "Let me get a good look at you. Damn, Gemma, you look hot!"

I gave him a swat on the arm. "I see that you haven't changed a bit." It was as if we had never missed a beat, instantly falling back into our usual banter.

"Don't tell me that you're here hoping I can fix this fancy car of yours?" he asked, nodding his head toward my car.

"Yeah, actually I was. I had no idea that you'd still be here though."

"What can I say? I tried the college thing for a while but really had no interest in leaving the lake. I took over for the old man a few years ago. I hate to disappoint, but Mercedes aren't really my thing. What the hell happened to it anyway?"

"I hit a deer the other day on my way up. So what are my options?"

"Does it drive okay?" he asked, running his hand along the dented hood.

"Yeah."

"Then I suggest you wait until you get back to wherever it is you came from and take it into a Mercedes specialist."

"I plan on spending the summer here. Is there anything closer?"

"The whole summer? Well, in that case, I can special order the parts and do it myself. But it'll take several weeks for the shipment. Does that work for ya?"

"Absolutely. Thank you, Logan. I really appreciate it."

"Anything for you, Gemma." He winked at me with his familiar charm. "Just leave the car with me today so I can see what kind of parts we'll need. Are you staying at your family's cabin while you're here?"

"Yep."

"I can give you a lift back to the cabin, and I'll bring the car to you when I'm done with the initial assessment. Come on inside so you can fill out the paperwork." He pulled his hat from his head, ran his hands through his blond hair, squinting from the sun's glare. "And . . ." He placed his hat back on his head and rubbed the stubble on his chin, with a conflicting gleam in his eyes.

"And what?"

"I have a surprise for you," he said with a mischievous grin.

He had piqued my curiosity.

I followed him inside as he continued past the office, through the main garage until we were out back on the patio. Three guys were laughing at something that one of them had said, sipping beer from the bottle, relaxing in the afternoon sun on worn patio furniture. This wasn't the surprise that I was expecting, although I wasn't sure what to expect. Logan cleared his throat, and all three men turned to gaze in our direction. Immediately one of them stood, and I felt my knees buckle as I realized who it was. A surprise indeed.

"Gemma?" Andrew asked, as if he wasn't sure I was real.

I felt tears sting my eyes as my heart filled with a familiar warmth, like coming home. "Drew?" I asked, wondering if my own eyes were deceiving me. I couldn't deny my heart though.

He walked toward me slowly, his blue eyes never leaving mine. He reached out his hand and cupped my cheek. "I can't believe it's really you." His voice was deeper, manly, sophisticated. His face was flawless, perfect white teeth, his bright blue eyes mesmerizing, much like I remember. His light brown hair was a little long around the ears, in need of a haircut, but styled purposefully to look like he had just stepped out of bed. He was taller than I remembered and thin, but muscular at the same time.

Once my head caught up with my heart, I jumped up and wrapped my arms around his neck. "Oh, my God, Drew. This is crazy. I can't believe you're really here." I felt his arms engulf me as we stood swaying back and forth in each other's arms, suspended in time.

Eight

I spent a few minutes catching up with Andrew and Logan, sipping the beer that they offered me as we covered only surface topics. We spoke of nothing important, nothing that meant anything to us. The other two men were good friends of Logan's and seemed friendly enough. I left the car in Logan's capable hands, and, the moment I hinted that I needed to get back to the cabin, there was a familiar sense of rivalry between Andrew and Logan over who was going to drive me home. Boys. Men. It didn't matter how many years had passed by, some things never changed.

Andrew was the one who drove me back to the cabin, given the fact that we were neighbors. Logan couldn't deny the convenience and practicality of Drew's gesture. We drove in awkward silence, both of us attempting—unsuccessfully I might add—to continue the insignificant conversation that we had started back at Logan's garage. This only emphasized the silence that grew between us. There were a million and one questions swirling around in my head that I longed to ask him, but I held back, knowing that it would only invite him to ask the same of me. I wasn't sure how much I wanted to divulge about my own life. I wanted to know so many things about his though. What he was doing here, if he worked for his father, if he was married or had any children, if he had spent all his summers here since I had last seen him.

Drew pulled his black Jeep into his own driveway, merely yards from my cabin and asked me if I wanted to come inside. Part of me wanted to spend more time with him, but I wasn't ready for the onslaught of memories that his cabin would surely bring. Running into him had caught me off guard, and I felt as if I needed a few minutes alone to process it all.

"I better not. I have a lot to do. I'm trying to get the cabin ready to sell, and, believe me, it needs a lot of work."

"I'm sorry to hear that. I mean, sorry to hear that you're selling the cabin." He frowned.

"I know. I'm going to miss it. But no one ever comes up to the lake anymore. I can't believe that my mom didn't list it years ago. Honestly it doesn't make much sense, given what he put us through, but I feel like my dad's the reason that she held on to it for so long. He just passed away, and now suddenly she wants to sell."

"I'm sorry to hear that as well, Gemma. Was he part of your life at all over the years?" Drew asked, knowing my dad had left us following a long stint of infidelity that resulted in my parents' divorce. Jacob and I never knew the full extent of his affair, and we never knew if my mother had asked him to leave or if he had simply left us.

"No, not really. He sent the obligatory birthday and holiday gifts, called us on special occasions, but I never saw him after he left. Of course there were always empty promises that he would visit, but he never made the effort. His lawyer contacted us when he died. Heart attack, I guess."

"It must be hard for you, knowing he's gone." There was no mistaking the tenderness in his voice, as if he still cared about me, though it had been a lifetime since we had meant anything to one another.

I shrugged my shoulders. Part of me wanted to tell him all my deepest thoughts and feelings, to divulge everything that lived inside me, like I would have back when he was my best friend. But another part of me knew that he didn't fill that role in my life and that we were no more than strangers now who happened to share a piece of our past.

"It's been hard all these years, wondering where he is and if he'll ever come back. I guess I have a sense of closure now, knowing that he's gone and that he'll never be a part of my life again." I told this to Drew knowing that I felt the opposite of closure, that I would live forever with the simple yet complex question of "Why?" That I would never be able to confront my father to get the answers to the questions that have haunted me over the years. The years that I struggled to understand how a father could be so loving, supportive, and present one day and the next just walk away as if his children had never existed. I had struggled with the notion that I wasn't good enough or that he hadn't loved me enough, and I know that this struggle still lives inside me—the root of all evil so to speak.

"Anyway, thanks for the ride," I said, trying to change the subject and to find a break in the conversation so that I could flee back to the cabin.

He shook his head back and forth, smiling. "Gemma Lang. I can't believe it." We both opened our doors at the same time and climbed out of the Jeep. "Can I walk you to the cabin?" he asked.

"Thank you but I can manage," I said, fidgeting with the shoulder strap of my purse.

He stood facing me in the driveway, his hands in the pockets of his jeans. "All right then."

"Bye, Andrew." I waved as I slowly made my way down the driveway toward the road that ran between our cabins. I stopped when I got to the end and turned to add, "Hey, Drew! It was really good to see you."

He stopped to look at me from the porch where he was about to step inside, a smile splayed across his face. "It was good to see you too, Gem."

I walked to my cabin with a smile on my face, remembering what it felt like to have this amazing boy in my life.

Nine

I could feel the rough skin of his palm against my mouth, the taste of salt causing my stomach to convulse. I struggled to breathe through my nose, the pressure he held against my mouth making this a difficult task. My heart beat hard in my chest, fear gripping my insides. He pressed his body against me from behind as he held one hand across my mouth and the other underneath my shirt against the bare skin of my stomach, his pelvis grinding against my backside. I could feel how erect he was, and my mind was frantic, trying to predict his next move.

I felt his whiskey-drenched breath against my neck as he spoke in hushed whispers in my ear. "You know you want this as much as I do, Gemma. Just be good and stay quiet."

The alcohol that I had consumed was clouding my thoughts, but the voice inside my head was screaming, "Run." I was frozen, my body heavy and unable to move. Why was this happening? He turned me around and pushed me down, hard, into a pile of brush. It caught me off guard, and, before I could even think to scramble away from him, he had his jeans pulled down and was on top of me. His weight was crushing me, pinning me in place, and I could feel stabs of pain where the sharp edge of rocks and branches pierced the skin of my back and bare legs.

My senses caught up with me, and I tried to wiggle out from underneath him, clawing at his face with my hands. He quickly had my arms pinned above my head with one hand as his other hand made its way up my skirt. I was no match for his six foot three, 220-pound frame. I felt helpless, and so I began to beg.

"Please don't do this. Please . . ."

***

I woke to a shrill cry, startling me, until I realized that it was coming from my own mouth. I was drenched in sweat, my heart pounding in my chest. The visions from my familiar nightmare flashing through my mind. I hadn't dreamed of him for years. Being here was bringing it all back. I had worked so hard to overcome what had happened, putting it all behind me so that I could move forward without the constant fear and the paralyzing memories. *Maybe coming back was a mistake.* I thought that I was stronger than this, that I had really moved beyond the past.

I was consumed in the moment with the fear and the shame, as if I had just experienced it all over again. I went to the bathroom and splashed cold water on my face, trying to wash the images from my mind. There was no way I was going to fall back asleep. I tried to read a book, but I was restless, unable to sit still or comprehend the words on the page that I was reading. The cabin was eerily quiet, and I could feel the fear settling in. Refusing to be prisoner to the crippling emotion that had controlled my life years ago, I walked down to the dock, hoping that the cool fresh air would clear my head.

The first thing I noticed as I headed toward the water was how bright the sky was. Once the road opened up, revealing the beach and the calm lake, I took in the full moon and the trail of light that it imprinted on the smooth water. I smiled to myself at the beauty of it. I stepped onto the dock and could hear the water slosh beneath my weight in the quiet of the night. I sat with my legs folded in front of me, in awe of the moon and everything that it illuminated in its wake.

I turned to glance at Monroe Manor. The lights were on, a sharp contrast to the darkness of the cabins surrounding it. My gaze wandered to the Monroes' dock, and I caught sight of a lone silhouette sitting at the edge, much like I was. I knew that it must be Drew, and I suddenly wanted to go to him. I stood and made my way back toward the beach, crossing the sand until I reached his dock. As I approached him, his voice rang out softly in the silence.

"I thought that might be you."

"I couldn't sleep," I admitted.

"Neither could I." He patted the space beside him, so I sat down, pulling my knees into my chest and resting my cheek on one knee so that I could look at him. In the light of the moon, I could make out the strong curve of his jaw, his long eyelashes, and the hollow point of his cheek where his dimple rests. His legs were dangling off the end of the dock, submerged in the water where he moved his feet in slow circles, creating tiny waves. His arms were straight at his sides, his hands tucked underneath his thighs.

"It's beautiful out here. I can't believe that I stayed away for so long. I really missed it," I said, unable to keep the deep sense of melancholy I felt from my voice.

"I really missed *you*, Gemma," he said as he turned to face me, his eyes glowing in the moonlight. "What happened between us anyway? We were so close, once upon a time."

I took in a deep breath. *Was this a rhetorical question, or did he really not remember?* Of course I would never forget, as much as I wanted to. But Drew's memory of that night was so different from my own. While that night was significant to me in more ways than I cared to count, I realized that it may not be significant to Drew at all. The thought clutched my heart as my therapist's words replayed in my head as a reminder. *It is not his fault, Gemma.*

"Wow, I don't remember you ever being this quiet." He laughed, pulling me from my reverie as I realized that I had never answered his question. "You seem so different. More reserved."

"I am different, I guess. You definitely haven't changed though."

"Oh, yeah, and how do you figure that?"

"Well, you're just as charming as ever and . . . straightforward. You still wear your heart on your sleeve." I smiled, remembering him from all those years ago.

"And you can tell this from the few minutes that we've spent together?" He smirked.

"Yep. You're still the same Andrew Monroe that I remember."

"Well, Gemma Lang, you are a mystery to me. But one that I intend to solve," he said, leaning toward me, gently bumping my bent leg with his elbow. His smile lit up his eyes as he spoke. My maiden name sounded so natural coming from his lips—twice now—but I hadn't been called that in so long.

"Walsh. Gemma Walsh," I corrected him and immediately wished that I hadn't. There was instantly an awkward vibe in the air that was not there before.

"Oh. Sorry. So tell me, Gemma Walsh, what is a married woman doing here all alone and unable to sleep in the middle of the night?"

I paused, looking out at the water. "Do you remember the time we were riding our bikes on the lake trail with Logan, and I fell off my bike and rolled down the embankment?" I asked, recalling a memory that had suddenly struck me.

"Yeah. What were we then? Twelve, thirteen?"

"Thirteen. I know, because it was the first summer that I spent here without my dad. Do you remember how scared I was? I think I knew I'd be fine, but everything hurt, and there was so much blood." I had cut my knee on a rock during the fall, causing a gush of blood that looked far worse than the reality, which had been only three stitches' worth of fuss.

"I was scared too. I remember wishing it had been me. It was hard to see you hurt. I was so protective of you."

"I think that was the first time I realized it. That you would always protect me. I remember how safe you made me feel while we waited for Logan to go get help." I hadn't even cried until Drew had carried me up the embankment and held me close. His compassion had completely dissolved my will to be strong; I had allowed my tears to fall along with the wall that I had always protected myself with. It was as if, until that moment, I had forgotten what it was like to completely depend on someone else to catch me when I fell, like I had once with my father.

And now as a new perspective hit me, I realized that, in some ways, I had forgotten how to depend on Ryan.

Instead, I had pushed him away, unwilling to share the burden of my failures. Although in the end, it was Ryan who had ultimately failed me. Just as Drew had eventually failed me on that night so long ago. A fresh wave of pain salted old wounds left behind by those who had disappointed me before, scars etched into my heart like tally marks.

I quickly swiped away a lonely tear that trailed slowly down my cheek before Drew noticed it. "I miss that," I said quietly.

"Miss what?" Drew asked, glancing over at me.

I focused my attention on the whirlpool that he was creating with his feet as he continued to kick them in tiny circles.

"Feeling secure," I muttered so softly that I could hardly hear myself. I hadn't meant to say the words aloud; it was just a stirring inside my head, a rumbling inside my heart. I knew Drew had heard me though as his feet stilled, causing a deafening silence. I was so wrapped up in the memory. The way Drew had whispered, "Friends to infinity," in my ear while he had held me close that day, feeling his love and strength wrap around me like a warm blanket on a cold night. Feeling certain that no matter what, Drew would always have my back. A feeling that, I sadly noted, seemed to come with consequences. As each time I let down my guard —accepting the vulnerability that comes with loving someone, really allowing myself to rely on another—the safety net was pulled out from underneath me, leaving me feeling more desperate and apprehensive then I had been to begin with.

"What do you mean, you don't feel *safe?*" he asked with concern.

I cleared my throat and pushed away my heart-rending thoughts. I turned to look at Drew and quickly changed the subject yet again.

"So, you first. What are *you* doing here at the lake, all alone, and unable to sleep in the middle of the night? Escaping the corporate world?" I asked, genuinely curious as to why he was here. I had assumed that he would be knee-deep in the family business, jet-setting around the world with a trophy wife on his arm. Although I couldn't really imagine Drew living like that, yet sometimes people change. I had just assumed that he would, once he was encompassed in his father's world.

"I guess you could say that. I'm taking a little break from *life* for a while." He turned back to the lake, his smile fading in the night. I understood the need to take a break all too well. That was exactly why I was here, not that I would admit that to anyone, least of all Andrew who had only been back in my life for a total of two seconds.

"So are you married?" I asked, my eyes falling on his left hand to check for a ring. Nothing, not even a tan line to indicate that a ring had once resided there.

"Nope," he answered, popping his *P* like a child. He did not elaborate, forcing me to pry.

"Divorced?"

"Nope," he said again, shaking his head from side to side.

"Gay?" I asked jokingly, but curiously. *You never know*.

This brought his face back to mine. He raised his eyebrows at me. "What do you think?"

I raised my hands up in surrender. "Hey, just checking."

"Okay. Your turn. Judging by the rather large diamond on your finger and your new last name, I'm guessing that you're married, right?"

I stared into Drew's eyes for a beat and then down at my wedding ring, as I twirled it around my finger with my right hand, completely at a loss. His question should have an easy answer, yes or no. But unfortunately I wasn't sure about my marital status. My marriage was in limbo. I felt a familiar stab of pain in my chest, one that I had been living with since the moment I had found Ryan in bed with someone else.

I thought back to the day that Ryan had proposed and had slipped this ring on my finger. It was a perfect spring day in Seattle, one of those days when people were thankful for the long, dreary months of rain, knowing that, without it, the surrounding beauty would not exist. I remembered feeling that sense of gratitude as Ryan and I strolled along Alki Beach, watching a young family as they played a game of Frisbee in the rocky sand.

"That could be us one day," Ryan had said as he squeezed my hand. I had smiled at him, imagining the two of us, surrounded by kids, sharing our life together. Nothing would have made me happier. Ryan and I had talked about marriage—always something just out of our reach— something we both saw in our future but not until we were finished with law school and had started our careers. We were both so focused on our goals, the finish line finally visible after years of running the race.

But that day Ryan had surprised me. Our casual stroll had ended at Salty's with a late seafood lunch on their waterfront deck. And on our walk back to the car along the same beachfront path, Ryan had stopped at our favorite spot so that we could enjoy the sunset that stretched across the uncharacteristically clear sky. The blue had faded to pink as the sun had dipped farther and farther toward the edge of the earth. Ryan had dropped to his knee and had presented me with this ring.

"Gemma, I can't imagine a day without you in my life. Promise me forever?" he had asked.

Stunned and overcome with emotion, I had whispered, "Yes," just as the sun had melted into the ocean, welcoming the night. And in that moment, Ryan had crased my past, filling my future with love and happiness and hope. I remembered feeling amazed at how much I loved him, my heart so full of joy that I thought it might burst. *Forever*. Forever turned out to be not quite long enough. I had left him, literally walked out on him. And whether or not I was going back still remained a mystery. Legally I was married, but in my heart . . . I wasn't sure.

I turned to Drew and gave him a simple reply. "Yes," I said, matter-of-factly, hoping that he didn't read too much into my delayed response.

"So why are you here?" he asked with unease.

"I told you. To fix up the cabin."

"So where's your husband?" he asked, almost accusatory.

"He's at home in Seattle. He's working." Drew's questions were leaving me flustered. I didn't want to think about Ryan or my marriage or what had happened. The reality too painful, the truth too humiliating. I tried to deflect Drew's questions with questions of my own, but he could see right through me.

"Okay, Gemma. I know that it's none of my business, but spit it out already. You're obviously not telling me something."

"You're right, Andrew. It is none of your business. And you aren't exactly being forthcoming about your life." I stood to go. It was late, or early, whichever way I wanted to look at it, and I was done talking. "Good night, Andrew." As I turned to go, he raised his hand in the air to wave good-bye as if saying "whatever" but never said anything or turned in my direction. This pissed me off even more. I walked back to my cabin with my arms folded across my chest, feeling like an irrational teenager—angry but for no apparent reason. *Damn that Andrew Monroe.*

*T*en

I sat on the porch swing with my eyes closed, enjoying the warmth on my skin from the late-morning sun. I was exhausted from a nearly sleepless night, getting a late start on the day.

"Peace offering?"

I jumped at the sound of his voice and opened my eyes to find Andrew standing at the bottom of the porch holding up a picnic basket.

"Jesus, Drew. You scared the living shit out of me," I said with my hand over my pounding heart.

"Sorry, I didn't mean to startle you." He laughed. "I felt bad about pushing you last night, and I wanted to apologize. May I sit down?"

"Be my guest." I motioned toward the porch swing, scooting over to make room for him.

"Coffee?" he asked as he set down the basket and began rifling through it.

"Yes, please." He handed me a coffee mug and filled it to the brim with steaming hot coffee from a stainless steel thermos.

"Cream? Sugar?"

"No, just black. Thanks."

"Good, because I don't have any," he said with relief. He handed me a red-and-white-checkered cloth napkin and then a warm huckleberry scone. My favorite.

"Oh, my God, where did you get this?" I asked.

"LuLu's bakery. I remembered that these were your favorite. Do you forgive me?" He cocked his head to the side, his smile igniting something inside me.

"I guess so. But only because you brought me a scone. I can't believe that LuLu is still in business."

"Yeah, she passed away a few years ago, but her niece has been running things for several years now. All the recipes have been handed down," he said as he bit into a scone.

I bit into my own scone and closed my eyes to savor the taste. "I think these are better than I remember." I devoured the entire thing in as little as three bites while Andrew and I sat in silence, taking in the lake as we sipped our coffee.

"So what's your plan today?" he asked.

"I wanted to pick up some paint and supplies from the hardware store, and start refinishing the outside of the cabin. But since I don't have a car, I may just sit here all day and do nothing."

"You're going to paint the cabin all by yourself? Why not hire somebody to do it?"

"I don't know. I kind of like the idea of doing it myself."

"Well, I'd be happy to take you to town, if you want," he said, hesitantly.

"Really? You don't mind?" I asked.

"Not at all."

We finished our coffee and drove to the hardware store where I picked up paintbrushes, paint pans, redwood stain for the cedar planks, and white paint for the trim. Andrew left me at the cabin with my purchases while he claimed to be in desperate need of a nap.

I spent the afternoon taping the trim around the doors and windows that I could reach, prepping for the long process of reviving the cedar siding that I planned to start the following day.

That night, while playing an old-fashioned game of solitaire at the dining table, I polished off a bottle of Merlot and let my thoughts drift to Andrew. It was hard not to feel attracted to him. His smile could light up the room. He was still the kind, gentle soul that I remembered, his father's cold, hard demeanor having no place in Andrew's heart. He was his mother's son through and through.

Eleven

The next morning I braved the dark confines of the garage, mentally talking my way through the spiderwebs to find the ladder that my grandfather had stored away. It was hard not to wish that Ryan was there to help with this task, knowing my fear of spiders and any other creepy-crawling thing that hid in dark confined spaces. I was married; I shouldn't have to wrestle with ten-foot-tall ladders and monstrous black spiders. I pushed aside my resentment of my situation and chanted in my head, *You can do this*, over and over, mentally psyching myself up for the task.

I emerged from the garage hastily, threw the ladder to the ground with a crash, and jumped around frantically. I ran my hands through my hair and over every inch of my body in a desperate attempt to brush off the multitude of spiders and their webs that I was almost certain were there. I heard a laugh from behind me and turned to find Andrew watching the embarrassing spectacle that I was making of myself.

"What the hell?" he asked, unable to hide the amusement in his voice.

"Get them off me," I screamed. I didn't have time to let the mortification of the moment sink in when I felt as if little eight-legged things were crawling all over my skin.

He only laughed harder. "Still afraid of spiders?" he teased.

He must have seen the fear in my eyes, so he walked closer and brushed his hands up and down my arms. He pulled something out of my hair. I wasn't sure what it was; I was too afraid to ask.

"There. Nothing on you. You're fine," he said with his hands resting on my shoulders, looking directly into my eyes, his voice calm and direct.

His touch raised the goose bumps on my skin to a new level, and I shivered at the sound of his deep, calming voice, so close to my face.

I stepped backward away from him, my cheeks ablaze in embarrassment now that I felt safe. "Thanks." I wrapped my arms across my chest, rubbing out the chill. "Where were you five minutes ago? I could've avoided this whole scene and sent *you* in there instead," I said, motioning toward the garage with my thumb.

He laughed again. "Sorry, but this was way more fun."

I punched him in the arm. He was wearing a pair of long running shorts and a sleeveless T-shirt. The muscles in his arms and shoulders flexed as my fist met his skin.

"Hey, I saved your ass from that big hairy spider crawling through your hair, and this is the thanks I get?" he said as he rubbed his arm.

I instinctively ran my hands through my hair again and shuddered at the thought. I pulled my hair back into a ponytail, securing it with the band that I had wrapped around my wrist. "What are you doing here, Drew?" I asked with my hands on my hips.

"I thought you might want some help painting. I don't really have anything going on. It could be nice to have a project. What do you say? Want some help?"

"You really want to help?" I asked, unsure of his motives.

"Yep." He gave me that closed-lip smile that showcased his dimples the most.

"Fine. Can you help me with this ladder?" I asked as he picked it up off the ground, chuckling to himself.

Twelve

We worked together the entire day, each with our own earbuds in place, listening to our iPods. Andrew was on the ladder, painting the upper portion, while I stood on the ground painting the lower portion. I had made us sandwiches for lunch that we ate on the front porch in the shade. We didn't speak much the entire day, but our silence was comforting and familiar, and I was thankful for his presence and for his help.

Each morning Drew dutifully showed up and took his place on the ladder as we worked our way around the house. With its color slowly being restored, the cabin was looking fresh and familiar, more like the way that I remembered it.

And the work was therapeutic like I had hoped it would be. Keeping my hands busy helped keep my mind off the things that had driven me here in the first place.

We had just finished the second coat of stain, and we stood back side by side with our paintbrushes in hand to admire our work. Sweat was dripping down my back underneath my tank top, and my cutoff jean shorts were speckled with red stain.

"Nice work, partner," Andrew said, raising his left hand while his right was still holding a paintbrush.

I raised my hand expectantly to give him a high-five, and he interlaced our fingers together instead.

"Thanks for all your help. I couldn't have done it without you," I said, slowly releasing my fingers from his. He was looking at me so intensely. Sweat beaded on his forehead, and he had a few days' worth of stubble on his upper lip and chin. He looked ruggedly handsome, and it was hard to turn away. Instead I ran my paintbrush down his nose, trying to break away from the awkward stare down that had us both frozen in place.

With a translucent red streak down his nose, he blinked, completely taken aback by my action.

I gave him a wicked smile, waiting for his reaction.

He quickly retaliated by running his brush across my cheek followed by a streak down my arm.

"Hey," I yelled as I ran away from him. We both rushed for the paint pan, dipping our brushes and flicking paint at each other, brushing red stain across the other's skin whenever the opportunity presented itself. I could feel the effortless grin on my face, stretching from ear to ear as the death grip that life had clenched around my heart loosened just enough to notice. I felt like the young girl that I once was, carefree and happy, spending the day with my best friend. Within minutes we were covered in red from head to toe and laughing breathlessly.

We both stilled at the same moment, and, with nothing else but a look between us—a voiceless communication that we had perfected long ago—we dropped our brushes and took off running for the beach, kicking off our shoes somewhere along the way. Our paced steps turned into a familiar race as we reached the dock. Drew was only steps ahead of me, and we reached the end at nearly the same time, both of us diving into the calm blue water. As I surfaced, trying to catch my breath, I was assaulted by a splash to the face. Drew was only a few feet from me, breathless as well, grinning like an idiot.

"Oh, you're going down," I said.

He only laughed at my pathetic threat and countered, "Bring it."

I splashed him back, square in the face, and, of course, this led to a full-on war. We both stopped at the point where we could hardly stay afloat, unable to catch our breath from laughing so hard. I swam toward him, calling "truce," and ran my hands over his face. Luckily the paint hadn't dried yet and washed away with each stroke of my hand. We were laughing in between breaths, treading water, as we wiped the paint off each other.

Suddenly aware of where our legs touched below the surface and the lack of space between our faces, I swallowed the desire that unexpectedly erupted from somewhere inside me. For a brief moment I thought that he was going to kiss me, his hand resting on my cheek, his blue eyes staring into mine—almost translucent in the bright sun. But the moment slipped by, and he swam away from me, his long strokes taking him toward his own dock. I was still out of breath and left alone to calm my pounding heart from whatever had just passed between us.

Exhausted, I stopped treading water and let myself drift below the surface into the cold dark depths of the lake, trying to clear my head. When I couldn't hold my breath another second, I slowly let air out of my lungs and pushed myself back toward the light, kicking ferociously, feeling the burn. I drew in a desperate breath once I felt the sun on my face. Wiping the water from my eyes, I opened them and nearly screamed. I was staring into Drew's eyes.

"Seriously, Drew, stop sneaking up on me," I panted, out of breath. I slammed my fist against the surface, splashing water into Drew's face.

He didn't even flinch, his features fixed with a solemn expression. "I should have kissed you that day," he said, treading water effortlessly just inches in front of me.

"What are you talking about?" I asked.

"That day at Indian Rock. That should have been our first kiss."

His words brought to mind the memory of the day in question. I knew exactly the moment that he was referring to. A hot day in August, the summer we had both turned sixteen. The last summer I had spent here at the lake with Drew, just days before our relationship had changed forever, our friendship ripped apart.

"I was just a kid, afraid of rejection. But, more important, I was afraid of losing you," he said, breathing hard.

The memory was crystal clear now, like a movie playing in my mind. We had hiked to Indian Rock, a huge cliff that emerged from the lake a few miles up the shore from our cabins, earning its name from the ancient drawings —which were believed to have been painted by Native Americans—that covered the face of the massive rock. Drew and I had climbed to the top with a six-pack of beer, talked, and then jumped off the landing into the cold dark water below. It was the first and last time that I had jumped off the rock, a popular adrenaline-inducing activity that every teenager had tried at least once.

"Why are you telling me this?" I asked, getting lost in

his icy-blue eyes, remembering the boy that he had been through the eyes of a teenage girl who had had a crush on her best friend. Although looking back, it had been more than just a teenage crush. I remembered the way I had watched him that summer each time he dove into the lake, taking in the new shape of his body. The boy that I had known had vanished leaving in his place over six feet of hard muscle and definition, rippled abs, and long toned legs. Even his jawline had become more defined.

And I hadn't been able to ignore the way he would watch me while I peeled away my clothes, stripping down to my bikini that I had finally filled out with womanly curves. Everything had slowly changed between us that summer, but neither of us had wanted to acknowledge it, both desperate to hold on to the friendship that had defined us for so long, a friendship that we had come to rely on like the air that we needed to breath.

Looking into Drew's eyes now, feeling my heart thumping hard in my chest with that familiar ache, that familiar need in my gut, I thought back to that day. The way Drew and I had both surfaced from that jump at the same time, the way my lungs had burned, as if on fire, after the long swim to the surface from the incredible depth that had swallowed us whole. It had been the most incredible, most exhilarating rush that I had ever experienced to date. I remembered screaming, "Holy Shit," once I had caught my breath.

And then I sensed something shift in his gaze. I had wanted him to kiss me then. I had closed my eyes feeling his breath on my face, anticipating the feel of his lips on mine. But as the seconds ticked by, I had opened my eyes to find him swimming toward the shore, feeling foolish for misinterpreting the signs, crushed that my feelings were one-sided, unreciprocated. And now, here he was, telling me what he should've told me all those years ago.

"I'm telling you this because I don't want to be afraid anymore. I don't want to lose you again without doing what I should have done that day." Reaching out his hand, he cupped my wet cheek, pulling my face closer as he tilted his head, closing the small gap between us. I felt his warm lips against the cold of my own, like a gentle caress. I shivered from the cold water that encompassed me as he softly urged my lips to part, deepening the kiss with his hand on the back of my head as our legs became entangled just below the surface.

Suddenly scared from the growing desire swirling in my gut, I pulled away before I was completely lost to him. Ryan's face flashed in my mind, and I instantly felt guilty, as conflicting emotions warred within me. I wanted this moment to be validated by Ryan's affair, but at the same time I could hear the old adage ringing in my head: *two wrongs don't make a right.*

"Drew," I whispered desperately, looking into his eyes to read his reaction. As if my breath had been stolen away, I couldn't finish my thought.

His eyes searched my face for a moment before he sank below the surface and swam away again. I watched him until he reached his dock, where he pulled himself up and walked toward the shore to Monroe Manor, disappearing into the wall of glass moments later.

I finally took a long pull of air, my first real breath in several minutes. Swimming to the edge of the dock, I climbed out, fighting the chill, and slowly made my way back to my cabin.

I wasn't sure what to feel or what to think. I can't deny the feelings that resurfaced from that kiss. Feelings that had been dormant in my soul all these years came crashing back in an instant. If only he had kissed me that day so long ago. If only I had known how he felt for me then. Things could have turned out differently. If only.

Thirteen

I set down my book in my lap. I was in bed, snuggled under
the comforter, trying to read until I fell asleep. I couldn't
concentrate on the words. All I could think of was Andrew
and the look in his eyes when he had kissed me. I brought my
fingers to my lips, remembering what it had felt like. It was
our first kiss—too little, too late—twenty years too late to be
exact. It had been decades since I had experienced a first kiss
with someone. It was amazing that, even at thirty-six, the
anticipation of it had felt the same as it did at sixteen.

I felt like a teenager all over again, and a smile crept
over my face. I felt giddy and happy but I couldn't deny the
dark cloud that loomed nearby. Andrew represented a part of

my life that I had tried to put behind me, but it still haunted me. And hiding here from my life didn't erase the fact that I was still married. Nothing good could come from this. And, yet, it was nice to have a distraction from the devastation that I had felt since the day I found Ryan in bed with that woman.

I thought of Ryan and wondered what he was doing at that very minute. Was he with *her*? There were so many unanswered questions, questions that I hadn't stuck around to ask. I hadn't wanted to know the answers then, the pain threatening to cripple me. I had felt weak in that moment. I hated the vulnerability of feeling powerless, the feeling that my life was out of my control. My chest ached from the realization that my marriage was most likely over. The realization that the choice to end my marriage might not be mine to make.

Ryan had apologized in several voice mails and texts, but I never really considered what his apology meant. Was he sorry for what he did, for hurting me? Was he wanting me back, or was he sorry that I found out, sorry for what he really wanted? Maybe Ryan had already made his final choice. Maybe I was just the last to know. Either way I didn't think I was quite ready to find out.

I tossed aside my book and turned off the bedside lamp. Sighing out loud, I rolled onto my side and closed my eyes. Andrew's beautiful face filled my mind again as the guilt festering in my gut reminded me that I should have been thinking only of my husband.

Fourteen

"Please don't do this," I begged.

I looked up into his eyes; they were dark and soulless, and I knew in that moment that my desperate words would not reach him. He was not the person that I knew; he was something else, and this realization brought my fear to new heights, paralyzing me.

Pain seared through my core as he took everything from me. My senses were overwhelming me. I could feel every inch of his skin where he touched me. I could smell his cologne, the whiskey on his breath. I could hear him grunt and whisper my name against my ear. It was all too much, and I prayed that it would end soon.

I'm not sure how long it lasted, seconds, minutes, but it felt like hours. Tears spilled down my cheeks as I cried in pain and fear. My arms ached from where they were pinned above my head. My legs were shaking from the unbearable weight of his body holding me down, and the pain from his thrusts was beyond anything that I had ever endured.

When I finally felt his weight lift from my broken body, I rolled to my side and vomited into the brush over and over again.

I heard him zip up his pants, towering over me as he said in a breathy voice, "You shouldn't have drunk so much, Gemma. You might regret this in the morning. Just remember that you wanted this as much as I did." I heard him chuckle to himself as he stumbled back toward the bonfire.

I tried to stand, but my body was shaking uncontrollably. I leaned against a tree and tried to straighten my skirt. Blood was trickling down my leg. I sat back down on the ground and sobbed into my hands.

***

I woke with tears on my pillow and ran for the bathroom, holding my hair back from my face as I vomited into the toilet. I sat on the bathroom floor, hugging my knees to my chest and sobbed for the sixteen-year-old girl who I had lost all those years ago. Being here was bringing it all back again. Drew was bringing it all back again. I had forgiven him years ago through extensive therapy, and I had forgiven myself, but I feared that maybe, deep down, I would never be healed, that I would never forgive, that I would never forget.

Fifteen

I hadn't heard from Andrew in three days, since the kiss. I wasn't sure what to make of it, but I wasn't exactly banging down his door either.

Logan showed up with my car sometime in the late afternoon. He had replaced the windshield, and had ordered a new bumper and front fender. I invited him in for an iced tea, and we spent an hour catching up on the big events in our lives that we had missed. We talked about law school, my wedding, and my job at the firm. We talked about his marriage to another local girl, the birth of his daughter, Zoe, his divorce, and the shared custody arrangement that he was suffering through. We didn't talk about Drew or that night so long ago.

As I was driving Logan back to Sal's Garage, we passed by Fred's, a legendary local hot spot that had been here for as long as I could remember.

"Let's stop for a drink," Logan suggested.

"I don't know. I really should get back," I said, although I took my foot off the gas pedal, and the car slowed.

"The Gemma I knew wouldn't have hesitated for a minute. Come on. Have a drink with me."

"All right, one drink," I said, as I pulled off the road and parked the car in the gravel parking lot. The place looked busy already, but, then again, it was one of the most popular bars on the lake. We took a seat at the bar, and the bartender approached us to take our order. She was blonde, the kind of bleached blonde that came right out of the bottle, with blue eyes weighted down by too much makeup. Her breasts spilled out of her hot pink Fred's T-shirt, and her skin was deeply tanned.

"Hi, Logan. What can I get for ya?" She eyed him flirtatiously, and he returned the favor, his eyes settling on her half-covered breasts.

"Hi, Scarlett. We'll have two Bud Lights and two shots of Patron," he said, raising two fingers in the air.

She nodded and walked to the other end of the bar.

"Wow, you really haven't changed a bit," I said, raising my eyebrows at him.

He laughed and shook his head at me.

Scarlett came back with two tall glasses of beer and then set two empty shot glasses on the bar before filling them to the rim with the clear tequila. Logan handed me one of the shot glasses and then picked up the other.

"To old friends and days gone by," he toasted before bringing the tiny glass to his lips.

"Here goes nothing," I muttered and swallowed the contents of my glass. The tequila was smooth but still burned my throat on the way down, and I instantly picked up my beer and drained half of it. Besides my love for a good wine, I wasn't much of a drinker, and I knew that I was probably already at my limit. Logan held up two fingers again, and Scarlett nodded from where she was standing, practically undressing him with her eyes.

"Oh, no, I think one shot is enough for me," I said, shaking my head as Scarlett walked toward us with the bottle of Patron in her hand.

Logan stood behind me, squeezing my shoulders, and leaned down to whisper in my ear, "Come on, Gemma. Loosen up. You're wound way too tight. I'm getting you loaded tonight." He kissed my cheek as I looked up at him. His smile was devious, and I knew there was no point arguing with him. I feared the hangover that I would inevitably have in the morning as I poured another shot down the back of my throat.

The sky was dark, and Logan and I were still drinking. The band had started to play, and I found myself dancing circles around Logan and singing at the top of my lungs. Maybe it was the effect of the alcohol or the company of an old friend—a very fun old friend—but I felt myself let go. There were no tests that needed to be taken, no trial that needed to be won, and no husband that I needed to please. It was just me, in the raw, having fun with an authentic smile stretched across my face, a warm flush in my cheeks.

A slow song started to play, and Logan pulled me into his arms midsentence, without missing a beat. I wrapped my arms around his neck and let him lead me in a gentle sway while I listened to him finish his story about the black bear that he had run into at the dump.

"I swear the damn thing was twice as big as the bear we saw on the trail when we were kids."

"What did you do?" I asked.

"Besides nearly shit myself?"

I giggled uncontrollably, resting my forehead on Logan's shoulder, feeling his chest rumble from his own laughter. And then, lifting up my head, I caught a glimpse of Andrew as he strolled in through the front door. Our eyes met briefly before he turned away and approached the bar. I watched him as he sat down on an empty stool, drained a shot of something, and then sipped beer from a dark bottle.

I felt a fluttering in my gut, and it took me a moment to realize that it was nerves. I was nervous. I wasn't sure what Drew was feeling after the other day. Was it a fleeting moment, brought to life from old emotions, or was it something new that was transpiring here and now? And were either of us going to acknowledge it, or were we going to act as if it never happened?

When the song ended, Logan and I made our way back to the bar. Logan spotted Drew and pulled me in his direction. "Well, look what the cat dragged in," Logan slurred.

"Hey, Logan. Wasn't expecting you two to be here." He lifted his chin toward us before taking a long pull from his beer bottle.

His eyes were cold and sad, and I couldn't help but feel that he wasn't pleased to see us.

"So how's your husband, Gemma?" he asked, his words laced with thick, harsh sarcasm as he avoided looking me in the eye.

So this was how he was going to play it? I could tell that he was drunk, and I wondered at what point he had become such a mean drunk.

"Logan, maybe we should go," I said, not wanting to risk my fragile feelings against Drew's wrath.

Drew reached out and grabbed my arm. "No, don't go. The fun is just beginning."

78

I wasn't comfortable with his tone.

He motioned for Scarlett, and she brought us three shots of tequila.

I was hesitant to keep drinking, but what the hell.

Drew raised his shot glass. "To the things that never seem to change, no matter how much time has passed." He tilted his head back and swallowed the contents of his shot glass.

I wasn't sure exactly what he was implying, but I could feel my anger bubbling just below the surface. Logan and I both finished our tequila.

"What the fuck is your problem, man?" Logan asked with his hands on his hips.

"Easy, Logan. No need to get all riled up," Drew said, holding his hand against Logan's expanding chest. Drew turned to me then, his tone still heavy with sarcasm, "Sorry, Gem. That was a dick thing to say." He took another drink of his beer, avoiding my eyes.

Logan shook his head back and forth, recovering from his sudden frustration, and leaned over the bar to talk to Scarlett. By the smile on her face, I could only imagine what he was saying to her.

I stood and watched the couples dancing in front of the stage, their hips and arms swaying in all directions while they shouted familiar lyrics in sync with the band.

Drew continued to stare with brooding eyes toward nothing in particular behind the bar.

When the music shifted to a slower melody, the band's own rendition of "Angel Eyes," I felt Drew spin around on his stool and grab my arm. I turned to look at him.

"Dance with me?" he asked. Before I could respond, he was pulling me out onto the dance floor. He drew me in close until my body was flush against his chest, holding my hand in his while his other hand rested on my lower back.

I rested my free hand on his shoulder and looked up into his eyes, trying to interpret his expression.

He pulled me closer, his cheek nearly brushing mine. "I'm sorry," he whispered into my ear.

"For what?" I asked, my voice competing with the noise of the band.

"For what I said, the way I acted. I walked in and saw you with Logan, and it brought back too many memories." He pulled back and looked me in the eyes. "He knows you're married, right?"

"Of course. And he doesn't feel that way about me anyway, Drew. He never did."

"That's what you think. I love the guy to death, I do. But he sleeps with everything without a penis, married or not."

I couldn't help but laugh at Drew's portrayal of Logan. Drew wasn't far from the mark, but that didn't change the fact that I didn't fall into the category of "everything without a penis."

"I might as well have a penis. He views me like he views you, as just one of the guys."

Drew's head fell back as he laughed, a huge grin spread across his face. "You're crazy if you think any man could envision you as one of the guys, Gemma. Look at you." He stepped back, keeping one hand in mine and the other still on my back, but his eyes scanned my body from head to toe. "You're gorgeous."

I hit him in the chest. "Stop. You're embarrassing me," I said, as I pulled myself flush against him, interrupting his perusal of my body. Inside I was high-fiving myself. *He thinks I'm gorgeous.* And then I thought of our kiss, feeling a familiar warmth flood my insides.

"You know I wanted you so bad back then, right?"

"What?" I asked, remembering that last summer that I saw him, feigning obliviousness.

80

"Oh, yeah. Wet dreams and all." He laughed, and I smacked the back of his head, playfully.

His voice grew more serious. "I wish that things would have turned out differently."

I swallowed the lump in my throat, his comment bringing me back to that night. A night that I wanted to forget. An instant chill swept over me, replacing the warmth that I had felt just moments before. My body tensed against his, and he pulled me in closer. Silence fell over us, and I sensed that he knew he had said too much.

The song was fading, coming to an end, and I stepped back, out of Drew's arms. "I need another drink," I said, as I made my way toward the bar with Drew on my heels. Logan was still monopolizing Scarlett's attention when I asked her for another round. She reluctantly turned from Logan's gaze to fill three more shot glasses, which she set down in front of us, filled two glasses with beer from the tap and uncapped a bottle for Drew.

***

I wasn't sure at what point I could not feel my lips, or my legs for that matter, but I was pretty sure that I consumed more alcohol than I had since college. The three of us closed down the bar. I hadn't had that much fun in years, and, for just a few moments—with our trio in full attendance—I felt like *that* girl again, the carefree girl who I used to be.

We piled into Drew's Jeep with Scarlett at the wheel. My head had started to spin or maybe the world around me when I heard Scarlett ask, "Where to?"

"My place, Kalispell Bay," Drew slurred.

We stumbled into Monroe Manor, and I was instantly assaulted with memories. Good memories. The place still smelled the same, reminding me of the early years when Drew's mom used to make huckleberry pancakes for dinner and read us stories in front of the fire on rainy days. When we were older and his mother was gone, Matilda—the Monroes' housekeeper and nanny—would make us French bread pizzas and chocolate milkshakes while we played pool or foosball in the game room. Although after Katherine passed away, we had spent most of our time at my cabin.

Scarlett's high-pitched squeal pulled me from my thoughts, and I looked up to see Logan chasing her up the stairs. The guy really hadn't changed—the ladies were still eating out of his palm.

Drew walked around the kitchen island and opened a cabinet, retrieving two glasses which he filled with water from the filtered tap. I walked over to the two-story-high windows that faced the lake. Although the few lights on in the cabin were dim, it was too dark to see anything outside other than a blanket of stars and a sliver of a moon. I could see my own reflection in the window as well as Drew's as he came up behind me. He handed me a glass of water once he was standing beside me.

"Thanks," I said, my heart thudding in my chest. My head was cloudy, and my body heavy, weighted down by the amount of tequila still running through my veins. But, on the inside, I felt light as a feather. I was floating on a cloud of something; I wasn't sure what. We stood in silence, staring into the night. It was hard to ignore the fact that we weren't those two kids anymore, best friends, seeing the two grown-up reflections in the window side by side. After several minutes had passed and our water glasses were empty, I turned from the window and walked into the kitchen. My steps still wobbly with intoxication.

"Well, I should go," I said, as I set my glass on the marble countertop.

Drew came up behind me, setting his glass next to mine; he grabbed my wrist and turned me until I was facing him. Without warning, he leaned down and kissed me, while drawing me closer with his arms wrapped around my lower back. Unable to process what was happening, my body took over, and I kissed him back as my hands found their way around his neck. He kissed me with such intensity, his tongue weaving around mine, that a moan escaped my lips. My entire body came alive under his touch.

He lifted me until I was sitting on the counter, and I wrapped my legs around his waist, my hands in his hair. For a mere thirty seconds, my hazy thoughts drifted to Ryan. I hadn't kissed anyone but him, like this, in so long that Drew's tongue in my mouth should have felt foreign, but there was something so right about the moment. Ryan's indiscretions filled my bitter heart, and I kissed Drew back with more determination. I could feel the hard definition of his chest pressed up against mine, his warm, strong hands on the bare skin of my back where he held me underneath my shirt. Desire pooled in my gut, heat building in my core, as I lost myself in him.

It wasn't long before he was walking toward the master suite with my body still wrapped around him. He laid me down on the bed, and my legs untangled from his waist as he pulled away from me. I felt the sudden loss of heat the moment his body left mine. I watched him in anticipation of what was to come as he pulled his shirt over his head and unbuttoned his jeans, letting them fall to the ground. I was mesmerized by the sharp cuts of his chest and abdomen, and the defined V that led to his man parts beneath his boxers. The man before me was more amazing than the teenage boy that I remembered, and I ached to reach out and run my hands over his body.

I sat up on the edge of the bed as he grabbed the hem of my tank top and began to pull it off. I raised my arms slowly over my head as he lifted it from my body. He interlaced our fingers and pulled me to stand in front of him. Tenderly sweeping my long hair from my neck, he slowly kissed me behind the ear, trailing gentle kisses along my neck, collarbone, and finally the top of my breasts, where they spilled out of black lace. I felt his hands reach behind my back and unclasp my bra, peeling the straps down my arms—one at a time—until it fell to the ground. His warm hands cupped my breasts firmly as his tongue found my mouth once again. My legs were shaky from the sensations that Drew's touch evoked, so I wrapped my hands around his neck to steady myself. My cropped skinny jeans were next as he pulled them from my body before pushing me back gently against the bed.

My thoughts were incoherent at this point. I was all body, all sensation, relishing in the way Drew made me feel. His hands and mouth worshiped every inch of me until I was reduced to a panting, pleading bundle of need, practically begging to feel him inside me. The incredible sensation I felt when he finally was inside me nearly sent me over the edge. He hovered above me, whispering my name with the first few penetrating thrusts, the passion between us escalating from slow and gentle to rough and urgent and then back again as he made love to me for hours. I lost sight of everything beyond Drew. Aware of only him as he moved our bodies from one place to another; shifting seamlessly from above me to beneath me and then behind me, taking and giving, his movements tender and yet demanding. His touch reminding me of what my body could do, what my body could feel. It had been too long since I had felt like this.

Sixteen

I awoke in the morning, my heart pounding in my head. The
sun was streaming in through the tall windows, and it took a
moment to remember where I was. My location was made
perfectly clear when my eyes found Drew asleep next to me.
The sheet was barely covering his manly parts. I took a
moment to watch his chest rise and fall with his breath; even
in sleep he was beautiful. My spotty memory from last night
filled my mind, and I jolted to a sitting position.

"Oh, my God," I muttered to myself. I suddenly felt
sick and not because of what I had done, but seriously sick. I
ran, completely naked, to the bathroom. Barely making it in
time, I threw up in the toilet. I splashed water on my face and

rinsed my mouth. *Ugh, why did I drink so much last night*? I thought. I wrapped a large fluffy towel around myself before returning to the bedroom.

I found Drew sitting on the edge of the bed with his face buried in his hands, the sheet wrapped around his waist.

I moaned and crawled back into bed, pulling the down comforter over me.

"I am so sorry, Gemma," he groaned.

"For what?" I asked, rolling onto my side, staring at his back and the way he was hunched over.

"For last night," he said, turning to face me, gripping his hair in his hand. "You're married, and I'm not *that* guy. I just . . . I don't know what came over me."

I propped myself up with my elbow and looked into his eyes. "Drew, don't apologize. Please, don't apologize. Last night was amazing, from what I remember anyway." Sighing out loud, I slumped back down on my back, my head sinking into the plush pillow and added, "My marriage is . . . complicated right now."

"What do you mean by complicated?" he asked, lying down next to me.

I looked up at the ceiling, contemplating how much to tell him. "I left Ryan. I walked in on him having sex with a woman from his office. In our bed." I rested my arm across my face, feeling ashamed and embarrassed.

"What did he have to say for himself?" Drew asked, his voice tense, tinted with anger as he leaned toward me.

"Nothing. I literally walked out on him, and I haven't spoken to him since." I peeked at Drew's face from underneath my arm. His jaw was tense, but his eyes were soft, etched with sadness.

"I'm so sorry, Gemma. You deserve so much better than that."

I slowly brought my arm away from my face and turned on my side to face him. "That's just it. As angry as I

86

am, it's just as much my fault as it is his. Our marriage has been strained for some time now."

"Do you still love him?"

"Yeah. But I don't know how to fix this. I don't know if I can ever erase that image from my mind, the image of him with another woman." I rolled onto my back again, feeling guilty for what I had done with Andrew. "And look at me. I'm no better."

Drew swept the hair from my face, tucking it behind my ear from where he now hovered over me, propping himself up with his arm. "Gemma, you *are* better than this. Last night was my fault. You had a lot to drink, and I should have left you alone. I just can't help the way I feel when I'm around you. I was too weak last night to fight it."

I looked up into his blue eyes, his gaze so full of love and adoration. Drew pulled my heart in two separate directions. Part of me loved him, loved him in a way that I will never understand, the way a person loves someone who once shared her heart and soul, someone who knew all a girl's faults and still loved her in spite of them. And the other part of me feared him. I feared what he represented, the painful memories that awakened in my mind in his presence, the resentment I had felt toward him for years threatening to resurface.

"I should go," I said, suddenly feeling overwhelmed.

"Don't go, Gemma. Stay with me, please. We can't take back what happened last night. Can't we just enjoy it a while longer?" He pulled me into his arms and held me.

I couldn't deny how natural it felt to be lying next to him, our bodies molded together. His touch ignited a fire inside me that had been burned out for too long, bringing the realization of just how dead I had been inside. I longed to feel alive once more, to see the world in color, to breathe again. I lay in his arms, feeling every beat of my heart, every breath that filled my lungs, fully aware of every newly awakened piece of myself . . . until I fell sleep.

Seventeen

I watched the dark beer bottle spin in the dirt, visible in the glow from the bonfire as I crossed my fingers in hope that it landed on me. It stopped, its long neck pointing toward Krista, a local girl with large breasts and a reputation to boot. I held my breath as I watched Drew lean forward and press his lips against hers. She was a little too eager to kiss Drew for my taste, and I felt confused by the jealousy that burned through my blood. Drew gave her the subtlest peck on the lips before pulling away. Her disappointment was palpable even from where I was sitting. Every kiss so far was subtle and innocent among the six of us who had dared to play spin the bottle, which was surprising with the amount of beer we were drinking.

It was my turn. I twisted my wrist and released the bottle, watching it spin around and around, hoping that it landed on Drew. I was desperate to kiss him and watching him kiss Krista had only made me want him even more.

"Oooh," the girls swooned as the bottle pointed at Logan who sat to the left of me. I sat waiting for a friendly peck but soon felt Logan's hand on the back of my head, drawing me closer as he devoured my lips with his own, prompting my mouth open. I felt his tongue slip inside and caress mine with expert skill. I got lost in his kiss until he pulled away moments later. I looked into his eyes as he sat back down in the dirt beside me, stunned that my friend had just kissed me like that.

I was abruptly pulled from the trance that I was lost in when Drew stood up, mumbling, "What the hell?" He kicked dirt our way as he stomped off.

I immediately stood and chased after him.

"It's just a game," I heard Logan yell at us.

"Drew? What's your problem?" I asked when I caught up to him at the tree line. We were at a party in the clearing, a popular spot for a bonfire and a night of drinking. It was surrounded by the forest and very secluded, only accessible in an SUV by a narrow dirt path.

He stopped to confront me, his face red and laced with anger. "What's MY problem? What was that all about?"

"It's a game, Drew. And that was all Logan. Not that it matters."

"You kissed him back. And it does matter," he shouted.

"And you kissed Krista, so what's the big deal?" I shouted back. I was so confused by his anger, my anger—the whole conversation.

"I didn't kiss her like that," he said, pointing toward the bonfire where our little game was being played.

"So what?"

He stepped closer to me, lowering his voice just a notch. "Don't you get it, Gemma? Don't you see what's happening here?"

"What?" I asked, feeling angry at him for shouting at me and causing a scene.

"Forget it. I'm leaving. Why don't you ask Logan for a ride home? I'm sure he'd be more than happy to give you one." Drew stormed off, climbed into his Bronco, and disappeared into the trees, leaving behind a cloud of dust. I started to cry. I wasn't sure why I was crying. I was so confused. I wasn't sure if I loved Drew or hated his guts. I stepped into the forest, surrounded by darkness and leaned against a tree. I just needed a few minutes to compose myself before returning to the fire. I could hear the voices of my friends fading in the distance as nature engulfed me, offering the privacy that I needed in that moment. Why was Drew so mad at me? What was happening between us?

I heard a branch snap behind me, but, before I could turn around, a hand clamped down over my mouth and a warm body pressed up against my back. The scream that escaped me was muted by his firm grip, but the fear swelled inside me—suffocating me as I struggled to breathe, fighting for every breath . . .

***

"No, . . . no, . . . no . . ." I screamed.

"Gemma, wake up, baby. Wake up."

I snapped open my eyes at the sound of his voice. Drew was shaking me awake. My body was covered in sweat, and I was trembling uncontrollably. He held me against his chest, rubbing his hand up and down my back, trying desperately to soothe me.

"It was just a dream, Gem. Just a dream."

My sobs erupted from his words; it wasn't just a bad dream. It was real, and my dreams were a vivid, detailed reminder of the nightmare that I had already lived through. He held me tighter while I cried. I was thankful for his comfort in that moment, but I knew that he was the reason it was all coming back again. His presence was too much, being here at the lake too much of a reminder.

When my sobs subsided, leaving behind only hiccuplike bursts of air—always the ugly aftermath of an emotional breakdown—I pushed Drew away.

"I'm sorry. I have to go," I whispered, as I frantically searched for my clothes that were strewn throughout the room. I pulled on my pants—not bothering with my panties —and my wrinkled shirt that was in a heap on the floor. With my bra and shoes in hand, I raced out of the bedroom, grabbing my purse along the way as I left Monroe Manor. I ran down the driveway toward my cabin, my bare feet aching from the sharp rocks in the road. I didn't let it slow me down. I reached my cabin—out of breath—and threw myself on my bed, hiding, in fear that Drew would follow me.

As expected, I heard him pounding on the cabin door a moment later. "Gemma, open the door. Talk to me. Please," he pleaded.

Realizing that I wasn't going to let him in, the knocking ceased.

"I don't know what that was all about, Gemma. But I'm here for you, if you want to talk about it." That was all I heard before he walked away.

***

I spent the day in bed, nursing my hangover, mourning my infidelity. Part of me felt guilty that I had broken my vows, but another part of me relished in the awakening of my soul, revived by Drew's touch. And I wondered if I could tell Drew my darkest secrets from that night, if I could trust him to be understanding without anger or judgment.

The way he had turned his back on me when I had needed him the most was almost as painful as the nightmare itself. I don't think that I could bear to lose him all over again. I feared the blame that he would direct toward me or the blame that he might place on himself. I knew all too well how the guilt would break him as it had me. I had blamed him for years until my therapist had helped me see who that blame belonged to. And yet it was still difficult to look at Drew and not think about the role he had played that night.

If he hadn't left me alone to cry in the woods, if he had trusted me enough to tell me how he felt in that moment rather than running away . . . But he was not the one who held me down against my will. He was not the thief who stole my virtue and my soul along with it; he was not the one who haunted my dreams. That was not Drew's fault. No, the one who held the key to my torment—my nightmares—was not Drew.

The blame belonged to his brother, William.

Bile rose in my throat from the mere thought of his name. How could I tell Drew that his only sibling, his own flesh and blood had raped me that night, the night that changed all of our lives?

The look of disgust and disappointment on Drew's face the morning after haunted my dreams almost as much as William's cold eyes. I had felt ashamed, dirty, but mostly broken as Drew said good-bye and stormed out of my life. Clutching a pillow to my chest, I tried to protect myself from the painful memories as I closed my eyes, succumbing to my exhaustion.

***

It was finally morning, and I stepped out of bed, exhausted from a sleepless night of ghosted whispers and phantom, brutal hands as the memory played out over and over again in my mind. I had squeezed my eyes closed tightly throughout the night, clamping my hands over my ears, trying to block out the image of his cold dark eyes and the sound of his voice whispering in my ear. I had fought it the entire night to no avail, as it was impossible to see, feel, or hear anything other than what I had in those shattering moments that I feared would haunt me for an eternity.

I took a long scolding-hot shower in hopes that I could wash his memory from my body. I scrubbed every inch of my skin until the raw pain was unbearable, and then I scrubbed some more. Even so, I could feel the filth on my skin, along with a sensation that it was seeping inside of me, through my skin, my body, my soul, leaving ruin in its wake. I pulled on a pair of sweats and a T-shirt and wrapped my wet hair into a loose bun.

In a desperate escape, avoiding my mother's questioning eyes and accusations, I ran to the beach. I sat in my favorite place, perched on the end of the dock, fighting against my despair. It wasn't long before I heard Drew walking toward me. It was hard to miss the sound of water sloshing beneath the slabs of wood that were floating on the lake, announcing Drew's approach.

I didn't turn to look at him, afraid that he would see the shame in my eyes. I wasn't sure what to say to him, and I felt the anger then, brewing just below the surface, slowly building. Part of me felt in that moment that he was the reason that it had happened in the first place. Emotions were running rampant inside me, and I could not grasp any one of them. I could not discern what it was that I was supposed to feel or what I wanted to feel or what I was afraid to feel. I felt too much.

Drew didn't sit beside me like he normally would have. I could hear him sigh in the still of the morning, his frustration evident in his silent brooding from where he stood behind me. I was expecting him to continue where we had left off the night before, still angry about my kiss with Logan—a part of the evening that now seemed so trivial. What I didn't expect was what he said next.

"I can't believe you, Gemma. Who are you? Obviously not the innocent girl who you led me to believe you were." His voice, hardened by sarcasm, could not hide the bitterness. I had never heard him speak with such disdain. I whipped my head around so fast, I felt a jolt of nerve sensations travel from my shoulder to my ear.

"William, Gem? Really? My own brother?"

His words sucked the air out of my lungs. I felt as if I might collapse right here on the dock where I sat. Before I could find words to convey my confusion and anger at his allegations, he continued.

"Don't you get it? You're not just my best friend, Gemma. I'm in love with you. I'm so in love with you, I can't see straight. That should have been me." He slapped his hands against his chest in anger as he shouted at me. "It should have been me!"

I flinched at his words and at the volume that he spoke them. I scrambled to my feet, using all my strength to stand tall and face him, despite feeling so weak and scared that my body trembled uncontrollably.

"Drew, it's not . . . it's not what you think," I stammered, tears spilling down my cheeks. "It wasn't . . . I didn't . . ." I tried to explain, the words threatening to push me off the cliff that I was standing on, afraid to say them, afraid of what it would mean if I did, afraid that it would be real.

"Forget it, Gemma," he said, shaking his head as he held up a hand to stop my incessant stuttering.

"Just listen to me," I screamed, pleading with him for a chance to explain.

"No. I don't really wanna hear the details. I just came to say good-bye. I'm leaving for school today. I can't stand to be here any longer."

A loud sob escaped me, and I folded my arms tightly across my chest as if I could hold it all in. I wanted to tell him what William had done, but I was scared. Drew was so angry.

"Please don't go." It was all I could say through my sobs.

"Bye, Gemma. Enjoy the rest of your summer," he scoffed as he walked back toward the beach, crossing the sand to his cabin. He disappeared moments later inside the wall of glass, and all I could do was stand there and watch him go.

I wanted to run after him, to make him hear the truth, to tell him that I loved him too. But I was frozen in place, paralyzed with fear, afraid of running into William. As if my heart wasn't already broken, I knew that I had just lost my best friend and the first boy who I had ever loved. And I needed him more than ever. I wanted to die in that moment, to end the pain and agony that was consuming me, and, in many ways, I did die that day—at least a part of me.

***

I opened my eyes gradually, overwhelmed with grief and a new sense of fear, rather than the jolting terror that usually woke me from my nightmares. I wiped the tears from my cheeks with the back of my hand, as I cried for the thousandth time over the moment that had replayed in my dream. And I wondered how I got here again, back to the scared sixteen-year-old girl who I had been. I had worked too hard—through years of therapy and self-reflection—to move on, to know my worth, to love myself again. And yet here I was, back at the scene of the crime—figuratively anyway—fighting with a fresh sense of self-hatred, fear, and anger. Not to mention loss—mourning everything that I had lost in that one night.

I considered myself a strong person, overcoming a traumatic event in my life and coming out on the other side a good person who lived an even better life. I was a lawyer, brilliant in the world of corporations and high-powered executives. I had made a small fortune, doing what I do best. I was proud of myself and all that I had worked for. And I had been happy and in love with Ryan, the perfect match for me, the other half to my whole, or so I had thought. I wanted for nothing, except the one thing that I couldn't seem to have no matter how hard I tried—a baby.

My perfect world was slowly unraveling, and I wanted to believe that it had all started the day that I had walked in on Ryan with that woman, but I knew it had started long before that. I had pushed away my husband, practically ran him straight into her arms. Of course Ryan had ultimately made the choice to betray me. We could have—should have—talked about our issues, our unhappiness. But my own fear of what I couldn't give him, the fear of Ryan realizing that I wasn't good enough for him—fear that stemmed from the night my self-worth was ripped from me—had driven a wedge between us. *I* had driven a wedge between us. My own self-loathing and insecurities had resurfaced at some point, leaving me to question everything that I had—or didn't have—and everything that I was.

It seemed as if I had come full circle, and I couldn't ignore fate's cruel knock on my door. I was back here again for a reason. Like I was being given a second chance to do it all over again, a chance to tell Drew what had happened. To set the story straight. And a chance for him to support me, to love me in spite of what happened. I wasn't sure if fate was giving us this chance for his benefit or for mine, maybe both, but I knew that I had to take it. I had to tell him the truth—eventually.

Eighteen

That night I dreamed that I was standing on the top of Indian Rock, afraid to jump, my heart beating loudly in my ears. I could hear my breath fill and empty my lungs, as if each one was my last. As I looked down into the cold blue water below, I could see a distorted image of Drew's face staring back at me. His expression shifted between hurt and disgust —as it was the morning when he had said good-bye all those years ago—to pure longing and satisfaction, the look that he held in his eyes while we were making love.

His voice called to me from somewhere in the distance—a throaty, whispery tone. "What are you afraid of, Gemma?"

The last thing I remembered before I was jolted from sleep was the image of empty dark eyes staring back at me as I fell from the rock, blackness closing in all around me. Wet. Cold. I woke, gasping for air, fighting for breath, as a fear of drowning shook my body to its core.

As dawn approached, I sat on the porch swing, hugging my knees to my chest with one hand and palming a steaming cup of coffee in the other. I frowned at the sight of my car parked in front of the cabin, wondering who had driven it here for me. *Logan or Drew*? I sighed at the thought of Drew. *What did the other night mean? What will happen between us now*? I was, after all, still legally married; this had to be a one-time thing. And, in my heart, as much as I wanted to pretend that it was over, I still pictured Ryan as my future, the father of my children. I may not be *in* love with Ryan, but, underneath the anger and despair, I definitely still loved him. There were moments when I wished that I didn't, but he had been my entire world for so long, and those feelings don't change overnight.

I wondered how many more days I could spend with Drew before I had to tell him what happened. I hadn't spoken of it in years. I had tried to bury it deep inside during high school, where it slowly killed me one day at a time, robbing me of sleep, happiness, and a sense of security. When I had started college, I had confessed for the first time what had happened to me during a drunken game of truth or dare with my roommate, Cassie, and two other friends who I had grown close to. I remembered how it had felt to finally say it out loud.

Lexi had admitted to having an abortion during her junior year of high school after choosing truth to avoid the dare of running through the commons of our dorm naked. Christy had revealed her deep, dark secret of a cocaine addiction that she spent most of her senior year recovering from in rehab. And I had blurted out that I had been raped by my best friend's older brother, instantly wishing that I had chosen dare. In that moment I would have gladly streaked through the commons than deal with the looks on their faces as they processed what my words meant.

They had asked a million questions, and I had answered them as best as I could, tears falling endlessly as I recounted each terrorizing moment. When they discovered that I had never told anyone and that I still had nightmares nearly every time I closed my eyes, they had suggested that I talk to someone, professionally, about it. I had been defensive at first, denying my need for help, but they had soon persuaded me.

Lexi was seeing a campus therapist, to deal with the guilt and shame of her abortion, and Christy had shared how much her therapist in rehab had helped her. And so a week later I had started seeing Dr. Shepley, a campus therapist who specialized in date rape and sexual assault. Dr. Shepley—or Jude, as I called her now—had been my therapist for nearly twenty years. She had slowly brought me back to life, and I still went to see her occasionally, but not as often as I probably should have—given all the failed attempts to have a baby with Ryan.

Ryan knew about my visits with Jude. He knew everything.

After a year of dating, Ryan had grown tired of the distance that I had kept between us intimately. I was having trouble with the sexual part of our relationship. I hadn't slept with anyone before, my one and only sexual encounter being the sole thing in my life that I longed to forget. Jude had insisted that I trust Ryan with the truth, assuring me that, if he really loved me, he would be understanding and patient. And, of course, she had been right. Ryan was amazing, and, when we finally did have sex, it was incredible. I felt as if he had taken something from William and had given it back to me, allowing me to feel a sense of power and control over my body again.

I never told my mom, only to protect her from the pain. There wasn't anything that she could have done, and I knew she would feel as if she had failed me, unable to protect me from William, someone who she had trusted and had loved like a son. This realization would have left her broken, and there was no reason to let it destroy both of us. I also feared that she would press charges or contact Mr. Monroe. I wasn't blind to the fact that it was my word against William's, and Mr. Monroe would have used his high-powered attorneys to protect his son and his name at all costs. I could not have survived any public knowledge of what had happened. I had just wanted to move on, to try to get my life back. And I had done just that. Yet here I was, reliving it all again, struggling with the decision to tell or not to tell.

The sun was rising in the clear blue sky, and I could feel the temperature rise as well. I retreated into the cabin to put on my swimsuit and pack a beach bag. Twenty minutes later, I walked down the road in my black bikini hidden beneath a black cover-up, large brim sun hat, and a bag filled with a water bottle, salted almonds, and a new historical fiction novel that I had bought months ago and had never had the time to read. Now all I had was time. Time to sleep, time to read, time to cook, too much damn time to think.

I laid a beach towel on the dock, pulled my cover-up over my head, and lounged on my stomach, propped up on my elbows to read my book. The sun felt warm on my skin as I listened to the gentle waves lap against the dock, slowly rocking me to sleep.

***

"You might want to try sunscreen next time."

I heard his voice, abruptly pulling me from my unexpected nap. It took me a moment to orient myself, but, realizing where I was, I quickly sat up. "Oh, my God, what time is it?" I asked, pulling my mangled hat from my head and rubbing my eyes.

"It's about two o'clock. And judging by the color of your back, I'm guessing that you've been out here for a while."

As soon as he mentioned it, I could feel the pain from the severe sunburn that spread across the skin of my back and the backside of my legs. I winced.

"Here I brought you some aloe vera cream. Let me put some on your back." Drew sat down behind me as I pulled my knees into my chest and wrapped my arms around my legs.

He pulled my braid to the side and over my shoulder, brushing my neck with his hand as he swept loose strands out of his way. This simple gesture felt so sensual, intimate. "Thanks." I gasped at the coldness of the cream and the feel of his hands on my skin.

"Sorry," Drew said.

"It's okay. Just cold." A shiver spread through me even though the sun was hot and intense. His touch evoked memories from two nights ago, when he had his hands, as well as his lips, all over my body. He gently massaged the cream into my skin, and I closed my eyes, savoring his touch. I felt his breath on the back of my neck and then his warm, wet lips as he softly kissed me behind the ear, trailing the tip of his nose down to my shoulder.

I froze and turned my head to look at him. "Drew. Stop."

"I can't control myself around you, Gem. You're so beautiful, you take my breath away." His voice was almost a whisper against my skin, sending chills through my body.

"We can't do this, Drew." I sighed. My words were coming from my head, a contradiction to what my heart was saying.

"I know." He sighed heavily. "You're right," he said as he shimmied to my left to sit next to me.

I reached for my black cover-up and pulled it on over my head, adjusting the thin fabric over my bare thighs.

Drew straightened his legs until his feet and calves were submerged in the water, and I did the same.

We both sat in silence watching a boat zoom by, pulling a teenage boy on a wakeboard. He jumped the wake, catching several feet of air before landing effortlessly behind the boat. The noise from the engine quieted as the boat's distance grew.

"It seems so cruel that we've found each other again after all these years, and yet we still can't be together." He sighed loudly again, our eyes never leaving the lake. "Maybe it was never meant to be. You and me."

I watched my feet as I kicked them slowly in the water, creating small waves that sloshed against the dock. I wasn't sure how to respond. I felt the same way. But I also felt that there was a reason that we had found each other again.

"Will you let me cook you dinner tonight?" I asked as I looked over at him, meeting his gaze. "We may not be able to be together in that way, but you're my friend, Drew. Let's focus on that. What do you say?" I bumped his arm with my elbow. "Bill Sherwood brought me a huge rainbow trout that he caught yesterday, and I have some fresh vegetables from the farmers' market." I tried to persuade him.

"You're really gonna give me the 'Let's just be friends' spiel after the other night?"

I flashed him my most innocent expression.

"Okay, friend. Sounds nice," he conceded.

He smiled at me, a real genuine smile that reached his eyes, and I was suddenly overcome with love for him. Not so much in a romantic way, but a deeper love that was embedded in my very core. He had been a part of my life longer than I could remember, and, though we had been apart for years, he had never really left me.

Nineteen

I slipped on a pair of gold hoop earrings, straightening my hair with my hands, as I took one more look at myself in the full-length mirror. I glanced at the flowing coral-colored dress that hung to my knees, contrasting nicely with my long golden hair that I had curled around my face. I left my feet bare and my makeup subtle, natural. I was fidgeting with the three-quarter-length sleeves of my dress when I realized that I was nervous. I was not sure what was bringing on these nerves. Maybe it was the idea that I was feigning friendship, when I knew that, deep inside, I harbored deeper feelings and a crazy attraction for Drew. Maybe it was the possibility that the truth might come out. Whatever it was, I had to get myself under control.

I went to the kitchen to distract myself with the task of getting dinner started. I had already prepared the fish, which I planned to grill outside on the back patio. A green salad—topped with Bosc pears, gorgonzola cheese crumbles, and chopped walnuts—sat in the refrigerator, ready to be tossed with a creamy vinaigrette dressing. I took the fresh summer squash, zucchini, and red potatoes that I had bought at the farmers' market, sliced them into thick pieces and placed them on a piece of foil. I brushed them with a creamy herb butter and set them aside to grill later with the fish. I felt so at home in the small kitchen where I had spent many days and nights helping my mother or grandmother cook. Or my favorite mornings when I stood on a chair and helped my grandpa flip his famous dollar-size hotcakes on the griddle.

I heard a light knock. Wiping my hands on a dish towel, I took a deep breath and walked to the door. Drew was standing on the porch, handsome as ever, wearing a navy polo shirt, khaki shorts, and a pair of brown leather flip-flops. His light brown hair was still damp but glistening with product in a messy style. I felt my cheeks heat as I took him in, my heart beating wildly in my chest.

He stepped inside and kissed my cheek. "Hey, beautiful," he said, as I felt his lips on my skin. "Here, I brought wine." He handed me a chilled bottle of Chardonnay.

I reached up and brushed a hand over my warm cheek where his lips had just been. "Thank you," I said, taking the bottle from his hand. "Would you like a glass?" I asked, as he followed me to the kitchen.

"Would love a glass." He smiled at me.

I set the bottle on the counter and rummaged through a drawer until I found an old corkscrew.

"Here, let me do that," he said, taking it from me.

I pulled two wine glasses from the cabinet, setting them down on the counter near Drew as he twisted the corkscrew until it was no longer visible. His muscles on his arm flexed when he pulled the cork from the bottle in one swift move. As he poured the wine into our glasses, something caught my eye. Black ink on the inside of his forearm. I couldn't believe that I hadn't noticed it before. When he set down the wine bottle, I reached out and held his hand in mine, turning his palm up until the tattoo was clearly visible. I ran my hand over the symbol, familiar yet different. I traced the bold black line with the tip of my finger. I looked up at Drew's face to find him watching me with a stoic expression.

"You got it too?" I asked.

He nodded, his eyes never leaving mine.

"It's different. What does it mean?" I asked, looking down again at the broken infinity symbol that was permanently etched in his skin, positioned lengthwise halfway between his wrist and elbow. Still holding his hand in my left, I turned the palm up on my right hand, holding my wrist alongside his.

He traced my tattoo with his own finger.

I had used the drawing that Drew had done when we were younger. The infinity symbol that we had promised to tattoo on the inside of our wrist, to mark our eternal friendship. We had never had the chance to get the tattoos, together, like we had planned.

But I had done it anyway—alone—when I had turned eighteen, needing to hold on to a part of Andrew. A part of my life that had once brought me happiness and security, a reminder that no matter what had happened, he would always hold that special place in my heart. I wanted to hold on to the Drew that I had known my entire life before everything got confusing and messy, before I grew to resent him, hate him, blame him.

Drew had made my design more feminine with ivy wrapping around the thin line, while the design he had drawn for himself was a bolder, more masculine English script from what I remembered. But what was on his forearm was not the symbol that he had designed years ago. It was different.

"It's stupid. I got this when I was eighteen." He shrugged, pulling his arm from my grasp.

His words brought my gaze back to his face. "What does it mean?" I asked again.

He looked straight into my eyes, pinning me in place. "It's to remind me that nothing lasts forever." The pain that I saw in his eyes broke my heart. The idea that this symbol reminded him daily of the way our lives had been torn apart back then, that he might live with bitterness and resentment in his heart, brought on a new meaning to the regret I felt about how things had ended.

He picked up our wine glasses, handing me one as he raised his in the air. "To reconnecting?" he toasted in a questioning tone.

I clinked my glass against his. "To reconnecting." I sipped my wine as I watched him down the entire glass before pouring another.

Drew helped me start the old grill and took over the cooking duties. "Manning the grill," he had called it, as if it was a man's job. We talked about all the neighbors as we stood near the barbecue, waiting for the fish to cook. Drew filled me in on all the recent gossip that he had learned since he had arrived, like the news that Mr. Hunter, who was well into his fifties, had left his wife for a woman half his age and now had a newborn son, or the fact that Jacob's old friend, Martin Basil, now went by Maureen after undergoing gender reassignment surgery.

He told me which families still came to the lake and who had sold their cabins to new families. I felt a familiar pang in my gut as he spoke of all the kids who we had grown up with. Most were married now and had children of their own. The idea that my childhood friends had children and were spending their summers here at the lake, recreating our memories, brought about a burning jealously that I couldn't deny. I wanted that more than anything. It was funny what we take for granted. The idea of getting married, being a mother. It was always the plan for as long as I could remember. But wanting something wasn't a guarantee. It doesn't happen that easily for everyone.

We sat down to eat at the table for two that I had set on the deck that overlooked the creek. We both began the meal in silence. I ate my salad first, while Drew focused on the fish.

As if reading my mind, Drew asked, "So how about you? Any plans for children?"

I swallowed the lump in my throat as I took another sip of my wine. My eyes settled on my finger, tracing the rim of my glass as I contemplated what to say. "We tried. Ryan and I, but I haven't been able to conceive. We've tried everything. In the end we finally settled on trying the old-fashioned way. Ya know, hoping for a miracle." I took a deep breath, remembering the last time that Ryan and I had made love.

My ovulation kit had confirmed that I was ovulating, and I had told Ryan as much. We had fallen into our usual roles, undressing ourselves, pulling back the bedding and laying down next to each other. My hands had roamed, finding what I needed and making sure that he was ready. It was hard to think about the emotional connection and sexual chemistry that had seemed to evaporate from our relationship.

The sex was only a method, a procedure, that was hopefully going to result in a pregnancy, a means to an end. We had held each other out of habit, shared only a few brief kisses as Ryan had spilled into me. I hadn't even had an orgasm. My thoughts had only centered around what was happening inside my body, actually visualizing his sperm fertilizing my egg—a technique suggested by my yoga instructor. Once we were done, Ryan had waited a few minutes before breaking our connection and then had kissed me on the forehead—a gesture that only confirmed my fears —and retreated to the bathroom to take a shower. I had placed two pillows under my hips and settled in for the hour that I would lie still with my hips elevated as I breathed deeply, continuing my visualization.

It was only a week later that I found Ryan in bed—the same bed that we had shared—with that woman. I felt an ache in my heart, thinking of how distant Ryan and I had become, unable to ignore the festering guilt from the sheer fact that it was somehow my fault.

"I'm sorry, Gemma. That must be so hard on you." Drew's voice pulled me from my thoughts. "Have you considered adoption?"

"Ryan's open to adoption, but I have my heart set on carrying my own child. I haven't been able to think about anything else." I was trying hard not to break down in front of him. "I want it so bad," I said, barely a whisper.

Drew reached over and rested his hand on mine, comforting me.

Our eyes met for a brief moment before I freed my hand from his, tucking a stray hair behind my ear. "And you? Kids in your future? Wife?" I asked, redirecting the conversation to him.

"Probably not," he said, swirling his wine in his glass before taking a drink.

"Why do you say that?" I asked, now curious how he seemed so sure of this.

"I don't know. I just don't see either in my future." He shrugged. "That was delicious, Gem. It was nice to have a home-cooked meal for once," he added, letting me know that the subject was closed for discussion.

"You're welcome." We cleared the table, taking our dishes into the kitchen. I washed while Drew dried, and we continued talking, this time about our childhood.

"I'll never forget the look on your face," Drew said while he shook his head back and forth, smiling at the memory. He was recalling a day when we had been catching frogs in the creek; I remembered it like it was yesterday.

"I still have nightmares about that. I can see it all clear as day. Reaching for that frog through the ferns only to realize that it was inside the mouth of a snake. Gross." I shuddered as the image flashed in my mind. The snake's head had been suspended in the air as it turned to look at me.

"You screamed so loud, my ears were ringing for hours. But the best part . . . the best part was watching you try to backpedal in the rushing current, falling right on your ass," Drew stammered, his words riddled with laughter. "You would have thought it was a cobra rather than a harmless garter snake."

I was trying to contain my own laughter as I imagined the scene through Drew's eyes; the image of me scrambling to get away from that snake, with a look of what could only be sheer horror on my face. "You know my fear of snakes, venom or no venom," I said as I rinsed a plate with clean water and handed it to Drew.

"I know. That look, though, classic," he said, shaking his head as he wiped the plate dry and set it aside.

Drew looked at me then, his features pulled into a dramatic fearful expression, mocking me. Tears were streaming down my cheeks as I laughed at the memory and Drew's ridiculous face. I was unable to wipe them away while my hands were submerged in a sinkful of soapy water, so Drew leaned in and wiped the tears from my face with the dish towel.

"That was *not* funny. I was terrified." But I laughed as I defended my reaction. "I still hate snakes," I said as I shuddered at the thought.

"No, I'm pretty sure it was funny," Drew said, beaming from where he stood beside me. He was standing so close to me that our sides were touching, and I was more aware of this than I should've been.

When the dishes were done, we both stood in the kitchen, unsure of what was next.

"Well."

"So do you . . ." I said at the same time. We both laughed.

"After you," Drew said, nodding toward me.

"I was going to ask if you wanted more wine. We could sit on the porch and catch the sunset?"

"That sounds great." He smiled, and I returned a grin, happy to have my friend back in my life.

We retreated to the front porch, swaying on the porch swing while sipping our wine. I had opened my favorite bottle of Merlot and had offered Drew my box of coveted mystic mint cookies. We sat in silence, taking in the canvas of colored clouds that were painted across the sky as the sun dropped slowly in the horizon. The lake was glasslike, offering a clear reflection of the sky above. The view never got old. Silence had fallen over us, Drew and I each lost in our own thoughts.

I could hear Drew chew quietly as he bit into a cookie. "I can't believe you still eat these. I haven't seen a box in years," he said with his mouth full.

"Me either. I found them at the General Store, on the same shelf where they always were. It was as if they were just waiting for me." I laughed. "I bought every box they had and asked the clerk to order more."

"Nice." Drew smirked and tossed another one in his mouth, not bothering to bite into it this time.

"Yeah, well, don't eat them all. I have a limited supply," I said, grabbing the box from his hands and biting into one myself.

"Remember when you used to hide a box of these in your Barbie case, knowing that Jacob would never find them there?"

I smiled at the memory. "Yes, I remember. And then we started hiding our beer there when we got older. In fact I wouldn't be surprised if there were still a few cans of Budweiser in that old Barbie case." We both laughed, remembering the good times, the simple days of our youth.

Drew reached over and held my hand, interlacing our fingers. "I missed you, Gem," he whispered.

Our gazes were fixed on the sun as its apex dipped behind the mountains, signifying the finality of the day— casting a dull haze of fire across the sky.

"I missed you too," I said, as I rested my head against his shoulder, savoring the peace of the moment.

Twenty

I had another bad dream. I knew that I should tell Drew the truth, but I was scared. We hadn't talked about his brother at all. We had talked about my brother, Drew asking me a million questions about Jacob. Where he lived, what he did for a living, if we were close. I had told him how Jacob was a free spirit, so different from me. He had gone to the Seattle Art Institute and immediately started his own company designing surfboards, skateboards, snowboards . . . every kind of board really. He traveled the world to places like Bali, Switzerland, New Zealand. He enjoyed extreme sports, spending his ample spare time surfing, skydiving, snowboarding, or whatever fulfilled his "ultimate rush" quota.

I told Drew that we were close but didn't see each other very often, between Jacob's traveling and my work schedule. Jacob always sent me a postcard when he reached a new destination, and I kept all of them, pinned up on a corkboard in my home office. We talked about my mother. Drew genuinely missed her, and that made me sad, to think that what had happened between us had kept him away from everyone in my family. We had even talked about his father and what a self-righteous ass he still was, but neither of us brought up William. I wondered where he was, what kind of man he had become, and what had happened between the two brothers. *Were they close or estranged or somewhere in between?*

Drew and William had once been inseparable. Only three years apart, they were thick as thieves. After Katherine had died, the light in William's eyes had slowly faded, until no one could recognize the boy who he had been. His father was hard on him, always comparing him to Andrew, and William had grown to resent Drew and his father. The trouble began not long after he had started the ninth grade. He had been expelled from several boarding schools, until his father had no choice but to send William to public school. He had continued to find trouble and eventually got involved in drugs. Their father had practically given up. He wasn't around much anyway; the boys were mostly raised by Matilda, who had been in their family since Katherine's diagnosis.

I knew, deep down, that the old William would never have hurt me the way he did. I knew, even back then, that William's drug abuse had turned him into someone else, the monster that had shattered my world that night. I always wondered if he was even aware of what really happened or had he been so drunk and high that he had imagined it another way. It was easier to believe that theory over the alternative. But regardless of his mental state that night, he did rape me, and I knew that it was only a matter of time before the subject of that night was brought into question.

William and that night were the only topics that Drew and I seemed to have skipped over, but I could feel the questions coming, the questions that were burning in Drew's mind, practically hanging from his tongue. He also seemed to be avoiding any questions about his life and why he was at the lake. I knew that he was keeping something from me, but, unsure of what it was, I was almost too afraid to ask.

Drew and I had spent nearly every day together. The weather was getting warmer now that summer was in full swing. We took long walks along the trail that led to the marina, where we would sit and eat ice cream sandwiches while we watched tourists launch their boats into the lake. We had gone sailing twice in the small catamaran that Drew's family owned, taking advantage of the gusty winds of early summer. We had spent a day hiking at Granite Falls. I had forgotten how beautiful it was, and we had searched for our shoes that we had nailed to the cedar shoe tree years ago. The shoe tree was famous, adorned with hundreds of different styles and colors of footwear that people had nailed to its trunk or hung from its branches. It was a silly tradition but had become a rite of passage, an offering of sorts. Drew tried to talk me into nailing up our shoes again, for old time's sake, but I refused to part with my two-hundred-dollar running shoes.

It was the Fourth of July. A sacred day of tradition at the lake. The weather was beautiful, uncharacteristically cooperating for a day of outdoor family fun and a night of fireworks. Traditionally it would rain on the Fourth of July, summer officially starting the following day. The neighbors were busy preparing dishes for the potluck dinner that we would share at dusk on the sandy beach. Drew and I never really discussed it, but it was assumed that we would spend it together on our beach, like we had countless times before while we were growing up.

I was baking a huckleberry pie, with the huckleberries that Drew and I had picked the day before, and had whipped up a macaroni salad using my mother's recipe. She was famous on the lane for this salad, and, in keeping with tradition, I thought that it was only right to bring it to the potluck. Logan was joining us and most likely bringing whatever flavor he was sampling this week. We couldn't keep up with his shenanigans.

Drew came by the cabin to help me carry my things down to the beach. We made our rounds, Drew introducing me to all the new families on the lane. The families who I did know introduced me to their spouses and children. Memories flooded my heart as I looked into familiar eyes and shared stories from our youth. Logan showed up just as we were all sitting down to eat. He had a young blonde woman on his arm. He introduced her as Shannon, and we invited them to sit with us.

There were at least a dozen children ranging in age from two to sixteen. I choked back my jealousy and instead immersed myself in their world. Playing beach games and building sand castles. One little boy in particular seemed to warm up to me instantly. He was adorable with tight curly brown hair, olive skin, and huge brown eyes. He wore a red cape and a matching shirt with a big *K* embroidered on the front.

When I asked him if he was a superhero, he stood up straight and proud, raising one hand in the air and proclaimed, "I'm the Kadenator!" He was the sweetest thing, his enthusiasm contagious, and I couldn't help but laugh at his ardent imagination. I sat on the beach with him as together we built "a planet" out of damp sand, and then I watched as he pretended to rescue it from an evil nemesis who was trying to destroy the universe.

I couldn't help but wonder if the parents all knew how lucky they were, to have a family. I bit my tongue when I listened to the mothers complain about the lack of sleep or the temper tantrums. It wasn't their fault. I was sure I would have similar complaints if I were in their shoes. I would give up sleep for the next twenty years if it meant that I could spend them with a child of my own. I could feel Drew's gaze on me throughout the evening, watching me play with the children. Every now and then, our gazes would meet, and he would smile, flashing me those dimples that I loved so much.

As the sun disappeared and the night sky grew dark, we all gathered around a roaring bonfire preparing for fireworks. I felt relaxed and happy, having spent the day with friends—old and new. I had even gotten to know Shannon pretty well, and she seemed smart and kind, a far cry from Logan's usual catch. I couldn't help but wonder where this road would lead me. Where I would wind up in the end. If my marriage was salvageable or if I would be alone. *If I couldn't save my marriage, would I ever be able to move on? And, more important, what would become of my dream of being a mother?*

It was hard to believe that I had been at the lake for over a month, each day drifting into the next unnoticed. I seemed to lose all track of time here without a grueling schedule to mark my days and nights. Maybe throwing my phone into the lake wasn't such a bad move after all. I was completely out of touch with work, my friends, my family. With Ryan. But for once, I didn't care. I knew that I would have to face Ryan soon. I knew that I would have to eventually ask the questions that would lead me to the truth. I was aware that I had a long, hard road ahead of me, but it was so easy to get lost here, to forget everything that was waiting for me back home. I would have to deal with it all soon enough, so, for now, I pushed aside these thoughts, unwilling to allow them to spoil the happiness I felt from the present days.

Twenty-One

I sat back in my beach chair, and watched Drew and Logan line up an arsenal of fireworks, their faces lit up like children in the light from the bonfire. They had driven to Canada the week before and had loaded up on fireworks for the occasion, spending hundreds of dollars. Drew wanted to give the kids a show to remember, but, watching him now, it was obvious that he was enjoying it just as much as they were.

The first set erupted into the sky, the thunderous explosion causing my heart to hammer in my chest as my eyes took in the spectacular array of colors lighting up the darkness. The children watched in awe as they cheered and begged for more. Drew and Logan continued their elaborate fireworks display, each one bigger and better than the one before, the grand finale taking my breath away. The crowd on the beach cheered, and Drew and Logan took a bow, before retreating back to the empty chairs near Shannon and me.

"So what did you think?" Drew asked as he sat down beside me and rested his hand on my leg.

"That was amazing. Well done."

"Thank you. It was fun, and I think the kids liked it." He beamed.

"Are you kidding me? They loved it," I said as I reached into the cooler next to me and grabbed a beer for Drew, twisting the cap off before handing it to him.

He tapped his bottle against mine and then took a long pull, wiping his mouth with the back of his hand when he was done. "Ah, isn't this great? Just like the old days," he said as we watched the kids roast marshmallows in the fire.

"Yeah, this is great," I agreed. And it was.

Kaden appeared before me, offering me a roasted pink Starburst on the end of a stick.

"Here try this," he said as I pulled the warm sticky blob from the stick.

I put it in my mouth and began to chew as a burst of flavor erupted on my tongue. "Wow, that's good," I said to Kaden as he beamed at me. "Thank you."

"You're welcome," he said, a blush spreading across his cheeks. He scampered away with his stick.

"Someone likes you," Drew teased. "Poor kid, I should warn him of your wrath now before it's too late." Drew had the biggest smile on his face, but I still flashed him an incredulous look as I punched him in the shoulder playfully.

"Jeez, Gem, stop hitting me already," he sulked as he rubbed his shoulder.

"Baby," I teased.

"Bully," he retorted. And I smiled at our familiar banter, feeling at home and grateful that I was here with Drew.

It grew late, and the families with young children slowly made their way back to their cabins to put the kids to bed. I said good-night to Kaden, promising to go swimming with him sometime soon as my heart swelled for this little boy. What I wouldn't have given to be tucking my own child into bed at that moment.

Eventually it was just the four of us. We sat around the fire, drinking and sharing stories.

"Gemma, you were so hot in high school," Logan teased while we were reminiscing about old times.

"Oh, stop." I giggled, a result of too many beers. "You were pretty hot too, Logan, but, of course, you already knew that."

"Yeah, no woman could resist what I had to offer," he said, running his hand down his abs until they landed on his crotch where he cupped his genitals through his jeans.

"You are such a pervert," Shannon said and slugged him in the arm.

"Yeah, you perv," I called out as I threw a bottle cap at him.

Drew laughed beside me and shook his head at Logan, unwilling to defend him.

"Hey, if I recall, Gemma, you didn't complain the last time I had my tongue down your throat." He was clearly teasing as he rubbed his arm where Shannon had hit him, but his comment hit me square in the gut, taking me back to that night.

Drew tensed beside me, his jaw taut, his hands in a death grip around his beer bottle.

Silence filled the air, heavy with tension. I tried to play it off, to go back to the light conversation that we were all engaged in just moments before. "Very funny, Logan.

Does anyone need another beer?" I asked, opening the cooler beside me, hoping to change the subject.

"I'll take one," Drew grumbled beside me. I doled out a beer to everyone except Shannon, who politely declined. I watched Drew drain the entire bottle before throwing it at the recycle bucket that sat ten feet from us. The bottle landed in the bucket and shattered, sending a loud clash into the quiet night.

"I'm out. Logan, you guys are welcome to crash at my place. I'll leave the side door open." Drew stood and started to walk toward his cabin. "Good night," he mumbled.

I stood to follow him, knowing that he was upset. "Drew, wait," I called out after him.

"Stay, Gemma. I'll see you tomorrow," he said without looking back.

I stopped and looked at Logan, debating on what I should do. *Give Drew his space or go to him?*

"Don't look at me, Gem. I don't know *what* his fucking problem is," Logan said, holding his hands up innocently.

I looked back toward Drew's cabin; he was almost to the door. I kicked off my flip-flops and chased after him.

"Drew, wait," I called out breathlessly when I had nearly caught up to him. He stepped into the dark cabin, and I followed him inside. I could see fireworks erupting into the dark sky on the other side of the lake through the wall of windows before me.

"Gemma, I need to be alone right now."

"That was a long time ago. Don't let Logan get to you," I said, still catching my breath.

"You're right. It was a long time ago, but I still feel angry when I think about that night. The jealousy that consumed me watching you kiss him like that. It was crazy, and I was so confused by it. I screwed up everything. I was just a stupid kid. But what *you* did . . ." His hands were fisted at his sides, his muscles straining underneath his shirt, the veins in his neck pulsed through his skin as he shook his head at me. His eyes burned in the dim light. "The hatred I felt for you the next day, when I had to listen to . . ." He stopped, unsure if he wanted to continue.

My gut churned, bile rising in my throat, knowing what he was going to say next. I folded my arms across my chest tightly, desperately trying to hold myself together, to keep from falling apart.

He ran his hand through his hair and looked away briefly, as if contemplating what he was going to say next. "I had this image of you. An image that didn't fit the Gemma that I knew, *my* Gemma. It made me sick, and I hated you. I had to listen to Will tell me how good you were. How good you felt when he fucked you." His words stunned me. He scrubbed his hand over his mouth as if he were shocked by his own words. But he had said them, he couldn't take it back.

Tears filled my eyes as I swallowed hard, the bile leaving a raw burn in its wake as it traveled down the back of my throat.

"I still don't get it, Gemma. Why William? He was a fuck-up. He was *my* brother. Why would you choose him? You were better than that. At least I thought you were. But maybe I was wrong. Maybe you weren't a virgin like you had led me to believe." He stood with his hands on his hips, spouting angry words at me, judging me.

And I just stood there in shock, letting his words wash over me, coating me with shame. I couldn't articulate what needed to be said.

I felt Drew's hands on my arms, gripping me tight—too tight.

"Say something," he demanded, shaking me. "Explain this to me. I'm tired of dancing around what happened that night. I want you to tell me why."

I was numb, unable to speak as I looked into his angry eyes, dark and intense.

"You broke my fucking heart, Gemma," he yelled, his hands still gripping me tightly.

Tears streamed down my face as I choked on my own sobs. Drew released me, and I sank to my knees, unable to stand on my own two feet. I buried my face in my hands, sobs raking my body.

"You have nothing to say?" he asked, still angry.

Why won't he stop? I couldn't take any more of this. I was breaking into a million pieces before him, and his venom continued to spill from his mouth.

"Why? Why did you fuck my brother that night, Gemma?"

I snapped. I couldn't take it anymore. I looked up at him, meeting his gaze as he towered over me. "I didn't fuck him," I screamed. "HE RAPED ME. WILLIAM RAPED ME." I fought for air, gasping for breath that wouldn't come. I had said it. I had finally said it. I struggled to take a few deep breaths, hugging myself tightly as I rocked back and forth on my knees. "Happy now? Please stop, just stop. I can't take this anymore," I whispered through the sobs that tore through me. My body shook with anger and despair, as I waited for his reaction, watching him through my tears.

"What did you just say?" he asked, his voice so quiet, a stark contrast to the volume at which he had shouted just moments before. Confusion settled in across his face.

"He raped me that night," I whispered, closing my eyes as I felt my words—the truth—escape me. I felt utterly exhausted all of a sudden.

"Will . . . What? . . . How? . . . Why didn't you tell me?" he stuttered, at a loss for words.

"I tried to tell you, but you were so angry, and I was scared."

Drew hung his head in defeat and sank to his knees in front of me. Tears welled in his eyes as he looked at me. I could see the pain and regret in the depth of his gaze as I watched a grown man's strength crumble, and it tore me apart inside.

"I'm so sorry, Gemma," he said, shaking his head from side to side. And, as if the last twenty years had just replayed in his mind, he buried his face in his hands and mumbled through his own tortured sobs, "Oh, my God, I'm so sorry."

I didn't know what to say. I couldn't absolve him; I couldn't tell him that it was okay. Because none of this was okay. It wasn't his fault, but his hurtful words were still fresh on his tongue, still echoing in my heart. We sat on our knees with our bodies facing one another but unable to look each other in the eye, unable to stop the flow of agony that spilled down our faces from the raw truth that was finally exposed between us. We were both defenseless from the grief that threatened to break us, as we relived all that was taken from us, all that was lost.

After what felt like forever, Drew wiped his face with the bottom of his shirt and finally spoke. "I don't know what to say. I hate myself for the way I treated you. I hate myself for leaving you that night. I want to kill Will. I want to kill him right now, this minute, for hurting you. I don't know how to make this better, Gemma. Fuck, all these years . . ." His voice trailed off, the pain robbing him of his voice.

I wiped my face with the sleeve of my sweatshirt. I reached for his hands and held them in mine. "Drew, look at me." I waited for him to raise his head and meet my eyes. "None of this is your fault. Please don't blame yourself. I've worked through what happened, and I'm okay."

He raised his eyebrows at me, unconvinced.

"Well, mostly okay," I said. "This isn't really William's fault either, Drew. He wasn't himself that summer, you know that. He was a mess, and I truly believe that he didn't mean to hurt me."

"But all that time, I hated you. And instead I should have been there for you, Gem. How can I not blame myself for that? And Will? Don't make excuses for him, Gemma," he pleaded, shaking his head. "My whole life, people have made excuses for him. He hurt you. How could anyone hurt you like that?" He ran his hands through his hair, gripping the ends forcefully in despair. "I want to kill him," he said through clenched teeth. He stood and walked away from me, pacing back and forth as he dragged his hand over his face several times. He finally stopped and placed both of his hands on a console table, leaning over it as if to calm himself.

I watched him as he sucked in long, deep breaths and blew them out forcefully—one after another. I didn't know what to say, so I just watched him as he broke apart before my very eyes, feeling my own tears fall endlessly down my cheeks. I didn't even move to swipe them away.

Without warning Drew suddenly let out an anguished cry as his arm swept across the top of the table, knocking everything in its path to the ground in a violent crash.

My heart stopped beating in the moment, startled by his outburst as the sound that came from his throat vibrated deep inside me. I could feel his rage as it rolled off his taut body in waves. I knew that he was moving through each stage of his grief in record time and that his anger was a valid part of it, but I also knew how that fury would burn through him, killing his soul a little piece at a time until he didn't recognize himself any longer.

"It won't change anything, your anger. I've been there, trust me. It won't change what happened," I said, surprised by my own voice.

He took another deep, but calming breath and knelt down in front of me again. "What do you want from me, Gemma? How can I make this better?" he asked in desperation, with a need to fix what was broken, to find a solution. It couldn't be fixed; there was no solution. I had learned that a long time ago.

"Just hold me," I whispered. Without hesitation, he scooped me up and pulled me into his lap. I placed my face against his chest, feeling his arms wrapped tightly around me as his hand gently brushed my hair to the side. I could feel his breath against my scalp as he rested the side of his face on top of my head, drawing me in as close as possible. His heart was beating fast and hard against my cheek, and I wondered if it was still his anger that burned through him or something else. Tears fell down my face as I remembered how badly I had needed this from him that morning, the morning that he had broken what was left of my heart. Maybe I could finally heal, maybe we could both heal together, and I could put this all behind me for good.

Twenty-Two

I woke in the morning in Drew's arms. We were lying on the floor just inside the door that led to the beach, wrapped up in each other, still fully clothed from the night before. We hadn't moved the entire night. Although somehow our heads were resting on pillows from the couch and a blanket had been thrown over the top of us. Drew squeezed me tight as I stirred. My head throbbed, and my face hurt from sinus congestion, most likely from crying all night. I stretched my body as much as I could with the way Drew was holding me. My muscles felt stiff and sore. When I looked up into Drew's face, I was surprised to find him awake and staring back at me.

"I can't believe that I slept like this."

"I didn't want to wake you," he said in a hoarse voice.

"Did you sleep?" I asked, worried by the dark circles under his eyes.

"Not really." He sighed and pulled my face against his chest once again, threading his fingers through my hair. And, as if he had been lying there thinking the entire night, waiting for me to wake so that he could say what was on his mind, he said, "I shouldn't have left you that night. I took you to that party, and we had all been drinking, and then I just abandoned you. I was supposed to take care of you, to protect you. I'm so sorry."

I wasn't sure what to say. I had blamed him for so long for that very reason, for leaving me that night. But I knew in my heart that it wasn't his fault, that he didn't deserve the guilt that he was fighting with now. "It's not your fault," I said, but as soon as the words left my mouth I realized how unconvincing they were. *Did I really still blame Drew?*

"I couldn't seem to let go of you the entire night. I may not have been there for you that night, but I will never let anything happen to you again." He squeezed me tighter, and I could sense his struggle with each jagged breath he took, each one causing his body to shake.

"It's not your job to protect me, Drew. It never was." I said the words, but I couldn't deny how safe I felt in his arms. I couldn't deny how much I needed him in this moment.

After several seconds of silence, he whispered into my hair, "You're wrong, Gemma. You're so wrong."

I pulled back, looking up into his eyes, and my heart broke at the fractured expression that I saw in his features. I longed to go back to the way we were before everything became so complicated, when the world was open to endless

134

possibilities, when Drew's smile alone could light up my life. He deserved every happiness, not all this pain and guilt from his brother's wrath.

In that moment my stomach rumbled loudly, and we both laughed. "I'm starving," I said. "Do you have any food around here?"

"I'm not sure," he said, shrugging his shoulders. "My housekeeper does all of the shopping, but she only comes in twice a week."

"Well, in that case, let's make breakfast at my place. Are Logan and Shannon here?" I asked as I sat up and pulled my hair into a ponytail.

"Yeah, they came in late last night. He supplied the pillows and blanket when he realized that I didn't want to move you." Drew yawned as he stretched, reaching his arms up over his head.

"Really? Well, leave them a note. They can join us for breakfast when they wake up."

Drew sat up slowly and rested his elbows on his bent knees.

"Let's go before I die of starvation," I said, nudging his arm with my elbow.

"Can I at least brush my teeth and change my clothes? I still smell like the bonfire," he said, pulling his shirt up to his face to smell it.

"Fine. Just meet me at the cabin when you're done," I said, standing up and realizing that I'd left my flip-flops on the beach.

"No," he said with urgency. "Wait for me. We'll go together. I'll just be a minute." Drew rushed to stand next to me, resting his hand on my arm, needing the assurance that I would wait, as if he didn't want to let me out of his sight for a minute.

"I'll be right here," I said with my arms folded across my chest. I plopped down in a leather swivel chair next to me, and Drew sighed loudly as he walked to the master suite to freshen up. I turned in my chair until I was looking out the wall of glass toward the lake. The sun was still low in the sky, and the water was completely still. It was going to be a beautiful day. A sense of peace came over me as a tear slid down my cheek. It was amazing that my body was able to shed another tear, having cried nearly the entire night.

But this came from somewhere else. I felt sad, a separate emotion from the despair that I had felt last night. Sad that I had stayed away from a place that had meant so much to me. I had missed the lake and everything that it had once represented. It was a new dose of regret—as if I didn't struggle with enough of that already. I wiped my face as I heard Drew enter the room. I slowly pivoted my chair around until I could see him. He was wearing a pair of khaki shorts and a fresh T-shirt. He looked tired and sad and . . . broken.

"Ready?" he asked, grabbing a baseball cap from a hook and placing it over his messy hair. He leaned over and scribbled on a notepad, most likely leaving a note for Logan.

I took a deep breath. "Yep. My shoes are at the beach though."

"I'll give you a piggy back ride. Come on." He smiled at me, and I couldn't help but laugh at his ridiculous idea.

"Seriously? I weigh a little more than I used to," I said as I walked toward him.

"Well, lucky for you, so do I." He turned his back to me and bent down. I jumped up on his back and wrapped my arms around his neck as he held my legs with his arms.

"Oh, my God," he said in a strained voice, as if he were struggling to hold my weight.

I hit him on the back of the head while we stepped out the back door. As soon as the door was closed, he took off running down the driveway toward my cabin, and I screamed the whole way, most likely waking up everyone on the lane. He reached my porch, breathless, and I hopped down from his back, laughing uncontrollably. It felt good to laugh, to release a different kind of emotion than the anguish of last night.

I left Drew in the kitchen, whipping eggs and warming up the skillet, while I stepped away to change into my yoga pants and a T-shirt. I pulled my hair into a fresh ponytail and brushed my teeth. By the time I came back to the kitchen, Logan and Shannon were sitting at the table.

"Good morning, you two," I said as I made my way back to the kitchen to make huckleberry pancakes, scrambled eggs, and bacon. Logan turned on the old stereo and immediately The Cars began to play. *I don't mind you coming here. Wasting all my time.*

"Wow, this brings back memories," Logan said as Drew poured hot coffee for everyone.

"Good memories," Drew said sadly, flashing me a half-hearted smile and looking directly into my eyes while he handed me a cup of coffee.

I smiled softly at him, as if to reassure him that we were going to be okay. I could feel this intense connection between us now that we were both caught in a web of truth and secrets, of perception and uncertainty, each of us knowing that we had to find our way out but not sure how.

We spent the day together, the four of us. Eating, talking, laughing. We even played pinochle for hours, a game that my father had taught us when we were young. It was a great day, despite the way that I would catch Drew looking at me with pure heartbreak in his eyes. I knew that I couldn't take away that pain for him; he would have to deal with it in his own way. The look in his eyes made it all real for me again, and I knew that I would have to deal with the pain all over too. I only hoped that the memory from that night didn't destroy us, that we could find ourselves again in spite of the pain and regret.

After saying good-bye to Logan and Shannon, Drew and I stood alone, unsure of what was next. It was already getting dark outside; the entire day had been spent with Logan and Shannon, leaving far too many things unsaid between Drew and me.

"Well, I guess I better head home. I'm beat," Drew said, standing by the front door to the cabin.

"Drew? Will you stay with me?" I asked. "I don't really want to be alone."

"Oh, thank God." He sighed in relief. "I can't stand the thought of being away from you right now." He pulled me against him, holding me close.

I closed my eyes and wrapped my arms around his waist, holding on to the moment as if it would be ripped away from me at any minute.

We took turns showering and then retreated to my bed. We lay awake for hours, staring at the ceiling as we shared memories from our childhood. We talked about his mother, and, for the first time, Drew was able to share his real feelings about her death and how it had destroyed their family, first his father and then his brother.

It was a new perspective through the eyes of the adult that he had become, but I couldn't help but picture Drew as a young boy, missing his mother. He told me how shameful it had felt growing up motherless and how cold his father became. He said that he missed my mother too and admitted that summer was the only time of year that he ever felt loved. It was lonely living at school without family. He had close friends there, bonding with other boys who were missing their families as well, but it wasn't the same. My mother, Jacob, and I were the only real family that Drew had had until that last summer when he had left for good. My heart broke at his words.

I asked him why he had never returned to the lake and why he had chosen this summer to come back.

"I couldn't face you or my brother again. And I was ashamed of the way I had treated you," he admitted. "It was just easier to stay at school."

"Why are you here now? What brought you back?" I asked, wondering what act of fate had brought us both here again at the same time after all these years.

"I needed a break from my life. I needed to remember who I was. This was the only place that I can remember ever being happy. So here I am."

"What were you doing before you arrived?"

"I was working for the company, under my father. I was never given any other choice. I was miserable. He's a ruthless, cold-hearted old man."

"I'm sorry, Drew."

"It is what it is. But I don't want to waste any more of my life that way. I want to be happy, and that's why I'm here. And finding *you*, here, after all these years, makes me happier than I could have ever imagined." He slipped his arm under me and squeezed me closer to his side.

I breathed him in and fought the urge to place my lips on his neck or the side of his face. I needed my friend right now, and I didn't want to complicate things. And I had to think about Ryan and the choices that I still had to make. As if reading my mind, Drew asked what I was going to do about my marriage.

"Are you going back to him, Gem?"

"I don't know. He hurt me, but he's still my husband. Even after everything, I can't deny that I still love him. I've loved him for as long as I can remember, fifteen years to be exact." *Almost as long as I loved you*, I thought. "That's nearly half my life. Love like that doesn't fade overnight. But being here with you changes everything. I feel different. I feel like I'm finding myself all over again. I hadn't realized it, but I've been lost for a really long time." A tear slipped down my cheek at this realization.

"I know the feeling," Drew said softly as he held my chin in his hand and gently kissed away my tear.

I gazed into his eyes filled with sadness, most likely a mirror to my own. We were both broken, each in our own way. We had each come home, to this place. I had thought that I was running away by coming here, but maybe I was here because I was searching for something. Drew and I had found each other in our quest for something more, and, maybe, if we were lucky—in the end—we would find ourselves.

Twenty-Three

Drew and I spent every day together as the heat of summer forged on. Each night I found myself folded into his arms in my bed, feeling safe and loved. We didn't plan it, and there was never any question of our plans, yet we just couldn't seem to say good-bye, even for just a few hours. It was as if we were making up for lost time, for all the years that we had spent apart when our friendship should have been held intact. That and I still sensed that Drew didn't want to let me out of his sight, as if he were protecting me, from what I wasn't sure.

My dreams had seemed to recede, finding their place somewhere in the back of my mind once again, as if telling me that Drew had finally set me free from the chains that had bound me for so long. Falling asleep in his arms, knowing that he knew the truth and still cared for me, was comforting and therapeutic in its own way. The boundaries of our friendship were never crossed; Drew was a true gentleman. Although there were moments when I longed to push those boundaries, I was afraid to complicate what was happening between us. I needed him too much to risk losing him again. And the fact that I was still married was reason enough to know that someone would get hurt in the end. And we had both been wounded enough.

We spent our days lounging on the back deck near the creek, talking or reading. Drew would sit on the wraparound bench with his feet propped up on a chair, and I would lay across the bench with my head in his lap. We talked about college, our jobs, and places that we had traveled. Of course Drew had been to several more countries than I had, and his recollection of the exotic places that he had visited was fascinating. One of the many perks of private jet and yacht shares. But none of that seemed to matter to Drew.

He told about his countless relationships that he'd had over the years. Most were forgettable, with the exception of the two women who he claimed to have loved. In the end, though, he had never loved them enough.

Drew and I were sharing intimate details of our lives, and I could feel the thick bond we had once shared snap back into place, but I couldn't deny the feeling that he was keeping something from me.

We talked about Ryan. How we met and what it was like in the beginning. It seemed like yesterday, and yet at the same time it felt like a million years ago. There was once a time when I couldn't imagine my life without Ryan in it. We pushed each other to be better, to reach for what we wanted. So, in many ways, we brought the best out in each other. Looking back, it was hard to believe that we had lost the ability to see the world with such clarity, the way we once had.

We couldn't even seem to see one another clearly, let alone the hustle and bustle of life surrounding us. We had lost our way, and I wasn't sure if we could find it again. And yet I still wore my ring on my finger and continued to rationalize why Ryan would do such a thing, still imagined that I could forgive him at some point. Unwilling to accept that this was really the end. Drew just listened, without judging, without offering up advice. Letting me work through it in my own way.

***

The morning of my birthday, Drew announced that he had a surprise for me. We had always celebrated our birthdays together at the lake, given that they fell two days apart. We had parted ways early that morning so Drew could prepare whatever it was that he had planned. I was anxiously waiting for his return; I wasn't big on surprises.

He finally appeared, looking youthfully handsome in his boarding shorts and a bright colored T-shirt. His crazy hair was hidden underneath a baseball cap. "Ready?" he asked, reaching for my hand.

"That depends," I answered hesitantly, folding my arms across my chest.

"On what?" He withdrew his hand, resting it on his hip instead.

"Where you're taking me."

"It's a surprise. Let's go." He ushered me toward the door as I grabbed my beach bag, packed for all sorts of possibilities. I patted the front pocket to reassure myself of the gift that I had tucked away there for Drew as we left the cabin. Drew led me to his dock where his boat was waiting, a twenty-six-foot Sea Ray, tied to the cleats where he had left it. It was a beautiful boat, fairly new, and equipped with all the bells and whistles, including the world's smallest bathroom and a wet bar.

Once we were settled in our seats, I asked Drew the obvious, "Are we going for a boat ride?"

"Not just any boat ride. We're going to Upper Priest." He beamed, knowing that he had touched a nerve with his response.

Upper Priest was a three-and-a-half-mile-long body of water connected to the lower lake by a two-and-a-half-mile narrow waterway known as the Thorofare. It had been designated a "scenic area" eons ago, which offered a certain protection for this portion of the lake. It remained virtually untouched, breathtaking, and tranquil, bearing white sandy beaches and swarms of wildlife. Drew knew this to be my favorite place to visit. It was an hour boat ride to the north even at an adventurous speed, deeming it an excursion for special occasions.

"Drew, you really know how to sweep a girl off her feet," I said playfully.

"Only you, Gem. Only you," he said with a triumphant smile while he flipped on the blower and untied the ropes that connected us to the dock. I pulled back my hair, securing it with a hair band in anticipation of the fast, windy ride as Drew started the engine and slowly steered the boat toward open water.

Moments later we were cruising across the calm lake, taking in the sights along the shore. I felt the wind on my face, the warm sun penetrating my skin. It was a beautiful day—perfect in every way.

"So can I drive this bad boy?" I yelled over the engine and the wind when we were nearly to the channel that spilled into the calm waters of Upper Priest.

"Be my guest," Drew said as he wrapped his hand around the throttle, gently pulling it back to slow our speed.

He stood from his seat and stepped back with one hand still on the wheel, as I slipped into the driver's seat and took control.

I held the throttle in my right hand, pressing it down as the boat gained speed.

"Easy there, tiger," Drew yelled in the same moment that he was thrown backward from the sudden momentum.

I laughed so hard that tears spilled from my eyes and were instantly blown away in the wind.

Drew shook his head and carefully sat down in the seat next to me.

I steered the boat in figure eights, enjoying the calm water that we seemed to have all to ourselves. My cheeks hurt from the grin that was stretched across my face. We reached the Thorofare in record time, and I slowed the boat until the wake was nonexistent. One of the many rules of the passageway, as well as Upper Priest—no wake.

Instinctively Drew moved to take control of the helm but I wouldn't budge.

"I got this," I said. And then added, "What's the matter? Don't you trust me?" I was feeling cocky. The truth was, I hadn't driven a boat in ages.

"It's pretty narrow. Are you sure?" he asked, hesitantly.

"Yep, I got it," I reiterated, as I pulled myself out of the seat and perched on the back of it for a better view.

Drew came to stand behind me, ready to grab the wheel at any moment.

The boat hummed as we puttered through the channel. It was hard to concentrate with Drew's front pressed against my back, his arms stretched against mine as he reached out from behind me to make small adjustments on the helm every few minutes.

I could feel his breath on my neck, and my heart accelerated with pure need. We had been cuddling in my bed every night for over a week, but, for whatever reason, this felt more intimate. At night we clung to each other, struggling to heal our past, fighting against the dark, our despair heavy on our hearts. But here, in the moment, there was no darkness, only light, and our despair was hidden away, replaced by freedom and joy.

Drew was forbidden fruit in this moment, and I suddenly longed to taste it. I turned my head just slightly, my cheek touching his as I tried to meet his gaze. He turned toward me in the same breath as our gazes locked. I leaned in to meet his lips, pure longing clouding any form of rationalization that I normally would have had. The lawyer in me always pleading my case in my head, anticipating the consequences of my actions. There was nothing but Drew in this moment.

Before our lips met, we felt a jolt, interrupting the moment as we both looked straight ahead to see that we had hit a large piece of driftwood. It wasn't serious, but it was enough to convince me that maybe Drew should take over. My head wasn't in it anymore, which could have proven to be dangerous. I reluctantly pulled away and took a seat across from him as he maneuvered the boat in silence.

Upper Priest was everything that I had remembered. It felt like we had happened upon a secret paradise, a fantasy that I had often entertained as a child. Drew beached the boat on a secluded stretch of pristine sand. It was our beach. Growing up we had always visited the same beach. I couldn't contain the huge grin on my face as I was assaulted with memories of this very place. I helped Drew with the blanket and large picnic basket that we set up on the sand. I raced to the tree line, searching for the old gray six-foot-tall tree stump that was lost to the taller evergreens that surrounded it. I ran my hand over the stump's bark, searching for the smooth surface where we had carved our initials. And there it was. *GL + AM, Best Friends to Infinity*. Drew came up behind me as I stared at it, lost in the memory.

"I can't believe it's still here," he said, reaching out to trace the letters with his finger.

"Let's add something while we're here," I said, feeling like a kid again.

Drew walked to the picnic basket and withdrew the corkscrew, handing it me.

I thought for a moment and then carved the words "and Beyond" with the current date below our initials. I smoothed my hand over the wood, cleaning away the chiseled pieces that remained and handed the corkscrew back to Andrew. We both stepped away and admired the old tree and the message, new and old that it bore.

"Why do I feel like Buzz Lightyear is going to land on the beach any minute?" Drew asked with a smirk.

"Very funny," I said with a smile, as I punched him in the arm.

I unpacked sandwiches, fruit, and chips from the basket while Drew uncorked a bottle of champagne and poured it into two glass flutes. Handing me one, he said softly, "Happy birthday, Gemma."

"Thank you, Drew. I can't remember the last time I had a day this perfect. And happy birthday to you too." I clinked my flute against his and took a sip. "I have something for you," I said, as I dug out the small wrapped box from the front pocket of my bag.

"Gemma, you didn't need to get me anything," he scolded with a frown.

"I wanted to, and it's more sentimental than monetary. I mean, what do you get a man who has everything?" I teased.

He looked at me intensely and whispered, "Not everything." I took a deep breath, feeling the weight of his words as I pushed the box into his hands.

He set down his glass of champagne, burying the base in the sand to keep it from falling over. The anticipation was killing me as he slowly unwrapped his gift. I had found my grandfather's old compass. A special trinket that had been at the lake cabin for as long as I could remember. Drew and I had once used it for all our adventures. My father had taught us to use it so that we could always find our way home from the woods.

I had had it engraved for Drew a few weeks ago with the infinity symbol. Underneath the symbol in a beautiful cursive font it read, *Some things are forever*. His tattoo still haunted me, the idea that he had lost hope in us along with so many other things in life, and I wanted to remind him that our promise was still alive, even though years had passed by.

He unveiled the compass as recognition flashed across his features. He turned it over in his hand and read the inscription before picking up the small note card that I had enclosed with it. "So that we never lose our way again," he read my words aloud. He looked at me then, his eyes full of emotion that I could not place. "Thank you. This is amazing," he said, gripping the compass tightly in his hand. "This brings back so many memories."

"I'm glad you like it. I wanted you to have it, to always remember." I smiled a solemn smile, overcome with so many different emotions.

"How could I ever forget, Gem?"

His words washed over me, warming me from the inside out as we stared into each other's eyes for a beat too long. I broke contact first, lifting my glass and finishing my champagne.

Drew rewrapped his gift and placed it inside the picnic basket.

We ate our lunch, finished our champagne, and stretched out lazily in the sun. The sun was warm, and I felt completely relaxed. For a brief moment, I felt guilty for leaving my life behind. I had left my husband, my work, my cases, my condo, my bills, my yoga class . . . all of it. I had been hiding away, neglecting my responsibilities, neglecting my life and everything that I had worked so hard to build. I pushed aside these thoughts and turned my head to look at Drew.

He was laying on his back, his chest bare, his tanned skin glistening in the sun. I took in the definition of his chest and abs, the small trail of hair that began between his pecs and led down his stomach, where it disappeared underneath his shorts. He had aged well and was possibly even more handsome than I had remembered. I wondered what he saw when he looked at me.

"What are you looking at?" Drew asked, startling me.

I blushed, completely embarrassed that I had been caught perusing his body from where I lay.

"Like what you see?" he teased, without opening his eyes or turning to look at me.

"Would it be wrong if I said yes?" I said, owning the fact that I had been caught checking him out.

He turned to his side, facing me, with his head propped up on his elbow, a complacent grin stretched across his tan face. "You think I'm hot?" he asked, and I instantly felt like we were sixteen again.

"Maybe," I answered stubbornly, channeling my inner-teenage self.

"Well, if it makes you feel any better, I think that you're *smoking* hot, especially in that black bikini."

His dimples were in full form from the shitty grin that was plastered across his face as he lay down on his back, closing his eyes once again, knowing what his comment would do to me, how it would affect me. Heat gushed to my cheeks, traveling all the way down to my toes, but not before making a special stop between my legs.

My need to push boundaries, to ignore lines that I knew I shouldn't cross, only taunted me more as the afternoon wore on. The flirting continued, and I couldn't ignore the way Drew seemed to invade my personal space throughout the day. The way he applied sunscreen to the places that I couldn't reach on my own, his fingers subtly brushing my breast as he rubbed sunscreen underneath the straps of my bikini top, his deft hands massaging my neck and shoulders—his hands on my skin were nearly my undoing. The way we swam together in the cool water, Drew adjusting my bikini strap when it was out of place as we found any excuse to touch one another. Lines were blurred, and our rekindled friendship hung on the fringe as something else took its place, something undeniable.

The wind was slowly picking up, and heavy clouds appeared from out of nowhere, obscuring the sun. I shivered as Drew announced that we should probably head back. The weather was shifting quickly. By the time we reached the channel it was sprinkling, the sky a canvas of dark clouds. We emerged into rough water from the Thorofare; white caps were painted across the dark surface as far as the eye could see.

"Hold on. I'm going to open her up, but it's going to be a rough ride."

Drew threw a navy sweatshirt at me that I pulled over my head, welcoming the warmth and the comfort. The boat sped up and bounced off each wave that we hit. I gripped the metal bar along the side of my seat, holding on for dear life. We were only halfway back when the thunder and lightning began. Bolts of lightning split the dark sky in half just moments before thunder crackled in the distance as the rain began to fall more heavily. I found myself counting in my head the seconds between the flashes of lightning and the roars of thunder. *One-one thousand, two-one thousand . . .*

The waves were rolling now as Drew steered the boat into them at an angle, the bow of the boat pointing to the sky before slamming down, allowing water to spill over the top. Drew gripped the wheel tightly, his knuckles white, as his gaze was fixed on the dreadful horizon. The white caps seemed to go on and on in the distance with no end in sight.

It reminded me of the time that my family had been caught in a bad storm coming back from our friend's cabin in Reeder Bay. Jacob and I had sat on the floor of the boat with our orange life vests secured tightly, hugging buoys as my father had driven the boat through four foot waves, heavy winds, and rain. We had gotten back to the dock before the worst of it. Fierce winds had capsized several boats, docks had been torn to pieces, and neighboring cabins had lost screen doors and roof shingles. Storms could be brutal at the lake, and I prayed that Drew and I made it back before the worst of this storm hit.

We passed Indian Rock, an obvious landmark, alerting us that the cabin was not far. It was hard to see through the thick rain. Drew had trouble mooring the boat as the wind was pulling its bow in different directions, and the waves were threatening to slam us into the dock. I jumped out and helped pull the boat alongside the dock, until it was aligned with the boatlift. Drew needed to get the boat out of the water and up on the lift to avoid damage during the storm. Wind was whipping through my wet hair, rain drenching my clothes and face as the storm roared on around us.

Once the boat was secure, Drew grabbed my hand and pulled me along as we ran up the dock toward his cabin. It took all our strength to run against the heavy wind, each step pushing us back, holding us in place. My heart was pounding in my chest from the exertion, the fear of the storm, and the relief that we had made it back safely.

When we reached the manor, Drew and I charged through the door, securing it behind us. The windows rattled in the wind; the lake was barely visible through the heavy rain. We stood silently still, catching our breath as we watched the storm tear across the bay. My hands were shaking as I struggled to pull the wet, heavy sweatshirt over my head. I felt Drew's hands on my arms as he helped peel the damp cotton from my body. Once my face was freed from the sweatshirt, I opened my eyes to find myself staring directly into Drew's, our heavy breaths the only sounds that could be heard over the storm. He pulled me to him as our lips connected urgently. His frantic hands were on my face, in my damp hair—gripping me, pulling me tighter against him. I was defenseless at his touch, my need to feel him in this way outweighing any reservations I may have had.

I hesitated for the briefest of moments when I felt his hands gripping the hem of my T-shirt. I moaned his name, and he pulled away. My eyes opened abruptly to find his intense gaze, melting me in place. "Drew?" I asked softly.

"I don't care that you're still married. I don't care about any of it, Gem. I need to be with you," he breathed, as if pulling away from me was causing him physical pain.

I whispered his name, but, before I could say anything else, he held his finger over my lips, his gaze piercing my soul as he whispered, "I love you, Gemma."

Without hesitation, I pulled his mouth to mine and showed him just how much I loved him in that moment. I couldn't say the words, but I could show him. He continued to undress me. Starting with my T-shirt, my shorts, and then he slowly untied my bikini top, letting it fall to the ground. I felt his hands on my breasts as I peeled his wet shirt off his chest and untied his board shorts.

Drew gripped one of my legs and then the other, placing them around his hips until I was suspended in the air, wrapped around him. He walked to the couch, holding me with his hands on my backside, laying me down gently, his mouth never leaving mine. He hovered over me until I pulled him closer, needing to feel all of him against all of me. Our movements were frantic, overdue, nearly desperate, as our denial dissipated in the heat of the moment. I was on fire, desire building inside me, ready to burst.

He pulled away, sitting back on his heels at my feet. All I could feel was my vigorous breath, the rise and fall of my chest as I watched him—watching me—while he took my foot in his hand and brought it to his lips. He very delicately kissed the inside of my arch, his lips following an invisible trail that led to my ankle, my calf, to the inside of my thigh. My body was tied up in knots, begging for release, silently willing his lips to continue their journey. He stopped and slowly lowered my leg back down to the couch. Hooking his thumbs into the sides of my black bikini bottoms, he pulled them down over my hips, his fingers grazing my skin.

Once that final piece of clothing was thrown to the floor, he crawled over me until our lips met. His mouth moved with mine, slowly and precise, as if he were cataloguing every detail in his memory—exuding more passion than I had ever felt before with just a kiss. My hands were feeling the curvature of his muscles along his back, trying to pull him closer—as if that were possible.

When my body began to plead with him to speed things up, he sucked my lower lip into his mouth and ran his teeth along it, keeping me at bay, escalating my need for him. I was ready to beg for more, craving the feel of him inside me. He pulled his face from mine causing me to open my eyes to look at him. When I did, our gazes locked intensely, stealing my breath. It was then that I finally felt him lower himself inside me, slowly at first until he thrust into me so hard that I gasped—his stare bore into mine as if he could see right into my soul. I felt exposed, vulnerable, as I felt him inside me in every way possible—the deepest way possible. My body, my heart, my soul.

We made love all the while the storm was raging outside, all around us. Nothing stood between us—not the past, not my husband, and certainly not the storm. It was just Drew and me. Together. At last.

Twenty-Four

Drew and I stayed on the couch, wrapped up in each other as we watched the storm move on. It departed just as quickly as it came, leaving a band of colors stretched across the sky in its wake.

"Can I ask you something?" Drew asked, as he traced lines on my bare shoulder with his finger. He was behind me, his front pressed against my back as we lay on the couch under the cover of a fleece blanket, watching the dark storm clouds that still hung in the east through the windows.

"I guess so," I answered hesitantly. I never knew what was going to come out of his mouth. Drew was fearless in that way, always up-front and honest.

He pulled my hair away from my face, and I felt his lips on my ear, distracting me momentarily. "Why corporate law?"

I sighed, relieved at the simplicity of his question. "I like the money and the power and the predictability," I said instinctively, having been asked this question a number of times over the years.

"Huh," he said, as his lips trailed down my neck delicately.

"What's that supposed to mean?" I asked, closing my eyes as the feel of his lips ignited fire deep in my core.

"I'm just surprised, that's all." His lips paused as he rested his warm cheek against mine, his breath caressing my skin.

"Why's that?" I asked, trying to focus on our words and ignore my body's commands. As Drew's bare flesh pressed against mine, it was hard to think of anything else.

"I guess you never really cared about that stuff before. I always imagined you practicing criminal law and putting away the bad guys. Taking pro bono cases because it was the right thing to do. That kind of stuff." He brought his hand to my hip and began tracing lines along my sensitive skin.

I could feel his deep voice resonating in his chest as he spoke.

I paused and thought about what he was saying. Seeing the girl who he remembered. I had once wanted to do something that would make a difference, to stand up for what was right. But that girl was lost and in her place was someone different.

"I wanted that too, but there's something so unpredictable in criminal law. There are too many surprises. I knew that I could work my ass off to try to make a difference, but, in the end, it's out of my hands. The verdict is rarely the right one. I like feeling in control. I like the power that consumes me when I fight for something bigger than me. Knowing that, no matter the outcome, no one's life is at stake. I don't know how to explain it." It was the first time that I had ever felt the need to defend my career path.

"I get it, Gem. I was just curious," he said, as he kissed me on the cheek and then on my neck again.

I took a deep breath and gave in to my body, knowing what it wanted, what *I* wanted. His lips found my shoulder as his hand reached around to cup my breast. I turned to face him, wanting—needing—to feel his lips against mine. I kissed him hard and deep as our hands explored the intimate venues that our bodies had to offer. Our conversation was lost to his touch. I was on fire, desperate for more, as desire consumed me.

"Feel free to take control at any time," he whispered, between breaths.

My mouth turned into a smile. "Smart ass," I whispered. But when our lips met again, I pushed him down, straddled him, and showed him just how much I liked to be in control. And by his symphony of moans, I could tell that he didn't have any complaints.

***

An hour later, we showered together, devouring each other again and again. We couldn't seem to get enough of one another. Our bodies finally demanded sleep, and I drifted away, nestled in Drew's arms with a lazy grin stretched across my face.

I felt Drew shake my arm gently and looked up to find him standing over me. The room was drenched in darkness; the night had fallen upon us while we slept.

"Come with me," he whispered and grabbed my hand, pulling me out of bed.

I had the sense to drag the top sheet off the bed and wrap it around me when I noticed that Drew was wearing a pair of loose mesh shorts that hung low on his otherwise bare body. I followed him quietly up the stairs, down the long hallway that led to the sunporch that opened up to the upper balcony. When I stepped into the room, bathed in moonlight, I was awestruck by the paintings that hung on a wire that stretched across the far wall. An easel was posed in the middle of the room holding a blank sheet of paper, ready and waiting.

"Drew," I breathed out. He turned on an upright lamp in the corner of the room that illuminated his paintings in soft light. There were at least twenty strung up on the wall, all amazing replications of the lake and its beauty. Drew had a gift; he always had. I felt so much emotion in his paintings, like each brushstroke represented something profound. It moved me.

"I turned this room into a studio," he said, as if he needed to explain.

I moved closer to take in the detail of each painting. "I didn't know that you still paint."

"I had forgotten how much I enjoyed it, until I came back," he said, standing in the middle of the room with his arms folded over his bare chest.

"You're amazing," I said, crossing the room to him. I reached up and wrapped my hands around his neck, letting the sheet fall to the ground as I kissed him tenderly. Drew showing me his work was like looking through a clear window, directly into his soul. I was so grateful and so proud of his talent, and so turned on.

His hands gripped my backside, pulling me closer to him as he kissed me hungrily. He pulled away a moment later, his gaze raking over my nakedness. "You're so beautiful, Gemma. Let me paint you, like this," he said, almost a plea.

I had never felt so loved and so wanted as I did in this moment. *How could I say no?*

"Where do you want me?" I asked, suddenly feeling a little shy and vulnerable.

He bent and picked up the bedsheet that was crumpled on the floor and led me by the hand to the chaise longue that sat in front of the balcony windows. "Here, lie on your side," he instructed.

I did as he asked, letting him make slight adjustments to my arms and legs.

He weaved the sheet around me, so that only parts of my skin were visible; my breasts he left exposed. My head was propped up with a large square pillow that rested behind me. One arm was draped above my head, my long hair splayed out all around it. My other hand rested across my middle. I felt sensual and beautiful and completely comfortable as Drew sat on a small stool behind the easel and began mixing paint on a small palette.

At first I had a hard time keeping a straight face—a smile threatening to erupt at any moment, but then I would look at Drew's face, and a sense of calm and peace would wash over me. He was so beautiful, his serious features visible from the moonlight that spilled in from outside. His eyebrows were pulled in tight in deep concentration, and he just barely bit down on his lower lip with his teeth. I wanted to reach out and run my fingers along his lips, releasing them, to feel his skin beneath my touch.

He was completely silent for a long time, and I wondered how long I would lie like this, how long it would take for him to complete this painting. My gaze never left his face, and, every now and then, our gazes would connect, causing my breath to still as I felt my heart pound in my chest. A slow burn was brewing inside me, the silent ecstasy escalating with each minute that passed by.

It felt like an hour before he finally put down his brush and moved toward me. I felt my breath hitch as he knelt down beside me. I was on fire, ready to burst from the anticipation.

He ran his hand along my hair, grazing my hand that rested above my head. Slowly, sensually, he leaned down and sucked my lower lip into his mouth, gently biting down with his teeth. I lay still, unable to move, barely breathing. His hands gripped the sides of my face as he moved his tongue into my mouth and kissed me deeply. I could feel it everywhere, my body thrumming at his touch.

When he finally pulled back, looking into my eyes with such intensity, I whispered into the space between us, "Did you get what you needed?"

"Almost," he breathed, running his hand along my bare leg that was slightly bent above the other. He started at my ankle and worked his way up to my thigh before his hand slid behind me and cupped my backside tightly, his gaze raking over every inch of my exposed skin. He stood and removed his shorts, letting them fall to the ground, and then slid in next to me on the chaise, pulling me closer to him.

I was ready for him, the buildup burning through my core, begging for release. He rolled me onto my back, pulling both of my arms above my head and held them there in his hand, gently, while his other hand pulled my left thigh up against his shoulder. He moved his hand to the cushion beneath us and rested his weight against it while he thrust into me, hard, his gaze penetrating me as much as his body, never wavering. My eyes blinked closed as I called out his name on a breath.

"Look at me, Gemma," he demanded.

I forced open my eyes as he held me captive with his fiery gaze and his body's demands. I felt my body explode with such intensity that it almost hurt, just moments before Drew found his own release, his gaze piercing me so deep that I could feel it in my soul.

Without a moment to recover, he pressed his lips against mine, fervently, releasing my arms in his grip to caress my face. I brought my leg down to rest beside his and ran my fingers through his hair, pouring myself into his kiss —giving him back everything that he had given me in that moment. As open as we were with each other, I couldn't help but feel that Drew was holding back, withdrawn, but the intensity in the room—in his gaze—felt like he had torn down the invisible wall around him, allowing me to see inside, to see all of him. In return I wanted him to feel all of me, now, in this very moment—so there was no room left for him to doubt how I felt about him.

Moments later, while we were enjoying the bliss, I asked him if I could see the painting.

"No," he teased.

I started to wiggle out from underneath him, and he wrestled me in place. When I finally broke free, I moved toward the easel, but he pulled the sheet that was still tangled around my body. I fell to the ground, laughing, as he rolled off the chaise and tackled me.

"I said no," he said, trying to rein in his laughter. "You always were a defiant little thing."

"*Pleeease*," I begged, nearly breathless from his weight that was crushing my lungs. I leaned up and kissed him on the lips, gently at first, but then I wrapped my hands around his neck and deepened the kiss until I felt him surrender. His body relaxed on top of mine and I slowly rolled him to the side until our positions were reversed. I could feel his need spring to life underneath me, and I knew that I had him right where I wanted him.

I continued to kiss him until he was rendered useless under my touch before making my move. I rolled to the side and broke free from his grasp all in the same moment, and lunged toward the easel. His hand caught my ankle, and I fell to the ground once again. When I looked up, I could see the painting from where I was sprawled out on the rug. I was instantly mesmerized, taken in by the beauty of the girl on the paper—all from Drew's hand.

"Oh, my God. Drew," I said, unable to break my focus away from the painting. I felt him release my ankle, and I stood slowly, captivated. He had captured every detail, every shadow, the way the moonlight struck my skin. But it was my face, mainly my eyes, that held me. It was as if he could see right through me—every fear, every dream, every loss, every desire. It was all there in my eyes. I was touched at the way he saw me; the beauty that I couldn't see in myself was here, written through his eyes with the stroke of his hand.

"It's beautiful," I whispered, still in awe at how well he knew me, how much of me was in this painting.

"*You're* beautiful," he said, coming up behind me, wrapping his arms around me while we both admired his talent. I felt his lips brush along my bare shoulder, and I shivered as my eyes filled with tears—overcome by him, the girl in the painting, this moment.

***

Days drifted into the next, and we had hardly gotten out of bed. We spent hours naked, loving every inch of one another. Drew was insatiable. And I couldn't complain.

At night we would cuddle in the warmth of a bonfire on the beach in front of Drew's cabin, admiring the blanket of stars above us. It was as if we could see every star in the galaxy from here. I loved getting lost in the vast canvas of night sky, imagining all the possibilities for my future.

It was late one night when we were lucky enough to catch sight of the northern lights. I hadn't seen the hazy iridescent colors since I was a child. The night's phenomena was mostly in shades of green, as if there were ghostly vapors swirling across the dark sky, but I could remember the vibrant purples, blues, and reds that we had witnessed years ago when I was just a kid.

Drew was sitting in the sand, leaning back against a large log that offered seating near the fire pit. I was resting against him, sitting in between his legs, wrapped in a blanket. I shivered against the chill in the air, and Drew wrapped his arms tighter around me.

"It's pretty amazing, isn't it?" Drew asked, referring to the northern lights. The night was quiet; the crackling of the fire and a distant frog's croak were the only sounds that could be heard.

"What causes this again? I can't remember," I admitted, my gaze locked on the transparent colors lighting up the sky.

"If I remember correctly, it has something to do with gas particles in the Earth's atmosphere and charged particles released from the sun's atmosphere." Drew raised his hands to the sky. "They collide and, ta-da, we have the northern lights." Drew wrapped his arms around me again.

"Very scientific, Mr. Monroe," I joked. "I think I like my dad's explanation better."

"Magic," we both whispered at the same time, remembering my dad and the tales that he used to share around the fire at night. I took a deep breath, fighting against the familiar ache.

Drew and I sat in silence for a few minutes, lost in memories.

"I tried to call him, Gem. But I think he's avoiding me." He leaned down and kissed me behind the ear.

I turned to look at him and asked, confused, "Who, my dad?"

Drew looked me square in the eye and said, "William."

I tensed at his name, and Drew's eyes grew solemn. I turned back to the fire, ignoring the pain in my chest, ignoring Andrew.

"I'm sorry. I just wanted you to know. I can't *not* confront him about this, Gemma. I can't just let it go."

Fear and uncertainty resonated in each beat of my heart. I was unsure of what this would mean. *If Drew confronted William, what next?* I couldn't imagine seeing him or even hearing his voice. I had closed the door on that part of my life so long ago, I wasn't sure that I could survive if it was opened again. I swiped at a tear that clung to my cheek as I considered what Drew would say or worse, what he would do once he reached William.

"Don't worry Gemma. Everything will be okay," Drew assured me. As my body trembled in his arms, he held me closer.

"I understand your need to confront him. But, Drew, I . . . I can't . . ." I struggled for the words.

"I know," he said, as he buried his face in my neck, kissing my skin lightly. "I know."

I crumbled in his arms, needing his strength and comfort more than I had ever needed anyone before. *What is happening to me?* He unraveled me. I was leaning on Drew, sharing my emotions with him, putting myself in a situation that I couldn't control, losing the tight grip that I kept on my heart. I wasn't sure what I feared more in the moment, my past or my future.

Twenty-Five

"What are you thinking?" Drew asked one afternoon after making love. My head was resting on his chest as he tucked my hair behind my ear, his finger grazing my cheek.

"Nothing." I was exhausted from the past hour that I had just spent with Drew, our lovemaking bordering somewhere between passion and porn.

"You can tell me, you know."

"I was just wondering how this would be—you and me—outside of this bubble that we've been living in." I searched his eyes waiting for his response. The truth was I was risking everything for these moments, and I was starting to question if it was worth it.

Being with Drew was the most amazing thing that I had done in what seemed like forever, chiseling away the years, leaving me to feel young again in the sense that I wasn't burdened with responsibilities or agonizing over consequences. I was just living in the moment, selfishly doing what I wanted, ignoring the lines between black and white, right and wrong—just enjoying the gray. But there *were* consequences, and I did have responsibilities, and I couldn't help but wonder where *this* was going—the erotic yet deeply emotional affair that Drew and I were engaged in.

Was this a relationship that would stand the test of time, a relationship that would define the end of my marriage? Or was this something else, a fleeting connection, a moment of weakness, a brief affair stemmed from a sense of retribution, past regrets, or what ifs?

My need to answer these questions, to gather all the data, to pluck off petals one by one—as if my fate could be that simple—was suddenly consuming me. I was tempted to back him into a corner, to force him to define what was happening between us, but I was afraid.

"Why would you want to leave the bubble?" he asked, as he threaded his fingers through my hair.

His blasé response stopped my heart. "Eventually I have to go back to my life. Where do you see *us* when that time comes?" I asked, cringing at the desperation in my voice.

"Let's talk about that when the time comes. You're not done with the cabin yet. The way I see it, you can't leave until it sells, and we still have a lot of work to do." He drew circles on my arm with his finger and kissed me on the top of the head.

I sighed and buried my cheek farther into the warmth of his skin, trying to ignore the sinking feeling that I had in my chest. The feeling that Drew and I didn't exist beyond this place, beyond the summer, beyond the lake. I closed my eyes and focused on the rise and fall of his chest, the way his skin felt against mine, and the fullness that I felt in my heart. The truth was, no matter how much I worried about the future, I felt happier in this moment than I had in a long time, and I silently scolded myself for analyzing it all rather than enjoying it for what it was, whatever *it* may be.

***

Drew and I continued to work on the cabin together. I couldn't help but notice that we were both dragging our feet, taking our time, dwelling on his comment. The end neared the closer that we got to finishing the small renovations of the cabin. I had hired someone to update the kitchen and bathroom, just small changes that wouldn't break the bank. Drew and I repainted the bedrooms ourselves and installed a new screen door in the back. We also restained the deck overlooking the creek, replacing a few weathered boards where needed. And the list went on and on, Drew always finding something else that needed to be done.

It wasn't long before I contacted an agent to list the cabin. I knew that I had a short window to sell before the summer vacation ended and visitors returned to wherever it was that they called home. Drew and I didn't discuss what this meant; we didn't talk about tomorrow or next week. I moved all my stuff into Monroe Manor, so that we could stage the cabin and leave it in pristine condition. It just seemed easier that way, given the fact that Drew and I spent every night together anyway. I was so caught up in the approaching fall, dreading the end of summer, and possibly the end of our relationship, that I hadn't really thought about the finality of selling the cabin.

When I had packed up all my family's treasured mementos and items that I couldn't part with, I sat back and looked at all the memories and wondered how so many years of my life could fit into just a few boxes. *How could I just let it go so easily, this place that felt like home and held all the secrets of my childhood?* If these walls could talk, they would tell the stories of my youth, my family, my happiness. . . . There was so much of me in the confines of this space. It was as if the stories of my life were written on these walls.

I stared at the large round table, in the center of it all with its mismatched chairs, and could almost hear the roaring laughter as we played a game of spoons or Risk or ate my grandfather's dollar-size hotcakes until our bellies were too full to move. I took in the stone fireplace and remembered all the nights we had roasted marshmallows, or the cold mornings that Jacob and I had spent sprawled out on the floor in front of it while we colored. I noticed the antique dark steel matchbox hanging from the mantel and could distinctly remember the sound made when my father struck a match against a rock of the fireplace each time he started a fire.

I snatched the matchbox from the nail where it hung and placed it in one of the boxes, thankful that I hadn't forgotten such an important item. Then I felt the deep regret of letting it go, wanting to box up the cabin itself and take it with me. But I knew that it wasn't just the cabin, it was everything. It was the people who had lived within it; it was the view of the lake, the sound of the gushing creek, the shade of the tall evergreens that towered above it, the quiet embrace of nature, the fresh scent of the forest, the memories of my father. . . . I took it all in and boxed it up in the depths of my heart where I would never forget. I wiped the tears from my eyes, overwhelmed with memories and the sense that I was saying good-bye to a part of my life, a part of me.

Drew came up behind me and pulled me against him. "Look what I found," he said, holding a pink-and-white Barbie case in front of me.

"Where did you find it?" I asked with a smile, as I wiped my nose on my sleeve.

"Under the bed. Open it," Drew said as I took it from his hand.

I knelt down and set it on the floor, unfastening the metal clasp and opening the case. I laughed so hard that tears were streaming down my face once again. Drew knelt down beside me and wiped my tears, laughing with me. Inside was a half-empty bottle of Southern Comfort, a label that I hadn't seen in years.

"You were right, Gem. We did leave behind our stash," he said, picking up the bottle and spinning it around to look at the label.

"I'm going to miss this place," I said with a sigh.

"You don't have to do this, ya know—sell the cabin." He placed the bottle back in the case, and I closed it, securing the clasp.

"I know. But no one comes here anymore. It's been the most amazing summer, but my life is in Seattle, and it's a busy life unfortunately. As much as I would love to, I just don't see myself having time to spend here."

"I guess you're right," he said sadly, trying to hide the pain in his voice. I wanted to scream at him, to ask him what he wanted from me. What all this meant for us and where this was leading. But I held it all inside, afraid that, if I painted him into a corner, he would only say what I feared, and this would be over sooner rather than later. So I said nothing, placing the Barbie case into a box, regretfully accepting the fact that this was most likely the last summer that I was going to spend at the lake.

***

As one day bled into the next, I found it unnerving that Drew never talked about the next step or what he planned to do. He had quit his job but had no desire to do anything else. I chalked it up to the fact that the next step didn't include me, and maybe he wanted to avoid the idea as well as the conversation of us being apart. I didn't want to think about it either, much less talk about it, but, with each day that passed, the uneasy feeling in my gut grew, and I feared what it was that Drew wasn't telling me. I felt it in the unanswered questions, the subtle way he dodged my questions or comments about his recent past or his future. The few times that he abruptly ended a phone conversation when I walked into the room, or sometimes he ignored a call altogether when he was with me, hiding the screen from view and assuring me that it wasn't important.

The insecure part of me was certain that there was someone else, but the rational side of me argued that it wasn't any of my business. I was still married after all. That was another subject that we seemed to skip over. My husband. My ring was still on my finger, glaringly obvious, like a gigantic pink elephant in a small room. I hadn't made any big decisions of course. Having avoided Ryan for over two months, I wasn't sure what choices I had left to make. And the fact that Drew hadn't asked me to decide my fate, the fact that he seemed to avoid the subject altogether, said more than enough.

For the most part, I felt happy here with Drew in our little world at the lake. Sometimes our little world included Logan and the steady parade of woman he entertained, or sometimes it included our neighbors—families who we had known for as long as we had known each other—but, other than that, it was just the two of us. I loved the simplicity of our days, Drew's playfulness, the bond that we shared from our past. I loved Drew deeply, and yet there were moments when the fear and uncertainty were almost too much to bear.

And then some days I missed Ryan. I missed our life, our predictable routine—at least our life before everything had become so strained. When we had more to say to each other than we had time to say it, when he would make me laugh so hard that tears would stream down my face and I would snort out loud, unable to suppress it but not caring, because Ryan and I were so comfortable with one another. The way we could finish one another's sentences, or the way we always drank out of the same coffee cup while we read the paper or our trial notes at the kitchen table before work.

But most of all I missed knowing what Ryan felt for me, and I missed the security of knowing that, no matter what, it was Ryan and me, always and forever. I was so confused and lost, feelings that I was so unfamiliar with. I always had a plan. I always knew what I wanted, and I went for it with the same conviction that possessed me in the courtroom. But now I was caught between two worlds, two wants, two needs, and I feared where that would leave my heart. The jagged fissure threatening to break it apart completely.

My mind was so distracted that I ignored the gnawing feeling inside that I was missing something. I couldn't place this uneasy feeling though, convinced that it must be tied in with my feelings about Drew and his evasiveness.

And then one day as I was sitting in my real estate agent, Rebecca's, office—pouring over her calendar to schedule an open house—it hit me. I frantically started counting the days, tapping the tiny squares with the pencil in my hand. Rebecca sat back with a puzzled expression as I counted over and over, realizing that I had not had a period since I had been at the lake. It wasn't uncommon for my cycle to be off after all the hormones and procedures, but I couldn't remember the last time that I had had my period. This was a strange realization for me, as I had obsessed over my cycle for years, knowing exactly what each day on the calendar meant in terms of my reproductive schedule. And I hadn't thought about it since I had arrived, as if I had given up on it altogether since my marriage could potentially be over.

"Are you okay, Gemma?" I heard Rebecca ask.

Without looking up, I grabbed my purse and started toward the door, mumbling on my way out, "I'm sorry, I have to go." I drove straight to the only pharmacy at the lake, which shared a building with the post office. A strange concept that I had always been puzzled by but, in the moment, I was grateful that a pharmacy existed at all.

I grabbed a test off the shelf. There was only one choice, and I threw a stack of bills on the counter, not bothering to wait for my change as I walked quickly to my car.

I pulled into Drew's driveway, grabbed my purse and the pregnancy test off the passenger seat, and made my way into Monroe Manor heading straight for the small bathroom just inside the back door.

I was a jumble of emotions while I waited for the results of this simple test. I couldn't ignore the crushing feeling that I associated with this routine; the results always the same, no matter how hopeful I was, no matter how careful we had followed all the rules. I felt that same fear now. My stomach twisted in knots as I glanced at my watch every few seconds. Part of me wanted to believe that this time was different because I hadn't been trying or praying or hoping. I hadn't been checking my temperature or counting the days, hours, minutes. . . . This time it could be different. And then I scolded myself for letting my mind go there, for letting the hope trickle into my heart.

I stared at the test stick in my hand, completely stunned by the pink plus sign. I had never had a positive pregnancy test before. Not ever. I instinctively placed my hand on my belly, imagining the life that could be blooming inside me at this very moment. I pushed aside the thought, unwilling to allow myself to think ahead, already preparing myself for the disappointment that would inevitably come. Surely there must be some other explanation.

Twenty-Six

The following day, I told Andrew that I had to pick up something in town, regrettably explaining to him that I needed some time to myself when he insisted on coming with me.

"Are you sure you don't want me to come with you?" he asked again, while he sat on the edge of the bed, watching me get dressed.

"No. I'll be fine. It's only a few hours," I said, avoiding his eyes.

"A few hours that you need, away from *me*. That's just great," he sulked.

I finished buttoning my sleeveless blouse and glanced over at him. I could see the hurt in his eyes as my words pushed him away, putting space between us that neither of us had wanted or needed until now. The truth was, I didn't want to be away from him for a single moment. But I had an appointment with an obstetrician in town—a modestly populated city about sixty miles southwest of the lake. Dr. Bradshaw, my fertility specialist, whom I had called immediately after seeing that plus sign, had referred me to a physician there when I refused to come home.

Dr. Bradshaw had said that I was most likely pregnant, that it wasn't completely impossible, that he had seen this happen plenty of times in his career. I couldn't talk to Drew about this until I knew all the facts, until I knew for sure. Part of me feared his reaction, feared what this would mean for us if I was, in fact, pregnant. But I was afraid to think that far ahead, afraid that this wasn't real.

***

"Well, there's definitely a baby in there," I heard her say as she moved the ultrasound probe over my lower abdomen with an almost-painful amount of pressure. Dr. Anita Pennings was an older woman with short, spiky gray hair and an easy way about her.

"See right here," she said, pointing to a round figure on the screen. "That's the head." She slid the probe a hint to the right and said, "And there's a hand."

I was in awe. I was pregnant and looking right at my baby. Getting a real glimpse of its head and hand and feet. It was incredible. Tears spilled down my cheeks, and, for a moment, I thought of Ryan. We had dreamed of this moment for so long, wanting this so desperately; the need to be parents had consumed us until it had ultimately divided us— breaking us apart. I was going to be a mother; I was finally getting exactly what I had wanted more than anything, but a small part of me ached for Ryan, knowing how bad he had wanted to be a father.

I wasn't sure what Drew wanted. He seemed completely uninterested in the idea of having children. Fate had a cruel sense of humor, but I wouldn't change the outcome. I wouldn't take it back. Maybe everything happens for a reason. Maybe Ryan's affair had a purpose. Maybe, just maybe, I was meant to be with Drew, even if only for the conception of this baby. We had had sex more times than I could count, and we had never bothered with protection. I hadn't really tried to prevent a pregnancy that my body had denied me time and time again, and Drew had never really asked.

"Okay, let's get some measurements, shall we?" Dr. Pennings asked, more as a statement than a question as she tapped a few keys on the ultrasound machine. "Well, it looks like your about twelve to fourteen weeks along, give or take. It's hard to say since you can't pinpoint the date of conception or your last menstrual cycle." She ripped a sheet of paper from the machine's printer and handed it to me.

I looked at her in shock. "Excuse me?" I asked. Clearly I must have heard her wrong. "What would my date of conception be if your calculations are correct?"

"Let's see," she said, picking up a chart and scanning it for a moment. "Sometime in May, but again it's hard to say. I'm going to give you the earliest due date possible just to be on the safe side."

My heart had stopped on *May*. The month that I came to the lake. The same month that I had tried to conceive a baby with Ryan, the same month that I had left my husband, the same month that I had drunken, mind-blowing sex with Drew. I had never considered that this baby could be Ryan's. I had just assumed . . . I wanted to scream. I had no idea who the father was. How could I have been pregnant all this time and not have known? I cringed at the amount of alcohol I had consumed and the medications that I had taken on occasion. I said as much to Dr. Pennings. She assured me that it was fine, that plenty of woman before me had similar concerns, and their babies were perfectly healthy.

As I left Dr. Pennings' office—after several blood tests—I pushed aside the huge issue and tried to focus more on the fact that I was going to have a baby. *I was freaking pregnant! How did this happen*? I was elated, in awe, nearly euphoric.

I drove robotically, following each curve that would lead me back to Monroe Manor, completely lost in thought. I had so many decisions to make and a sudden deadline as the baby's due date of early February was now marked on the calendar. My mind was whirling as I drove back to Andrew. I knew that I had to tell him that I was pregnant, but I was scared of what this would mean for us.

Not only had Andrew never expressed any interest in having children, but he seemed to detest the idea. Uncertainty clouded my mind as I considered what I should do. Do I tell Ryan? Can I forgive him for what he did, and, more important, do I want to? Would Ryan still want me if this baby was Drew's? And will Drew want me at all, knowing that I was pregnant? I was finally getting the one thing that I had wanted more than anything in my life, and my joy was tarnished with these questions, tarnished with fear of how this would change things for Drew and me.

***

As I walked into Monroe Manor, I set down my purse and car keys on the kitchen island, calling out Drew's name. I found each room empty as I slowly walked through the first floor, peering around every corner, searching for Drew. My excitement was masked by the dread that hung in the balance from the anticipation of telling Drew that he was possibly going to be a father. I stood at the wall of glass and looked out, scanning the deck, the beach, and finally the dock.

My heart skipped a beat or two when I spotted Drew perched on the end of the dock in only a pair of shorts. His beautiful tanned skin stretched tightly across the cut of his muscles as he leaned back, his hands splayed out on the dock, supporting him as he looked out across the lake. His hair was wet, and beads of water rolled down his back as if he had just finished a swim moments before. He was beautiful. The magnitude of my love for him hit me full force. I walked slowly toward him and sat down only inches away, dangling my bare feet in the water.

"How was the drive?" he asked without turning to look at me.

"It was fine," I said, looking down at my feet as I kicked them back and forth in the water.

"Did you find what you were looking for?" he asked in a clipped tone, a double-edged sword exposing how hurt he was.

"Drew, I didn't need to buy anything, and I didn't need time to myself. I'm sorry that I lied to you." He turned to look at me, and I looked dead into the limpid blue of his eyes, feeling guilty for keeping something from him—again.

"We said that we wouldn't do this, Gem. That we would always be honest with each other."

"I'm being honest *now*," I admitted, wanting desperately to ask him if he was being honest with me but afraid of his answer.

"Well, what was today all about then, Gemma?" he asked, the hurt still in his eyes.

"I'm pregnant," I blurted out before taking a deep breath to prepare myself for his reaction.

I could see his mind processing my words, his gaze unflinching as he stared deep into my eyes, the rise and fall of his chest heavier, strained. My heart was on the verge of crumbling the longer he stared at me in silence, my worst fears hovering, waiting for confirmation. My own chest was heavy, my breath long and labored, as I searched his eyes for some kind of warning of what was to come. The world around us was at a standstill—a dead calm—while I hung on his every breath.

"Say something," I whispered when I felt like I couldn't hold on another moment, the anticipation nearly shredding my heart in two.

He reached out and caressed my cheek with his hand, as his mouth turned up into a lopsided smile. "That's incredible, Gem. I know how much you want to be a mother, and, just for the record, you're going to be an amazing mom." He brought his other hand to my face and kissed me so deeply that I could feel it in my bones.

I felt wet tears on my cheeks as relief flooded my heart. I had been so afraid of his reaction that I had not fully accepted my new reality, this miracle that was growing inside me. My heart filled with love for my unborn child.

Drew pulled back gently and wiped away my tears with his thumbs. I saw the genuine smile on his lips and heard the reassuring words that he spoke, but something in the vacant, solemn depth of his gaze extinguished my earlier sense of relief. I didn't elaborate on the rest, on the fact that Andrew may not be the father. I didn't say another word about pregnancy or babies or how rare and unexpected this news—this gift—was.

The look in his eyes bore the truth of what he felt in his heart, the one place that he could not hide from me, and, though I wasn't sure exactly what that truth was, I knew him well enough to feel completely shattered in that moment.

I pulled away from him abruptly and stood, running back toward the cabin. I could hear him calling my name, his voice getting closer as I reached the side door. "Gemma, what's wrong?" he asked when he reached the door. I continued to the master bedroom, tears blurring my vision as I grabbed my suitcase out of the walk-in closet and laid it open on the king-size bed.

"Gemma, what in the world is going on?" he asked, breathless, with his hands on his hips.

I began to pull clothes from their hangers, stuffing them in my suitcase as quickly as I could. I didn't bother with folding them. I just wanted to get out of here, to figure out what I was going to do, but I couldn't stay here anymore. I couldn't stay here with him and pretend anymore. I was a grown woman with real responsibilities and now even bigger responsibilities, and I couldn't afford to act like a teenager anymore, to play this game with him.

I felt his hand on my arm before he whirled me around to face him. He wrapped his hands around my arms to hold me in place. My gaze was focused on his chest; I was too hurt to look into his eyes again, afraid of what I would see.

His voice was calm and direct. "Gemma, talk to me. What are you doing?"

"Stop, Drew. Just let me go. I want to leave. I can't stay here anymore," I said as I tried to pull away from his grasp.

He only gripped me harder, as his voice became more demanding. "You're acting crazy. Slow down and talk to me." He was gritting his teeth in frustration.

"Talk to you, Drew? Talk to you? What do you want me to say?" I asked, finally looking into his eyes. What I saw was unexpected—complete agony . . . regret . . . sadness. I paused, my chest heaving as I lost myself in his eyes. "You want me to be honest with you?" I whispered. "Why don't you try being honest with me for once, Drew. I know that you're keeping something from me. I know that you don't want this baby," I choked out.

Once again he was silent, hesitant, torn.

"Whatever," I said, feeling so angry with him, with his silence. I slipped from his grasp and walked to the bathroom, throwing everything that was mine into a bag. A bottle of my Chanel perfume fell to the floor in my haste and fractured into pieces, the ear-shattering sound of glass against tile jarring my determination as its fragrant content pooled at my feet. I bent down to pick up what was left of the bottle and gasped as I cut the tip of my index finger on its sharp edge.

I stepped back and collapsed to the floor, holding my finger to my lips as blood slowly seeped from the cut. I looked at the broken glass strewn about and felt as if it was my heart, spilled out all over the floor—shattered. I brought my hands to my face and sobbed, my devastation getting the best of me. It was all too much. This news, Drew's silent rejection, and all the uncertainty that swirled around me. It was just too much.

I heard Drew approach me. He cradled me to his bare chest and stood, carrying me to the bed and setting me down. I continued to sob, only partially aware of him and his movements. He reached for my hands and pulled them from my face, blotting my blood-soaked finger with a tissue. I watched him through downcast eyes as he unsheathed a Band-Aid and wrapped it around my cut with gentle hands, before handing me a clean tissue to wipe my eyes and nose. I cringed at how pathetic I must look to him, falling apart over a cut on my finger. Although we both knew this was about more than just a cut.

Lifting my chin with his finger until our gazes met, he said in the gentlest tone, "I love you, Gemma. *That* is the honest-to-God truth." And then he kissed me, holding my face in his warm hands. I surrendered to him completely, as I ran my fingers through his hair, pulling him closer to me. Moments before I was ready to walk out of his life and never look back, but feeling him against me, tasting him on my lips as he kissed away my despair—I would take what I could get, even if it was just for one more night. But deep down inside I was hoping that wouldn't be the case.

He slowly pulled my shirt over my head. I heard my suitcase crash to the floor as he pushed it aside and lay me back on the bed. His movements were gentle, but there was a palpable intensity behind every touch, every caress. We lay beside each other, just kissing, as I felt Drew's hands trace every inch of my exposed skin, as if he were memorizing every part of me. Our breaths were quick and heavy, in sync, as our need for one another grew. Our desire building, our tender kisses becoming urgent, nearly desperate for more. Clothes were removed with swift movements and thrown to the floor until there was only skin against skin.

His mouth wandered from my lips, grazing my collarbone and settling lower. I felt my breast fill his palm as he held it gently while his tongue circled my nipple until it puckered under his wet lips. I arched my back, pushing into his touch as my body yearned for more of him. He brought his lips to rest just below my belly button, his hands caressing my slightly protruding belly, and, for just a moment, I was hopeful that this was his way of showing his acceptance for me and this baby. His momentary tenderness melted away as he gripped my thighs in his hands, lifting them as he buried his face near my core, his tongue lapping at my flesh.

"Oh, God, Drew," I called out as all my senses gathered at my center, leaving the rest of my body weightless and numb in his hands. My fingers gripped his hair tightly, holding him against me as I completely let go. Shudders racked my body as I rode the wave of the climax, fueled by the intense emotions of the day. I rested my hands above my head as my heart beat wildly in my chest. I felt Drew kiss his way back to my lips. I could taste myself on his tongue, and, without giving me a chance to recover, I felt him fill me with one strong thrust as another orgasm rocked through me. He was relentless as he made love to me for hours, intensely yet poignantly.

His hands were on my skin, grazing the peripheral of my body but his touch was penetrating, reaching me somewhere deep inside. I could feel him everywhere—my heart, my soul, my mind. And, as lost as I was to him in this moment, I couldn't ignore the pending darkness that lurked in the depths of my being. In a place where only intuition and suspicion could survive, a place where we push our unwanted gut instincts—hoping that they're fallacious and only stem from our own insecurities. That darkness threatened to invade me as the intensity in Drew's touch and the pain hidden behind his closed lids screamed good-bye.

Twenty-Seven

It was early; the sun had only just begun to awaken the day, as I slowly opened my eyes to find the bed empty. I felt the absence of Drew's embrace and sat up slowly, expecting to hear him in the en suite bathroom. But the room was completely quiet. I pulled on my panties and one of Drew's sweatshirts that was draped over the back of a nearby chair and walked through the cabin in search of Drew. I instinctively went to the windows and looked out at the lake, discovering him on the beach.

He was standing on the shore, barefoot, in a pair of running shorts and a sweatshirt, skipping rocks in the calm water. A thin layer of fog hovered over the surface of the lake, the rising sun just barely penetrating it, melting it away at the edges, exposing only the shoreline. A sure sign that fall was just around the corner. Drew crouched down to search for more rocks in the sand, before standing and throwing each one into the smooth surface of the water with expert skill. He looked so lost; his face held an expression of a thousand unspoken words.

He was struggling with something; that much was obvious. I took a deep breath as I continued to watch him, knowing that whatever he was mulling over in his mind had everything to do with me, with us. *Was he being forced to choose? What was he keeping from me, or rather who was he keeping from me*? I thought of my marriage—of Ryan—and asked myself if I was ready to let it go, to let Ryan go. *If I had to choose, right now—this minute—to move forward with Drew or to try to salvage my marriage with Ryan, no matter who the father of this baby was, who would I choose?*

I knew in my heart that I loved Drew. The love that I felt for him could not be defined, or neatly labeled and placed in a box. It was boundless and unconditional, a force that pulled two souls together under extraordinary circumstances. He was my past, but also my right now. He reminded me of who I really was behind all the titles, the fears, and the secrets. He made me feel alive again, made me want to be a better person. He made me feel like that little girl who had the world at her feet, full of possibilities—ready to take on the world.

His heart was massive, and he wore it on his sleeve, as if he feared nothing. He saw the world for all its simplicity, unwilling to see anything more than the true heart of the matter. My heart was torn as I still loved my husband; I knew this to be true for the sheer fact that I still felt so hurt by what he had done. And when, for the first time, I heard those words, "You're pregnant," all I could think of was

Ryan. That I was finally getting my chance at the life that I had always dreamed of, but Ryan had always been part of that dream, that life.

But could I forgive him? Could we ever go back to where we left off? And this led me back to Drew. *What did it mean that, after all these years, we were back here again?* In this moment, watching Drew on the beach, feeling so conflicted, the thought of letting him go tore me apart inside.

I ran my hand over my belly, imagining this baby inside me, picturing its tiny face, delicate fingers, and toes. I was plagued with so many uncertainties, but one thing was constant and unequivocal—I loved this baby and wanted nothing more than to be a mother. And deep down inside, a part of me wanted this with Drew. I envisioned a quiet, simple life with him. One that would allow this baby to grow and bask in unending love from both a mother and a father, giving him or her a stable environment that I had known growing up, that Drew and I both had once known until unfortunate circumstances had changed all that.

It was as if gravity had pulled us both here, to this place at this exact time, and I couldn't seem to defy the force of it. I couldn't ignore the significance. I knew I wanted this, and, yet, I feared what it was that Drew wanted and what he was struggling with.

I continued to watch him, committing every one of his features to memory. The strong curvature of his jaw, his light brown hair jetting toward the sky in complete disarray, giving him a sexy edge. His perfect smile and deep-creviced dimples that awarded him a youthful appearance. The cut lines of his body, his breathtaking and beautiful physique that I had grown to know so well. He was incredible as a man, but what I loved the most about him was the boy who I still saw in his eyes. The boy who I remembered and loved like family for so many years. He meant everything to me. Everything.

He glanced up to the cabin and caught sight of me watching him. Our gazes locked for an instant, and I gave a little wave from where I stood at the window. He smiled back before he turned to toss one last stone into the water. He rubbed his hands together, shedding the sand from his palms, and slowly made his way up the beach toward me.

My breath caught as he walked through the side door and scooped me into his arms, holding me tightly against him as he kissed my neck, growling playfully against my skin. I laughed quietly and kissed him on the mouth, unable to resist feeling closer to him.

"Good morning," he whispered against my lips as what he had done to my body the night before played through my mind, causing a heated blush to spread across my cheeks.

"Morning," I whispered back. I felt his hand reach down and grip my backside, covered only by a lacy pair of panties.

"Nice," he mumbled as he kissed me again.

I pulled away when I felt his intention shift, knowing that we needed to talk before our bodies spoke for us. "Drew, we need to talk," I said as I crossed my arms over my chest, bracing myself for whatever was to come.

He took in a deep breath and blew it out through his nose before responding. "Okay," he said with resolve, as he sat down on the arm of the couch.

"You can't keep avoiding the future, Drew. I need to know what *this* is," I said waving my hand between us. "I need to know what you want."

"What I *want*?" he asked with a smirk. "As if it's that easy," he mumbled.

"What do you mean by that?" I asked, as I squeezed my folded arms tighter across my chest.

"What do *you* want, Gemma?"

His gaze was boring into mine, and I couldn't tell if his question was accusatory or inquisitive. I was fumbling, unable to read him, dreading each word that we exchanged. I hesitated for only a mere moment. "I want you," I said with an unwavering stare. "And I want this baby. With you. No matter who the father is." I saw a flicker in his gaze as my last words spewed from my mouth before I could take them back.

"What do you mean, no matter who the father is?" He squinted his eyes at me, questioning everything now. And I wanted to kick myself for admitting that to him before he could tell me if he saw me in his future. I guess it was better that he knew the entire truth before I forced him to make a decision.

I took a deep breath and instinctively brought my hands to my belly, as if I needed to protect him or her from whatever came next. "This baby was conceived in May, Drew. It could be Ryan's or yours. It's too close to tell for sure." I searched his eyes, waiting for his reaction.

He stood and began to pace in front me, scrubbing his hands over his face as I heard him take deep, ragged breaths.

I stepped closer to him and reached for his arm to stop his pacing. "I can't take this anymore, Drew. Tell me what you want."

I saw so much pain in his eyes, it nearly brought me to my knees as he remained quiet once again, conflicted.

"TELL ME WHAT YOU WANT," I screamed in frustration, throwing my hands up into the air.

He gripped his hair in his hands and said quietly, "I want *you*, Gem."

I waited for the blow, knowing that a "but" was coming.

Shaking his head back and forth, throwing his own hands in the air, he said it. "But I can't do this."

Tears spilled from my eyes as his words crushed my heart and whatever hope I had left for us. I folded my arms tightly across my chest once again, trying to comfort myself against the agony.

He was suddenly angry, tears filling his own eyes. *"God dammit,* I can't do this," he yelled as he looked upward, as if he were actually talking to God.

I was so confused. He was saying one thing, but his body was saying something else entirely. And he was so angry, but not at me. I stood in silence and waited for him to explain himself.

"It's too late, Gemma. Don't you see? I was okay with this. I had made peace with this before I came here. I never expected to see you, to be here with you. I don't want to leave you," he said through his own tears as he stepped toward me.

"Drew, what are you talking about? You're not making any sense. I love you. I want to be with you, wherever that may be. We can raise this baby together," I said reaching for him.

He stepped away from me, gripping his hair forcefully again. He let out a loud groan in frustration. "God, I'm so angry," he yelled into the space around us before he lowered his voice and looked me straight in the eye. "Gemma, you have to go back to Ryan. Especially if this is his baby. I can't do this with you."

"Do what with me? Raise a baby? Is that what you're saying? You don't want to have a baby with me?" My need for him to clarify what he was saying, what he was feeling, was overwhelming. I didn't want to let him go.

"I won't put you through this, Gemma. You have to go. Go back to Ryan."

He was beginning to scare me. He wasn't making any sense. I knew that he loved me, but I was unsure of what was tearing him apart inside. I was falling apart inside too. His words were leaving me stranded somewhere between hope and despair.

"Drew? What are you saying? I love you. Please don't do this," I begged, desperate for him to see how much I wanted this life with him.

He paused in front of me and reached out to cup my cheek in his hand. He looked into my eyes with the gravest sincerity. "I love you too, Gem. More than anything in this world." He brought his hands to my nearly flat belly, and I covered his hands with my own as he continued. "And I already love this baby inside you, whether it's mine or not. But none of that matters." He shook his head as he turned away from me, as if he were unable to face me any longer. "*None of it matters*," he screamed at no one as my heart broke from his distress.

"Why, Drew? Tell me what's going on. Is there someone else?" I asked, staring at his back as I cried for him, for us.

He whirled around, with tears running down his cheeks. "There's never been anyone else, Gemma. It's always been you," he whispered.

His gaze was so intense, burning right through me. But the desolation in his eyes told me more than I wanted to know. I knew it was coming, the truth that he had been keeping from me. The truth that I was desperate to know but scared of what it would mean for us, knowing that whatever he said next would tear us apart for good. Seconds ticked by, as we stood in silence. My heart was already crushed, bleeding for him as I felt its heavy beat inside my chest, *thump . . . thump.* I watched his lips when he began to speak as I hung on his every word.

"I'm dying, Gemma. I came here to die. I never expected to see you, to be with you again. I'm so sorry. I should've told you. I'm so sorry."

His words echoed in my mind, pulling me into a dark abyss.

"You can't stay here with me. You have to go back to Ryan." His words were growing distant as blackness settled in all around me. I reached for him and felt him envelope me in his arms. I looked up but could no longer see his face, his voice barely audible and so far away as he whispered, "I love you, Gemma. I'll always love you . . ."

Panic consumed me; my breath became shallow. My heartbeat pounding in my head was the only sound that I could hear as my world swirled around me, sucking me further into the blackness. I could no longer feel Drew against me, and so I frantically reached out my arms, tried to close my palms around something, anything, but came up empty. *Drew . . . Drew . . . Drew.* I was screaming his name in my mind, but there was no sound. Only darkness.

Twenty-Eight

"Gemma? Gemma? Can you hear me? Baby, wake up."

I could hear his muffled voice in the distance, but it wasn't the voice that I wanted to hear. I reached deeper into the crevices of my mind, searching for its meaning. *Why was he here?* My reality was fading, its once vivid colors dwindling into the background of my mind as his voice became louder and clearer. I desperately wanted to go back to where I had been, back to Drew's arms.

I tried to squeeze my eyes tighter, tried to focus on his face—the strong curve of his jaw, the blue of his eyes mirroring a bright cloudless sky, the crazy brown hair that he let fall where it may, his strong voice, his words . . . I felt the sharp pain in my chest as I remembered his words, *I'm dying*.

I choked on a sob in my throat as Ryan's voice became closer, clearer. I realized that the image of Andrew, the feel of him, the sound of his voice . . . was gone. Andrew was gone. I blinked once, twice, blinded by the brightness that invaded my sight. Where everything was once so clear, it was now blurry and out of focus. I had felt weightless just moments before, but now gravity was pulling me back to the center of the earth as I slowly became aware of my surroundings.

"Oh, my God, Gemma," Ryan said with tears in his eyes.

His face was slowly coming into focus. My eyes scanned the room, bright white walls, machines, a white board with my name written on it along with numbers, charts.

Confusion settled inside me. *Where was I? Where's Andrew?* I tried to speak to convey my confusion, but nothing happened; there was no sound.

"It's okay. Don't try to talk, honey. Just relax." Ryan's words did nothing to alleviate the anxiety that was suddenly building in me. I needed to know what was happening. I could feel my lungs fill and empty, and my heart beat deep in my chest. But I couldn't feel much else. I tried to wiggle my toes or my fingers but could not feel them. And then I remembered the baby. *I was pregnant. Or was I? What was happening?*

"Baby," I croaked, my strained voice sending a thousand splinters to the back of my throat.

"The baby is fine, Gemma. Everything is fine. You came back to me. Oh, God, you came back to me," Ryan said, as he brought my hand to his lips and kissed it adoringly.

I wasn't sure of anything in that moment, but his words brought me back to that day. The image of him with

192

that woman burned into my mind. *Had I come back to him? In what regard?* I attempted to turn away from him, unable to sift through the dull but varied emotions that struck inside me but was only able to direct my eyes away from him. My baby was okay. A flutter of hope surged though me, as I held on to the only thing that I could seem to make sense of in that moment.

A brief moment passed or maybe several minutes before I heard a foreign voice calling my name. I turned my gaze to the sound of the voice to find a tall older man in a pair of blue scrubs and a long white lab coat.

"Gemma, I'm Dr. Selzman, your neurosurgeon. I know that you must feel very confused right now, but I want you to try to relax. I'm going to explain everything to you in a moment, but first I would like to conduct a physical exam, if that's okay?" He waited for me to respond, as if I had a choice in the matter.

I nodded softly, the slight movement causing pain to ricochet through my head and down my neck. I winced.

"Are you in pain?" Dr. Selzman asked.

I nodded again, closing my eyes against the pain.

"I'll give you something for the pain in a moment. Can you open your eyes for me?"

I slowly peeled open my eyes again and blinked when he flashed a bright penlight into my line of sight before he held my eyelids open with his fingers.

"Follow the light please," he said.

I did as he asked. I followed his instructions and answered his questions with a subtle nod or shake of my head. With each minute that ticked by, the fear swelled inside me as I tried to imagine what all this meant, what had happened, and why Drew wasn't here by my side.

Once he was pleased with my physical response to his exam, Dr. Selzman began to explain how I came to be in this bed, in this state.

His words were precise and clear as he explained that I had been in a car accident, thirty-one days ago. I had hit a deer which had somehow sent the car into a tailspin until it smashed head-on into a tree. I had hit my head on the windshield at impact when my air bag failed, causing a severe head injury. The rest of my body was unscathed, but the severe swelling in my brain was nearly fatal. I had been in a coma for nearly a week, but he had to keep me in a medically induced coma thereafter when I began to regain consciousness before the intracranial pressure was reduced. He was finally able to lift the drugs, allowing me to wake up. He went on to explain that the numbness I felt in my extremities would recede over time once the medications were completely bled from my system.

They had discovered that I was pregnant, only a few weeks at the time, and thought for sure that my body would naturally miscarry from the trauma. But miraculously the pregnancy had remained viable. They had just heard the heartbeat for the first time yesterday, and the baby seemed healthy and thriving. The doctor had every reason to believe that I would make a full recovery, and they would continue to monitor the pregnancy carefully. He warned that I wasn't out of the woods yet as I was barely eight weeks into the first trimester, but he was hopeful.

"You still have a long road ahead of you, Gemma. Right now all you need to worry about is getting your rest. We'll take care of everything else," Dr. Selzman reassured me.

His words washed over me as I tried to absorb the shock of what had happened. I had been in an accident; I had nearly died. I tried to think back to the accident, but everything was still a little fuzzy. Thirty-one days. The accident was thirty-one days ago. My mind locked on the memory of the deer lying in the middle of the road, hitting my head on the windshield because I had removed my seat belt for that brief moment. Although I had been fine. I had finished my drive to the cabin. It was just a deep cut and an annoying headache. Every moment from that point on flashed through my mind as I tried to make sense of everything.

And then it hit me. My terrified screams while the car spun out of control. Seeing the tree come at me in full force, as if it was happening in slow motion. Knowing that something very bad was about to happen, the overwhelming fear that ripped through me. And Ryan's face—my last thought that I could recall.

The cabin. Drew. Everything. *Was it all a dream?* It couldn't possibly have been a dream. It was so real. I felt things that I hadn't felt in a long time. *And the pregnancy? How could I have known that I was pregnant if it hadn't been real?*

I was overwhelmed with relief that I was alive, that my baby was real and growing inside me, and yet I was full of grief as if I had lost something. And, in a way, I had. I had lost Drew. I closed my eyes and conjured his face from my recent memories. *How could this not be real? What we shared?* Tears wet my cheeks as I felt a tightness in my chest, a pressure slowly building, clenching my heart tightly. I wasn't sure of anything in the moment.

A sudden need to find Drew consumed me. I had so much to say to him, so much that he needed to know. I tried to sit up, but I couldn't move. My useless body felt the weight of a thousand pounds, and I knew that I wouldn't be leaving here anytime soon.

I heard Dr. Selzman ask if I had any questions, his broad forehead lined with concern as if he sensed the panic rising in me. I couldn't seem to form any words on my tongue so I merely shook my head. As he left the room, I was aware of Ryan at my side, reaching for my hand again.

"Gemma, did you hear that? You're going to be fine, and we're going to have a baby," he said ever-so-softly.

I couldn't move my hand from his touch, but I pushed against the pain and the invisible chains that held me in place and turned my head to the side, slowly, away from him. I couldn't look at him right now, in this moment, when all I could see was Drew's face. I couldn't forget what Ryan had done, how he had hurt me. It was frustrating to not be able to convey my thoughts to him or move my body in protest, and I was so tired. I closed my eyes, shutting it all out, welcoming the darkness once again.

Twenty-Nine

I woke in a panic. I wasn't sure if I would ever get used to waking up in this place. Each and every time, it took me a few minutes to orient myself. The stark white walls, the antiseptic smell, the constant noise muted by eerie silence. Each day I gained back more of myself. I could move my extremities, talk, sit up with assistance. The physical recovery was my biggest challenge, Dr. Selzman kept reminding me, but I wasn't so sure. I couldn't help but wonder when I would laugh again or when I would find peace in the knowledge that my baby was going to be okay.

Ryan took longer breaks from my side when he realized that his presence was anything but comforting. I couldn't seem to move past this resentful anger that took root inside me and seemed to grow with each passing day. The worst part was that I wasn't even sure what or who I was angry at. My thoughts centered on Drew and the day when I was strong enough to find him. I had used Ryan's iPhone to search the Internet for "Andrew Monroe" and for contact information for the Monroe Enterprises' offices.

After several phone calls to offices around the globe, I had finally been told that "Mr. Monroe was on a leave of absence, and it was unsure when he would return." These words echoed in my mind, oddly familiar. I had tried to contact Andrew's father, but he was impossible to reach as if I were trying to call the President of the United States, rather than the president of a multibillion-dollar enterprise. I refused to contact William, although his name had popped up in several of my searches. He wasn't linked to Monroe Enterprises in any way that I could tell, but I refused to find out more information about him.

I had found a number for Sal's Garage and had left a message for Logan, but I hadn't heard from him either. And so I was left with the wait, my patience wearing thin, as I focused on my recovery so that I could leave this place and find Drew myself. I didn't care what it took; I was going to find him.

I heard a knock on the door to my room that sat slightly ajar—the nurses' best attempt for my privacy. They had moved me out of the ICU last week—now that my condition was no longer "critical"—to a step-down unit where I was still being closely monitored, but it was more peaceful, less intense. This allowed me the ability to eat real food, rather than being fed through an IV and a feeding tube. And it allowed my family to fill my room with a beautiful array of flowers, which my mother brought in every three days to "keep things fresh," as she liked to say. And that is what she held in her hand now, a beautiful arrangement of wildflowers, as she stepped into my room quietly.

"Good morning, sweetheart," she chimed as she busied herself arranging the flowers in an empty vase and filling it with water from the small sink in the corner of my room. She set them on the table at the side of my bed and leaned over to kiss my forehead. I inhaled her perfume— Beautiful by Estée Lauder. My mother's signature scent. "Jacob called. He said he'd call your room later today. The time difference in Sydney has made it difficult for him to reach you."

I nodded. I missed my brother. As much as I wished that he was here to help me sort everything out, I knew that he would think I was completely crazy. He was also Ryan's biggest fan. Jacob called and emailed Ryan more often than his own sister. They were extremely close, and I was sure that Jacob would only encourage me to work things out with Ryan, his loyalty showing no boundaries. Jacob was in the middle of a huge project on a movie set, his strict three-month contract keeping him from flying home to be by my side. My mother had kept him updated on my progress during the entire month that I was in a coma, assuring him that there was nothing he could do, and to stay and finish his job.

"I brought you some new magazines that I thought you might like," she said in a cheerful voice, as she pulled them from her bag and set them on the tray that hovered over my bed.

"Thanks, Mom," I said in a flat tone, immediately feeling guilty for showing so little regard for her and her efforts. The truth was, I had enjoyed my mother's company, which is more than I could say for Ryan's. I could be myself around her and talk openly about my recovery. I didn't, however, talk to her about Drew or what I think had happened while I was in a coma. It sounded crazy even in my own head; saying it aloud would only cause my mother to question my sanity.

"Oh, Gemma." She sighed as she sat down on my bed, facing me. She pulled to the side the long scarf that hung from my nearly bald head—the aftermath of several brain surgeries that required my hair to be shaved off—and ran her finger delicately across my cheek. "What is it? When am I going to get my Gemma back?"

Her compassion and her words "my Gemma" broke something apart inside me. I hung my face in my hands when I felt the tears running down my cheeks, evolving to fully fledged sobs in a matter of seconds. I felt her hand on the back of my shoulder, comforting me, encouraging me to let it all out. I had been focused, stoic, numb for days, and her words had flipped a switch, turned on all my emotions at once. The pain encompassed me then, wrapped itself around me, unrelenting as I cried.

After several minutes of silence, while emotions tore through me and spilled from my eyes, my mother handed me a tissue. I wiped my eyes and nose, and balled the tissue in my hands tightly, my eyes focused on my hands. "I don't . . . I don't know what to do," I choked out between hiccups of lingering sobs.

"About what, Gemma?" she asked softly.

"About Ryan, the baby, Andrew," I answered in incoherent mumbles, staring at the damp tissue in my hands that I twirled around my fingers nervously.

"Andrew?" she asked, as if she had heard me incorrectly.

I looked up into her eyes, taking in the lines that webbed around them, the dark circles painted like shadows of the life that she had once held there. I took in the worried expression, the sorrow that she hid so well behind her cheerful disposition and realized the price that she had paid as well, for my accident, my near-death, my life. I instinctively held my hands over my belly, knowing that one day I would know what that felt like.

And maybe I already did. The vulnerability that came from being a parent, the cost of knowing that you would give your own life to keep your child safe, bear their grief and pain as if it was your own. And so I launched gently into what had happened, or what I thought had happened, between Drew and me. I spared only the more intimate details and the truth of what was revealed between us from our past, describing what I felt in each moment.

"And now here I am, left wondering what was real and what was just a dream, and what it all means for me, for Ryan, and for our baby," I said through my desperate sobs, as my mother just sat and listened as the crazy story poured from my heart. "Do you think that I'm crazy?" I asked.

She reached out and took my hand in hers. "Gemma, listen to me. I don't think you're crazy at all. I think that your mind and your heart were fighting like hell to keep you here, and this . . . dream . . . or whatever it was, did just that. It kept you here with us, fighting. If you need to find Drew, honey, then I understand. But don't be disappointed when you find him. He's not the Drew from your dream and maybe nothing like the Drew that you remember. He could be happily married with kids, or he could be just like his father. It's been years. You don't know what you're going to find.

"I know that Ryan hurt you, and you feel like you may never be able to forgive him, but he loves you, Gemma. He loves you so much. He never left your side, not for a minute, for thirty-one days. That speaks volumes. He made a mistake, but he loves you, and he chooses *you* just as much today as he did when he married you. You're going to have a baby. You're being given a second chance. With Ryan, this baby, with life. Consider this before you shut him out for good. That's all I ask."

I listened to her words, knowing that she was right in only the way a mother can be. This infinite wisdom that seems to grow the older she gets.

I wiped at my eyes again. "What if I can't? Forgive him?"

"You will, eventually. It takes time, but when you love someone the way that you love Ryan, everything eventually falls into place again."

"Did you ever forgive Dad?" I asked. We had never talked about him, about what happened between them. And I saw the surprise in her eyes from my question.

"That was different," she said, pausing as if to collect her thoughts. "It wasn't a one-time mistake with your father. It was years of lies and several different long-term affairs. I loved him so much, and I loved our family even more. I think that I could still have found it in my heart to forgive him, to take him back after everything, but the difference is, Gemma, your father didn't choose me in the end. He didn't choose *us*."

I absorbed her words as the fossil of pain my father had left resurfaced. "Why didn't he choose *us*, even if he didn't choose you?" I asked, my voice mimicking the words of my thirteen-year-old self. The question that had haunted me all these years was finally answered. He had been the one to leave. I had always hoped that it was my mother's decision. That my mother had asked him to leave. That he had hurt her and she was unable to forgive him, pushing him out of our lives with vengeance.

"He loved you and Jacob more than anything, but your father was never good at facing things, and I think that the guilt of breaking our family ended up destroying him. Literally destroying him."

I took a deep breath, trying to squelch the occasional sob that still rocked through me.

"Don't let your emotions from this . . . dream . . . get in the way of your marriage, Gemma. Focus on what you know to be real."

She squeezed my hand and kissed me on the forehead, a mild gesture letting me know that this conversation was over.

"I'm going to grab a cup of coffee downstairs. Can I get you anything?"

I shook my head, my mind reeling from her words. *Real.* The problem was I didn't know what was real. Dream or not, my feelings for Drew felt real. More real than the rest of my world at the moment, and I couldn't deny that.

"I'll be right back," my mother said in her singsong voice, as I watched her walk from the room.

***

The next day as Ryan sat in the chair beside my bed, tapping furiously on his laptop, my mother's words and the unspoken promise that I made to her rang in my ears. I set down my magazine in my lap and looked at Ryan. I took in his flawless features, trying to remember the man that I had fallen in love with. The cocky, dreamy baseball player. The smart, funny, and extremely compassionate law student. The patient, sensual, and incredibly talented lover. The honest, devoted friend. And eventually, the attentive, romantic, and loving husband. The other half to my whole.

His usually cropped and perfect brown hair was a little longer than usual and unruly, as he had continuously run his fingers through it while he was working. His face was perfection, even with the slight stubble that dotted his upper lip and chin. His broad shoulders and chest were still as sculpted as the day we met, although his middle had grown a touch softer with age. A subtle flaw in his otherwise perfect physique, but one that I loved. His fingers stopped typing as he looked up, his warm brown eyes capturing my gaze.

And we were frozen in the moment, our gazes locked, holding so much promise between us, each of us afraid to look away. He gently closed his laptop and set it aside without averting his eyes. A single tear bled from the corner of my eye and slowly dribbled down my cheek, followed by another. He slid onto the bed, facing me, our gazes still searching, pleading. I felt the bed shift and dip as he leaned in and wiped my tear with the tip of his thumb.

I closed my eyes briefly at his touch, and, in the same moment, I felt him crash against me. His arms finding their way behind me, as he raised me up and held me against him. My arms reached out and held him around the neck as I buried my face on his shoulder. Tears fell endlessly now as I felt the pain and regret and sorrow in his embrace. And the relief for this moment that passed between us, whatever it may be.

"I love you, Gemma," he whispered into my ear, and his breath on my flesh sent shivers rippling through me. We hadn't held each other in what felt like forever. I couldn't remember the last time we had connected like this. It was long before the accident, long before I found him in bed with another woman. Maybe since the devastation of our last failed attempt to conceive.

"I love you too," I whispered against his shoulder. And I did still love him. I was just so hurt. Hurt from his choice that day, hurt from all my failures. I wished it was simple. Forgiving him, forgiving myself. I wished I could snap my fingers and the image of him betraying me would be gone, the pain would be gone. And we could start over, together, with our baby.

"I'm so sorry," he said.

Anger ripped through me at his words, robbing me of the moment. I drew back and looked into his eyes, feeling his betrayal all over again. Wondering how he could love me and yet consciously make that choice, the choice to sacrifice our relationship, our promise to one another. How could he be so reckless with my heart? The thought made my stomach convulse, and I held my hand over my mouth instinctively, shaking my head back and forth, unable to absorb any more pain from what he had done.

"I can't lose you, Gemma," he whispered with a fresh wave of fear in his eyes.

I beat my fists against his chest as hard as I could, which wasn't very hard from our close proximity. "Why would you do that to me? To us?" I yelled. "Why?" Desperation fell from my lips in a mix of anger and sadness. "You broke *us*. You broke us," I repeated, my words getting lost in a new string of sobs as I buried my face in his chest. He held me tightly in silence, and I could feel his own tears on my skin as we finally faced the pain of what he had done and the pain of what we had become.

Thirty

I was on the verge of being discharged. My grueling physical therapy was finally proving a purpose as each day I took more steps without the use of a walker, my legs finally functioning like they were meant to. It was a slow process, and my patience was tested time and time again. I focused on Drew's face, knowing that once I was released into the world —come hell or high water—I was going to find him.

So with each painful step, with each exercise that my therapist pushed me through, I visualized what I would say to Drew when we were finally standing face-to-face. I continued to call his office, and I left numerous messages for his father, all to no avail. I'm not sure why, but I knew that I had to go to the lake. I felt drawn there. Maybe it was my dream or the fact that I was supposed to be there, had it not been for the accident, but I had a strong sense that I would find Drew there.

I tried to prepare myself for whatever I might discover when I did find him, my mother's words heavy on my mind. I just wanted a chance to tell him the truth, a chance to have my friend back in my life. I tried to prepare myself for the wife and children that he may have or the cold-hearted man who maybe he had become. But all I could see was the Drew from my dream. The kind, gentle soul who —even after all these years—still loved me.

So I pushed myself as if I was moving toward Drew with each step, and I focused on the baby as well. Knowing that my health was a vital component to my baby's health.

The baby was growing, and my doctor was happy with the few pounds that I had gained. My stick figure, dangerously malnourished from the coma, was starting to fill out here and there. I was ready for the curves that pregnancy would bring. I craved the swell of my belly, full of the new life that I had dreamed of for so long. It still didn't feel real, even as I watched the little blob dance and shift on the ultrasound screen, or as I listened to the sound of its strong and steady heartbeat fill the room. It didn't feel real.

But in the quiet and stillness of the night, when I found myself alone, I would caress my flat belly as I talked to the baby in the encouraging and loving tone only meant for a mother. I found myself wondering about epic thoughts like the existence of God or fate. I had lost my faith in these things over the years, unwilling to believe that a God would allow someone to suffer as much as I have, to deny me one of His gifts when He seemed to give them so freely to the least likely contenders like teenage girls, crack addicts, and women who possessed not one motherly trait in their body.

I also refused to believe that I was not meant to have a child or to be a mother. Refused to believe that such was my fate. But now I felt that there was some kind of lesson to be learned, a hidden agenda. That everything happened for a reason. I'd dissected my dream over and over again, wondering its purpose, its meaning. Wondering why Drew would come back to me, even if in a dream, all these years later. *What did it mean?* I wasn't sure, but I knew that I had to find him. To make sense of it all.

Within all these thoughts in the quiet hours of the night, as I held my hands over the life blooming inside me, I found hope.

***

Ryan and I spent hours talking, trying desperately to connect in some way, to bring back what we had lost. He broke down and told me about his "mistake." How it was a momentary lapse of judgment, a moment of weakness, just that one time.

"Why would you take her to our home? How could you do that in our bed?" I asked, finally facing the questions that I had avoided as long as I could. I was sitting on the edge of my hospital bed with one leg drawn up underneath me. "It was the biggest slap in the face, Ryan. Why not a sleazy hotel?"

Ryan sat in the chair near the bed, hunched over with his elbows resting on his knees. "It wasn't like I planned it. I had spilled ketchup on my shirt at a lunch meeting. We were at that little Bistro down the street, so I stopped at home to change my shirt before going back to the office. Sasha came up with me."

I cringed at the sound of her name. I preferred to leave her nameless. "Please don't say her name," I demanded holding my hand up, interrupting him.

"Sorry. But she followed me into the bedroom and came on to me, very aggressively. I'm not blaming her. But it felt so good to feel wanted. I got caught up in the desire, the connection."

I felt that sick feeling in my gut. I wanted him to stop talking, but I knew that I needed all the facts or I would never be able to forgive him. I knew that I would always wonder.

"I wasn't thinking. Obviously," he added.

"Oh, you were thinking all right, just not with the right part of your body," I mumbled.

But inside I felt the guilt flood my heart. I had been so distant and emotionally unavailable for so long. I had shut down and had completely shut him out in the process, carrying the burden myself when he would have gladly shouldered the weight.

"I deserve that, Gemma, I do. But don't forget that we're supposed to be a team. And you pushed me away. I felt like I had already lost you."

"Don't put this on me. I didn't force you to sleep with her. You did that all on your own," I said in a raised voice, pointing my finger at him in anger. I hated the bitterness that I felt in my heart. It was so much easier to be angry and petulant than face the real issue. "You obviously had feelings for her or at the very least felt attracted to her. This didn't just happen. Was it really just the one time?"

He sighed and buried his face in his hands for a moment and then looked back up at me. "Yes. I swear it was just the one time. But there was a lot of flirting leading up to it, which I considered completely harmless at the time. Now I realize how inappropriate it was. I'm sorry. I would take it back in a heartbeat. I never wanted to hurt you. It meant absolutely nothing. I love you so much, Gemma. God, it was the biggest mistake of my life. My biggest regret."

They were only words, but I knew Ryan well enough to know his torment and his guilt, his suffering. I knew he loved me, and he was *choosing* me, choosing our family. I wanted to forgive him, to forgive myself, and to move on, but I didn't know if I could. The pain of it all was still so raw. I prayed that my mother was right, that time did heal all wounds.

Thirty-One

The next morning, I took a walk, holding the railing tightly as I shuffled slowly down the familiar hall of the transitional care unit. I reached the end, staring at a door to the stairwell. *What the hell*, I thought. And decided to push myself a little. I was wearing cropped black yoga pants, a loose-fitting pastel T-shirt, and running shoes. My hair had been slowly growing back; my mother had styled it in a short, spiky cut. *What I wouldn't give to have my long blond waves back.*

I looked less like a patient today and more like a visitor as I pushed the heavy gray door open and ascended the stairs, one at a time as I gripped the railing with a steady hand. I reached the next floor and pushed through another door that opened to yet another hallway that bore the same antiseptic smell, constant movement, and hushed voices. I walked slowly, peeking into each open door as I passed, wondering what each patient was suffering through. *Was it cancer, an illness, elective surgery*? I looked up and felt my feet nearly crumble beneath me.

William.

I gripped the railing tightly as my breath caught in my throat.

His tall and bulky frame filled the doorway of the next room that I was about to pass. He was stepping out into the hallway, just a few feet from where I stood. His dark hair was gray at the temples, his blue eyes sad but held some measure of warmth—so different from the cold depths that had haunted my dreams.

For years I had envisioned this moment, rehearsed what I wanted to say. But now my mind was utterly thoughtless, my scripted words nonexistent. My body was a flurry of activity though, anything but quiet. A sheer layer of sweat arose on my skin; my heart pounded in my chest—*thump, thumping* in my ears—my stomach churned, bile rising in my throat as I felt a slow tremble travel through my limbs.

I couldn't seem to look away, my wide eyes staring at him in disbelief. He turned and looked at me; his initial expression conveyed confusion, but, as sudden recognition reached his eyes, he looked just as shocked as I was. We stood in silence, my gaze unflinching, for what felt like forever as the sound of my heart rose to a crescendo. My face flushed with heat. Before either of us could utter a word, my eyes wandered inside the room that he had been exiting. It was then that I saw *him*.

I balled my hands into fists, digging my short fingernails into the skin of my palms until I felt a sharp, stinging pain where they broke through the surface, proof that I wasn't dreaming—again. For a fleeting moment I was elated, stunned that he had been here all along, in the same hospital, just one floor above me. *What were the chances?* I had found him, and my once-still mind was now a jumble of emotions and words that I longed to convey to him. The moment split, burst in two, as his condition finally registered somewhere inside me.

My feet were suddenly moving faster than my mind could process the scene. I pushed William aside as I entered the room. Throwing myself against *him*, uninhibited by the number of tubes and wires that protruded from his still body. I sobbed onto his chest, soaking the pale blue hospital gown that covered his ashen skin, desperately hoping that *this* was the dream, that this wasn't real.

"No, no, no," I sobbed. "No, Drew," I whispered. As if I already knew why he was here, the glaring reality weighing down my heart like a two-ton brick. And that was when I heard William's deep voice from behind me.

"Gemma? What are you doing here?" William asked softly.

Hearing him say my name, almost took me back to the woods. I could almost smell the unmistakable scent of smoke from the bonfire, the smell of whiskey on his breath. Almost. With Andrew lying motionless on the bed before me, I pushed it all away and buried it deep inside, reverting my focus to the more important matter.

"William," my voice cracked and I cleared it before I spoke again. "What's wrong with him?" I asked without taking my eyes from Drew.

"He has an inoperable brain tumor, like Mom. He refused any kind of treatment and signed DNR forms against our wishes. He's . . . gone, Gemma." His words were broken as he struggled to keep his emotions in check. "We're just waiting for him to take his last breath." I could sense the exhaustion in his voice and maybe grief.

"I'm too late," I whispered to no one, just words suspended in the thick air that surrounded me. Tears streamed down my face as my love for this man slashed through my heart. *Wasted*. That was the word lingering on my tongue, filling my mind. These emotions, the love, the grief, all the years we had spent apart. Wasted. "It isn't fair. . . . It isn't fair," I repeated in a breathless whisper. And then I felt it, the anger, boiling inside me, threatening to spill over. I stood and faced William, no longer paralyzed with fear but overwhelmed with my disdain for him and what he had done.

"YOU," I yelled, the word coming from a place deep inside me, a voice I did not recognize. "You did this," I continued to yell, stalking toward him. I slapped him across the face, the sound echoing in the quiet of the room, drowning out the machines and monitors. He instantly raised his hand to his cheek where my handprint was marked in red across his skin, branding him. "You took him from me. You ruined us. You ruined *me*. How could you, William? How could you?" My resolve was faltering, and I knew that it was only a matter of time before I fell apart, my anger surrendering to my grief, breaking me wide open.

"GET OUT," I screamed. "You don't deserve to be here. You don't deserve to grieve for him," I said, pointing toward the open door, ignoring the part of me that had once loved William like a brother, ignoring the part of me that was reminded by the fact that he was Drew's brother, flesh and blood, heart and soul. With a solemn look in his eyes, he turned and walked out the door. I collapsed into the chair near Drew's side, my head on his chest, sobbing once again while my body shook from the adrenaline that had pounded through me.

When my devastation began to ebb, I pulled my face back to look at Drew. He looked older than he had in my mind and yet the same. Still beautiful. I longed for him to open his eyes, to get lost in their icy blue depths, to see him smile at me with those signature dimples. I caressed his cheek and his arm, reaching for his hand as I intertwined our fingers. I imagined my touch melting into his, wondering if he could feel me, if he sensed that I was here.

I willed him to open his eyes or to squeeze my hand —anything to signal that he knew it was me. Nothing. Still holding his hand, I brought it to my lips and gently kissed each knuckle, closing my eyes to savor the feel of his hand against my cheek. As I opened my eyes, I was suddenly aware of something on the underside of his arm, halfway between his elbow and wrist, black ink. I gently turned his arm until it was clearly visible, the tattoo from my dream— the broken infinity symbol. *It's to remind me that nothing lasts forever.* His words echoed in my mind with such clarity. *Was this part of the dream? Am I really awake? How is this possible? How could this be real?* Chills coursed through me, leaving tiny bumps along my skin as I considered the possibilities, felt the weight of the coincidence.

***

I stayed by Drew's side for hours; the hospital staff came and went, quietly making their assessments and writing in their charts. I replayed our time together in my head over and over again, rationalizing the idea that we had both been drifting in a place between this world and death, together. And that somehow what we had shared was real . . . somewhere.

The more time I spent thinking about it, the less crazy it seemed. I wasn't sure how else to explain the tattoo and the fact that I knew I was pregnant and the coincidence that Drew was in this bed, dying just as he had told me in my dream. It couldn't have been just a dream. I was hopeful that somehow Drew knew what had happened, that he knew how

I felt about him, that we had some sense of closure. . . . I had to believe this to be true.

The sun was fading, casting shadows outside the window of Drew's hospital room. A nurse in pale blue scrubs entered the room quietly. I wondered if they were trained to tread so lightly. They seemed to enter and exit rooms like ghosts, floating in and out as if they were never there at all. Her soft voice startled me, pulling me from my thoughts.

"Are you a patient here?" she asked.

I looked up, confused by her question.

"You have a hep-lock. I just assumed that you were a patient," she clarified.

"Oh," I said, raising my hand to show the IV site that was taped to my skin. "Yeah, I'm a patient downstairs, in 412."

She nodded as she hung a new IV bag on a pole and attached it to Drew's own IV that was threaded in the vein of his left arm.

"Is there any chance that he's going to be okay?" I asked.

"I'm sorry. I can only discuss his condition with immediate family," she said with a sense of empathy. "You know you should probably head back to your room. You've been here nearly my entire shift."

"Yeah, you're probably right," I said, wondering why no one had come to look for me. I squeezed Drew's hand one more time and then stood. My vision blurred, and my body swayed wearily as my weight settled to my feet. I grabbed the arm of the chair and held on to balance myself.

"Are you okay?" the young nurse asked as I felt her hands on my arm, forcing me back into the chair.

"I'm dizzy and a little weak," I replied.

"Just sit. I'm going to get you a wheelchair and have someone escort you downstairs." I couldn't protest. I knew there was no way I could make it downstairs on my own.

Moments later a tall, young man arrived with a wheelchair, helped me into it, and whisked me down the hall toward the elevator. As we passed the waiting room, I saw William sitting with his head tucked into his hands. He looked up just as I passed. I couldn't deny how broken he looked, but I refused to feel sorry for him after what he had done.

"Gemma," he called out, standing quickly and walking toward us as we waited for the elevator.

"I can't do this right now, William," I whispered, swallowing the lump that had suddenly formed in my throat. I heard the *ding* of the elevator, and the doors slid apart. My escort stood, holding the elevator doors open, while he waited for William and me to finish our exchange.

"We need to talk, Gemma. Please just hear me out," he pleaded as he stood awkwardly with his hands buried in the pockets of his faded jeans.

"No," I said firmly. It was all I could say before I broke down again. "Let's go," I whispered to the boy waiting to take me to my room. He wheeled me into the elevator, spinning me around so that we faced forward, and I caught William's gaze right before the doors closed. As the elevator screeched to a halt just one floor below, I felt the tremble take hold of me as William's dark eyes blazed in my mind, haunting my very soul once again.

Thirty-Two

I returned to Drew's room every day that week during my walks, my daily exercise encouraged by my physical therapist. Only my mother knew the truth as to my whereabouts as I disappeared for hours at a time. And then one day as I sat by Drew's side, still willing him to open his eyes—my hope never faltering—I somehow knew that this would be my last visit. I was not sure how I knew, but I felt it. Maybe it was the way my gaze locked on his face, and I couldn't seem to look away, as if I was memorizing every feature—storing it away—adding it to the image I held there of him as a boy.

He looked so peaceful laying there, more still than I had ever seen another human being before. I longed for him to open his eyes, to see him smile, flashing me those dimples that I loved so much. I wanted to believe that our time together was real, and I felt a pang in my chest for all the wasted time. All the years that we could have been in each other's lives. *What were the chances that we were both here at the same time*? But a moment too late. How cruel fate could be.

If only I had been here sooner, if only I had awoken sooner. We could have said all the things that needed to be said. I reached for his hand, holding it in mine as tears streamed down my face. I leaned down and kissed his cheek, resting my face against his skin. I had to believe that my time with Drew was real. There was no other explanation. *That* had been our chance to say what had needed to be said, to feel what we had needed to feel, to be who we had needed to be. To say good-bye. But I would never know for sure. And this fact gripped me with such uncertainty and regret that I feared it would never let me go.

The next day I shuffled in to Drew's room, and found the bed empty and stripped, as if he had never been there at all. I shouldn't have been surprised; I had felt the end draw near the day before, but my breath still ceased in my chest, the overwhelming loss knocking the air from my lungs even though I had known that this moment was inevitable, that he was already gone. I sat in the chair where I had rested by his side that entire week and cried. The same young nurse, who I now knew as Annie, came to my side and gently rubbed my back.

"He finally went late last night. He's at peace now," she said, as if her words would comfort me. But all I could feel was fate's cruelty once again and my hatred for William. I knew that it wasn't his fault that Drew was gone, but I needed someone to blame. I needed someone to blame for this pain and grief and anger that was filling me to the brim. Before it spilled over, leaving me empty, I ran from the room as fast as my weak and damaged legs would carry me.

Coincidentally I was discharged that very day. Ryan was prepared to take me home, back to Seattle. But I refused, insisting that I needed some more time. I wanted to stay with my mother for a while until I was stronger. Ryan felt defeated but gave in to my wishes. He didn't have much of a choice.

When my mother and I were settled into her car, I took a deep breath and said what had been on my mind since I had learned that Drew was gone.

"Take me to the lake," I said, almost a demand.

"Gemma? You need to rest. We're going home, and, when you feel up to it, then we'll go," she said as she gripped the steering wheel tightly, looking in my direction where I sat with my eyes fixed on the parking lot ahead.

"No, I need to go now." Something in my voice must have changed her mind because I heard her sigh and start the car. When we pulled out onto the highway, we were heading north, toward the lake.

I felt a strong sense of déjà vu as the car veered around each corner. My mother slowed as we rounded a sharp curve, and I realized that this was the scene of the accident. I remembered feeling anxious that I was almost there and then getting the text from Ryan. I remembered my screams as I felt the car skid across the road—the moment when my reality split, my mind finishing my journey while my body fought to hold on.

"I came here, to this place, many times while you were in a coma. I don't know why. I would sit on the side of the road and pray. I just wanted my baby girl back. I couldn't help but feel responsible, sending you up here alone in your condition." My mother wiped the tears from her eyes as she pushed her foot on the gas pedal, and we moved on from the place where I had almost lost my life.

The moment passed, and I was unable to say anything. Unable to think about what it would have meant if I hadn't woken up. I placed my hands across my belly, imagining the world without me, without this life growing inside me.

We drove slowly down the dirt lane that led to the cabin, pausing at the larger potholes in the road. As we were passing Monroe Manor, I opened the door and lunged out, hearing my mother's protests as I shuffled down the driveway toward the back door. I turned the knob but it was locked, I banged on the door as if someone would be there. Nothing. I followed the walkway that ran alongside the cabin toward the beach. Cupping my hands around my face, I veered into the large windows that faced the lake. No one was there, but everything looked the same as I remembered. Some of the furniture was different than in my dream, but still I couldn't help but look at the couch and remember what it had felt like when Drew had touched me.

Tears filled my eyes as I turned and looked out at the lake. Without much thought of where I was going, I walked down the beach and out to the end of my dock. It was a beautiful and warm summer day, but I shivered at the chill that invaded me. It was as if I had just stood in this very place yesterday, and yet it had really been years since I had been here. It was hard to believe that I hadn't recently breathed in the clean scent of the pine-filled air or looked upon the mountains in the distance or felt the cool water of the lake on my feet. *It had to be real*, I kept repeating in my mind.

I walked up the lane to my cabin and stopped dead in my tracks when I took in the exterior. It was just as I saw it last. Cedar-red siding, freshly stained, a bright white trim outlined the large front windows. My mother was perched on the restored porch swing, swaying back and forth, watching me with worried eyes. It was all as I had left it, just weeks before, not the twentysome years that had supposedly passed since I had been here last. My heart beat with trepidation, as I walked slowly to the porch.

I looked at my mother with questions in my eyes that I could not articulate.

"I don't know what to say, Gemma. Someone did us a kind favor, that's all. Don't go looking any further into this," she said, as if I had asked the question in my mind out loud. The front door sat ajar, and I made my way up the steps and through the threshold. I wasn't sure what to expect, what I might find. Inside, the cabin was the same from my childhood. The air felt damp and musty. The kitchen remained untouched, dust coated the red Formica countertops and the white sheets that covered all the furnishings. The memory of my arrival was so fresh in my mind—the smells, the touch of the fireplace, even the dusty white sheets that I had carefully removed one at a time. But here everything sat, untouched. Except the fresh paint that coated the outside walls.

I pushed open the back screen door and stepped out onto the deck overlooking the creek. The deck was still in poor shape, boards protested under my feet with pleas to be replaced, the paint faded and peeled away at the edges. I felt a panic building inside, an urgency to find something that made sense, a sign that would confirm my instincts. I ran back inside, my slow and heavy body betraying me with every step. I frantically searched through the chest of drawers in the hallway, looking for my grandfather's compass. Wanting it to be absent from where it had rested for nearly twenty years, wanting it to be gone because I had gifted it to Drew.

I was compelled by my dire need for some sort of sign from God or fate that my time with Drew was real. And just as I was sure that the compass was amiss, my hand felt the familiar cold round surface. I withdrew it from the drawer, my heart beating heavy in my chest, as I turned it over in my hand. I swept my finger over the smooth surface, lacking the inscription that was there when I last remembered holding it in my hand, the day that I had given it to Drew. That day, from my dream, when Drew and I had spent time at Upper Priest, replayed in my head.

Clutching the compass tightly in my hand, I flew out the front door and walked next door to Bill and Ann Sherwood's cabin, pounding on their door, until Bill appeared before me. He had been a kind man growing up, and, as I stood staring into his startled face, I could see the same kindness in his eyes. He was nearly bald now, with only patches of gray above his ears, and his belly protruded over the top of his belted khaki slacks.

"Can I help you?" he asked. Before I could answer, he glanced behind me to see my mother walking toward us. "Bethany? Gemma? Is that you? Well, I'll be damned. I haven't seen the likes of you for years."

Skipping the pleasantries, I launched into the reason I was banging down his door. "Bill, I need you to take me to Upper Priest."

"Upper Priest? Why in heaven's name do you want to go up there?" he asked.

"I saw your boat tied up on the dock. Please, I need to go there right now." My rushed words sounded crazy even to my own ears, and I worried for a moment what he must think of me.

"It's nearly noon, Gemma. That's a long trip," he said, scratching his bald head as if he still had a full head of hair.

"Please, Bill, it's important." I felt my mother beside me then.

"Bill, good to see you," she said, as she shook his hand. "I'm so sorry for this intrusion." She turned to me. "Gemma, what is this all about?"

"Mother, please, I need to go to Upper Priest."

"I was going to go out for a little fishing today anyway. I guess we could venture up north for a bit," Bill said.

"Oh, thank you, thank you," I said, holding my hands together in front of me with the compass pressed between my palms.

"I'll just get my things and meet you at the dock," he said, sensing my urgency.

I turned to walk toward the beach as my mother was suddenly in step beside me.

"Gemma Rose Lang, I swear I don't know what's gotten into you."

I suppressed the need to correct her, to remind her that my last name was Walsh.

***

The long boat ride north was uneventful. The water was calm for a late summer day, but it was midweek, and not many boats were on the lake. I sat quietly as my mind wandered to moments that felt like last week as my mother and Bill made idle chitchat, filling in the twenty-year time gap that spanned between them. When we finally navigated through the Thorofare, I directed Bill to the beach where Drew and I had always spent our time. Before the boat was completely beached in the sand, I jumped from the bow and waded through the knee-deep water. I followed my heart to the tree and held my breath as I stepped close enough to read the words carved into its bark. *GL + AM, Best Friends to Infinity*. Nothing more, nothing less.

My heart broke. A part of me had wanted the new carvings to be here, the words that I had added that day. I wanted so badly for something—anything—to be real. I wiped tears from my cheeks with the back of my hand as I reached out and touched the words that marked a time in my life that I would never get back. He was gone. Drew was gone. And my recent memories were nothing but a dream, a rare coincidence. My heart threatened to break wide open in that moment, but I pushed it back, fought against the grief. Not here. Not now.

On the boat ride back to Kalispell Bay, I closed my eyes and let the wind beat against my face, my silent tears whisked away before they could be felt on my cheeks. The boat's motor filled in the silence that had fallen over the three of us. I heard my mother's earlier whispers, explaining to Bill the recent trauma that I had endured, as if to excuse my absurd behavior. Neither of them knew quite what to make of the situation.

After helping Bill loop the boat ties through the cleats on the dock, I wandered slowly up the dirt lane toward the cabin. My mother and Bill trailed behind me, giving me my space. I heard my mother ask quietly about the cabin's new paint, and I whirled around, waiting for his response.

"Little Andrew Monroe, bless his heart, done that all himself. He asked me to keep it to myself of course. It took him weeks. I guess he was already pretty sick by that point. But nonetheless he showed up every mornin' and worked himself to the bone . . ." His words faded at that point as all I could hear was the beating of my heart in my ears, pounding steadily, as I pictured Andrew on the ladder, painting the siding of the cabin. His smile lighting up his eyes as we worked side by side, getting to know each other once again. He had been here.

"Poor thing . . . So sad what happened . . . just like his mother . . ." Bill's voice barely registered as I continued walking toward the cabin, tears stinging my eyes. I walked to the back and dropped down on the concrete step of the back porch. I hung my head in my hands, and the grief spilled out of me in steady waves, thrashing against the walls of my heart. I wasn't sure how long I sat here, mourning Drew and the loss of the time that I thought I had shared with him.

The blue of the sky had turned to an orange and pink haze, almost glowing through the treetops. I stared at the height of the evergreens that bordered the back of the cabin, obscuring the copper creek that I could hear clearly as it streamed in a steady rush over rocks and fallen logs, fighting its way to the open waters of the lake that waited just around the bend. I noted the mossy earth that lay at the foot of the trees, flourishing in the shade the evergreens provided. And that's when I noticed fresh soil, turned over in a heap beneath the trees, as if someone had been digging around in the dirt.

Curiously I rose from the step and walked over, kicking the dirt around with my foot. And without another thought, I fell to my knees and buried my hands in the cool, damp soil. Assaulted with memories of a day long ago when Drew and I had dug a hole in this very place. Choosing a spot at the birth of the tallest tree so that we would never forget. *How could have I forgotten?* A renewal of energy shot through me at the prospect of finding our time capsule that we had buried long ago. I felt it, the thermos, at my fingertips and tunneled deeper into the earth until it was free. I wiped the dirt from the steel container and slowly twisted off the lid, already picturing what I would find.

The thin colorful threaded friendship bracelets that I had weaved for us, the laminated picture of Drew and me that I had used as a bookmark in all my Beverly Cleary *Ramona* books. Drew's Susan B. Anthony silver dollar—that he had been hesitant to part with—and a newspaper clipping that we had cut from his father's *Priest Lake Herald* on that day, secured in a sheet of plastic wrap, for a time reference. As I shook the thermos, the contents dumping into my lap one at a time, I recognized all these items—except one.

A foreign piece of treasure, secured in a plastic bag. I could see my name written in neat print on a folded white envelope. I carefully peeled open the plastic seal and pulled the envelope from the bag. I ran my fingers over my name, *Gemma*, before sliding my index finger under the sealed flap and retrieving the folded paper from inside. With unsteady hands I slowly unfolded the paper, my mind bouncing back and forth between sheer curiosity and fear.

It was a letter dated two months ago.

Dear Gemma,

If you are reading this, then I was right about you, and I am most certainly gone. I figured that, upon hearing the news, you would come to this place that once meant so much to us both. This is my cowardly way of saying good-bye. I didn't have the heart to disrupt your life. To become a physical presence in your life again, knowing the plans that God had in store for me. And the last thing you need is to endure another good-bye. I did check up on you, just to make sure that you were happy and that your life was what you deserve. It seems that you are very successful and married to a good man. And from a distance, you seem happy. And I hope that you are—happy, that is. The one thing I am sure of, you are beautiful. Like take-my-breath-away beautiful. But then again, you always were.

When I was diagnosed just like my mom had been, I knew that this was the end for me. I came here, back to the lake, to live my final days. I couldn't think of anywhere I'd rather be. I miss you. I miss us. My one regret in this life—letting you walk out of it. I should have fought for you, fought for my best friend—the closest thing that I had to a family since I lost my mom. I was a stupid kid, blinded by my emotions and then my pride.

And so I wanted to say that I am sorry. I'm sorry that I didn't live up to the promises that we had made to each other. For what it's worth, you have been with me, in my heart, every day since I last saw you. And I will carry you with me into the next life.

I do not fear what is to come. I have made peace with my fate. I long for the quiet, an escape from the pain. And I know, somehow, that I will be with my mom again. And maybe I'll be able to watch over you, to know you in a way that I haven't in a long time.

I painted the cabin, my final gift to you, in hope that you will come here again, to this place, with your own family.

And my parting words, for what it's worth: Let go of your regrets and truly live —you deserve every happiness.

I love you, Gemma Rose Lang. I'll always love you.

Remember me ...

Your Friend to Infinity ... and Beyond,

Andrew

Tears fell in rapid sequence, leaving wet swirls on the paper, soaking through the black ink that spoke the words of Drew's heart. The idea that he was here recently, thinking of me and didn't reach out to me, couldn't pick up the phone and call, and the idea that I was too late, filled my heart with painful regret. And in the same moment, Drew's words stared at me from the paper in my hands. *Let go of your regrets.* I clutched the letter against my chest, drawing comfort from the fact that Drew had held this same paper in his own hands only two months before. I reached for the picture of us. A close-up of our faces, taken by my mother on a bright sunny morning. My large front bucklike teeth and freckles, wet blond hair falling in chunks around my eyes. Drew's perfect round face, full cheeks dawning the biggest dimples I had ever seen and clear blue eyes shining light like the heavens. Our bright smiles were so authentic, full of promise and possibilities, unaware of what lay ahead. We didn't have a care in the world. Why would we? We had each other.

Thirty-Three

My mother convinced me to get in the car though I was reluctant to leave. I sat in the front seat, with Drew's letter still clutched to my chest, finding some semblance of comfort by keeping his words close to my heart. The thermos and its contents were tucked away in my purse. The trees swept by outside my window, nearly lost to the approaching darkness as we drove down the highway in complete silence. My mother slowed as we passed by the gas station, the General Store, and Sal's Garage.

"Stop the car, Mother!" I yelled as I caught the movement of someone closing the large garage door at Sal's.

Without question, my mother slowed the car and pulled off into the gravel lot where my gaze was fixed. I opened the car door and walked toward the dark figure, praying that it was who I thought it was. My heart stopped when I saw the familiar blond hair and hazel eyes. I knew I was supposed to believe that I hadn't seen him in years, but I felt like I had seen him yesterday. He looked exactly how I had imagined.

He began to walk into the shop through the smaller door before he looked up at the last minute and spotted me.

"Can I help you?" he asked, oblivious that it was me. I couldn't blame him, I hardly recognized myself in the mirror since the accident, and he hadn't seen me since high school.

Frantic, afraid that he would walk away and I would never see him again, I called out to him. "Logan." My voice broke, and I cleared my throat and called out once again. "Logan."

He stepped away from the doorway and out into the night at the sound of my voice. He stared at me for what seemed like forever until recognition finally flashed across his face. "Gemma? Is that you?" he asked, unsure.

"Yes. Logan, it's me." My heart was clamoring in my chest, tears threatening to spill from my eyes, now that he was standing right in front of me. Under the floodlights, I could see how broken he appeared. He looked much older and tired and sad.

"Oh, Gemma, I can't believe you're here," he said as he pulled me to him, wrapping his arms around me. "Did you come for Drew?" he asked.

I nodded against his chest as my tears soaked his T-shirt. I wanted to tell him everything in that moment. About the accident, my dream, Drew. But I couldn't find the words beneath my grief.

"The service is the day after tomorrow. You'll be there, right?"

I hadn't thought of that. I was so distracted with proving my dream to be real, I hadn't thought about his funeral. My chance to say good-bye, to pay my respects. His father would be there . . . and William. I took a deep breath.

"I'll be there. Where is it?" I asked.

"Here. Ten o'clock. At the little chapel on the hill that overlooks the bay. It was what Drew wanted."

"Did you see him? He was here?" I asked as I pulled away from him, looking into his eyes.

Logan nodded. "Yeah, he was here for about six months." Logan hung his head, resting his hands on his denim-clad hips. "Damn stubborn ass, wouldn't let anyone help him."

I attempted a smile and said, "Sounds like Drew."

A car horn sounded in the distance, and I looked behind me to see my mother flashing her lights. "I better go. That's my mother. We're heading back to her house tonight, but I'll return for the service. I have so many questions and so much to tell you. Can we catch up then?"

"Of course." Logan pulled me back into a hug. "It's so good to see you, Gem."

"It's good to see you too," I said, wiping the tears from my eyes as I stepped away. I reached out and cupped his cheek for a moment, memorizing his familiar face. "Bye," I whispered and walked swiftly back to the car and my impatient mother, still holding Drew's letter in my hand.

***

Exhaustion settled into my bones, pinned my heart to the inside of my rib cage as I stepped out of the car at the chapel. Wind whipped through my short blond hair that stood on end while I looked out at the view. You could see the entire south end of the lake from this spot, including Kalispell Island. I could see why Drew would want us to honor him at this chapel, in this place. It seemed fitting that the sky would be a mess of dark clouds today, in the middle of summer, threatening rain. I wondered if Drew believed in God, in the end.

We used to ponder the idea of His existence when we were younger, after Katherine had died. I think that Drew needed something to believe in, an idea that he could hold on to that brought a sense of purpose to his mother's death. But neither of us could imagine that there was a God that cruel. Now I hoped that Drew had found that belief and purpose in his own death, that maybe in the end he had found a sense of peace.

Emotions rocketed through me. I was unable to fight them. I hadn't been able to sleep or eat the past few days, anxiety haunting me about this very day—saying good-bye to Drew and being in close proximity to William. I wasn't sure how I was going to make it through the day, but I had to come. *How could I not?*

I heard my mother beside me seconds after the slam of her car door. "Are you ready, Gemma?" she asked.

"Can I have a minute alone? I'll meet you inside," I said as I turned to look into her eyes. I could feel her sadness from where I stood; it was written in her eyes. Drew had been such a special person in our lives for so many years. She insisted on coming to pay her respects, and I wasn't able to drive myself.

"Sure," she said as she squeezed my hand tightly in hers and turned to make her way into the small church. I took a deep breath, filling my lungs with the clean pine-scented air, my thoughts a swirling mix of memories—old and new. I whispered into the wind, hoping that my words would carry on its wings to the heavens or wherever Drew might be now.

"Drew, I'm sorry that I didn't tell you. I'm sorry for it all. I hope that somehow you knew the truth and that you find peace in knowing that I loved you then and that I love you now. It *was* always you. It will always be you."

I held my hands over my belly, feeling a sudden surge of strength, knowing that life and death were so full of mystery and miracles. I couldn't sort it all out in my head, to make sense of it all in this moment, but I felt that everything happened for a reason, that everything in life had a purpose. Who we meet, who we love, who we lose, . . . it all had a purpose. I had been thinking this for a while now, needing to believe in something myself. Grasping at anything that could fill the void of explanation for recent events.

My accident, my dream, this baby, Drew's death . . . I closed my eyes and raised my face to the clouds, feeling the wind against my cheeks, imagining that Drew was somehow reaching out to me, that he was here with me. Tears wet my cheeks in the same moment that tiny raindrops fell from the sky. A small smile reached my lips, a heartbreaking smile. It was silly but I wanted to believe that I was feeling Drew's tears on my cheeks, mixed with my own.

Get a grip, I thought to myself as I opened my eyes and wiped away the moisture, careful not to smudge my mascara any more than it already had. I brought my hand to my lips, kissed the ends of my fingers and blew it out into the air, sending Drew a symbol of my affection, just like I had done so many times when we were young. Saying good-bye was always so hard at the end of the summer, so Drew and I had started a simple ritual. He would stand at the end of his driveway, and I would stand in front of my cabin. We would blow each other a kiss across the lane just before I piled into my family's car and drove away.

"Never say good-bye," he had said to me once.

And so we never did, until that last morning on the dock when he had said good-bye, breaking the first of the many promises that we had made to each other.

I straightened my black shift dress, brushed a hand through my short, wind-blown hair, and walked slowly to the church, focusing on the steady rhythm of my heels clicking on the pavement with each step.

The service was beautiful. I sat between my mother and Logan. The crowd was small, thirty to forty people, close friends and family, just the way Drew would have wanted it. The priest read from a short script, a depiction of Drew's life and personality, which he nailed to a tee. I silently wondered if Drew had written it himself. His mother's sister read a poem that brought tears to my eyes, but it was the music that really gutted me.

One of Andrew's closest friends from boarding school, Lucas, played a few songs on his acoustical guitar. His voice flowed through me as he sang a simple and beautiful arrangement of "Fix You" by Coldplay, which was so Andrew. But the words stabbed me right in the heart, as if Drew was speaking to me in some way. When Lucas began playing a slow, melodic version of "Free Fallin'" by Tom Petty, I could barely suppress the sobs that raked through me.

I could see Logan, from the corner of my eye, lean forward and bury his face in his hands. This was one of Drew's favorite songs, but now, as I listened to the words, I felt a connection to their meaning, as if Drew was telling me that he was sorry and that he had somehow known the truth. It was almost too much. This was most likely all in my head, but he had taken the time to bury a letter for me in our time capsule and painted my cabin when he had barely had the strength to stand. Anything was possible. He knew I would be here, somehow, even though it had been years since we had seen one another.

238

My eyes wandered to the first pew where Drew's father and William were seated. A beautiful woman with long dark curly hair was seated next to William with her hand in his. Beside her was a boy, a young teen, who shared the same dark curly hair. And beside the boy was a young girl, half his age with light brown hair that fell down her back in waves. My gut tightened as I considered the possibility that this was William's family. Of course even he would have children. The unfairness of it all filled me with the bitterness that I was familiar with, but then I remembered the miracle growing inside me as I wrapped my arms across my belly, protecting him or her from everything that I felt in that moment.

After the benediction Drew's casket was carried outside to the cemetery that stretched out to the edge of the hill. A small white tent was set up over the burial site. I walked out, flanked by my mother and Logan, our arms intertwined.

From where I stood, I could see the view of the bay again, and I couldn't help but think that Drew had picked the perfect spot. He would be laid to rest, with his favorite view stretched out before him. But, most important, those that came here to grieve him would be reminded of the beauty of the lake. I was sure that Drew knew that such a view might bring them comfort.

The burial service had ended, and I honestly couldn't recall a single second of it as I was lost in my own thoughts, a cold numbness growing inside me. Only a few of us remained afterward. Most everyone had left to attend the reception at Monroe Manor. I couldn't seem to leave, as if something was drawing me to this spot. I stood a few feet from the grave, morbidly staring at the crew of workers as they filled the hole where Drew's body lay, motionless, in a wooden box. It all seemed so unfair at the moment.

"Gemma, are you ready?" I heard Logan ask from behind me.

My mother had gone ahead to the reception when Logan offered to drive me himself.

The rain had stopped sometime during the service, and now the sun was starting to peek out from behind a mass of dark clouds. I couldn't answer or move to acknowledge him in anyway, as if my body was bolted in place.

"Come on, Gemma," Logan said, as he wrapped an arm around my shoulders and tried to steer me toward the car. I reluctantly let him lead me away from Drew, my feet growing heavier with each step. I leaned my head against Logan's shoulder, welcoming the comfort. As we neared the driveway of the chapel where the cars were parked, Logan's voice vibrated in my ear where it rested on his chest.

"Hey, Will. I thought you had already gone back to the cabin."

I jerked my head up at the sound of William's name and met his eyes in the same instant.

"I need to talk to Gemma," he said nervously.

"Sure, I'll give you both a minute," Logan said as he began to step away from me.

"This is neither the time nor the place, William," I said through a shaky voice, reaching my arm out to grip Logan around the waist, holding him in place. I didn't want to be alone with William. I couldn't handle the fear and anxiety that had suddenly crept up on me just from the sound of his voice.

"We need to talk about what happened that night. Please just let me explain, to try to make it right."

Tears spilled down my face as the nausea settled in at his words. "Make it right? How can you make it right? You destroyed me that night. I trusted you. You were like a brother to me. How could you?" I choked out.

Before William could respond, Logan stepped out of my reach, toward William. "What the fuck? You son-of-a-bitch!" Logan yelled seconds before he wound his arm back and connected his fist with the side of Will's jaw. The sound echoed in the vast space around us. Seconds later he did it again, but this time his fist landed in William's gut, causing him to grunt loudly as he fell to his knees. He was doubled over with his arm across his abdomen as he held up his other hand to stop Logan from another advance.

It all happened in slow motion. Logan, breathing heavily, was in a rage and began to approach William again with the intent of kicking him while he was down.

"Stop, Logan," I screamed as I stepped in between them. "Please don't do this," I pleaded, holding my hand against Logan's chest. This was not the place. We were here for Drew. They shouldn't be fighting like this.

Logan stopped in his tracks and leaned over, bracing his hands on his knees as he tried to catch his breath.

William sat on his knees in the dirt, holding his gut. I saw tears running down his cheeks, the left side of his face bright red—almost purple—as he spit a mouthful of blood in the dirt beside him.

We were all panting, the intensity of everyone's emotions filling the space around us, the air almost too thick with tension to breathe.

Logan's strained voice broke through the sudden silence. "This is about that night. In the woods. Isn't it?" he asked, staring directly in my eyes from where he was still hunched over.

I didn't answer his question.

"There's more to it than what you told me, isn't there? It was him. And this asshole actually . . ." His voice trailed off, unable to finish his sentence as he put the pieces together from that night so long ago.

I could only nod, unable to voice the confirmation.

"Son-of-a-bitch," he said again as he shook his head from side to side. "I could fucking kill you right now," he growled, directly at William.

"I know. I deserve that. Believe me, I do," Will said, surprising me with his words, his admission, the self-hatred that I could sense in his tone.

From where he sat, on his knees, in the dirt, he turned to me then. "Gemma. There's no excuse for what I did. I was fucked up. I was so high and wasted that night, I barely remembered what happened the next morning. But I could hear your pleas and cries in my head the next day. I knew that I had done something awful, that I had hurt you."

"How could you tell Drew that I wanted you, bragging to him about sleeping with me after what you had done?" I asked, disgusted with him.

"I was scared. I thought for sure that you would tell Drew. I knew that if I hurt him enough, he would hate you and leave. And I was right."

"You make me sick," I said, angry tears making their way down my face. I wiped them away roughly, mad that I was allowing myself to cry in front of him.

"I know. I'm sorry. I couldn't live with what I'd done. I nearly overdosed several times, trying to make the guilt and pain go away. When I finally made it through rehab, I wanted to find you, to turn myself in, to make it right."

Part of me, deep down inside, beneath all the anger and hatred, wanted to pity him. I wanted to feel for him and everything that he had gone through, but my empathy was overpowered with the pain of all that he had taken from me.

"Why didn't you then, William?" I yelled at him through the torment and tears, as I lunged at him with my hands fisted at my sides. "Why? Why? Do you know what you did to me? You broke me! You broke me!" I screamed at him, as my body shook with rage and heartbreak. Logan wrapped his arms around me then, pulling me into his chest protectively.

"It's okay. It's okay. He can't hurt you anymore. Just breathe."

242

I tried to focus on Logan's calming voice, tried to slow my breath as I sobbed into his chest.

William continued to speak. "I would have turned myself in, but Janelle was pregnant with my baby. She needed me then, and my son needed me. It wasn't about me anymore, or you, Gemma. For once people were depending on me, and I had to do the right thing, *for them.*"

His words resonated somewhere deep inside me. *How could I fault him for choosing to be a father, for turning his life around?*

"Don't think that I moved on and forgot about what I had done. I have agonized over it all these years. When my daughter was born . . ." He broke down in sobs, his head shaking side to side as he gripped his arm over his stomach in pain.

"When my daughter was born, I kept thinking of you and knew that, if anyone ever hurt her the way that I had hurt you, I would kill them. I felt like a monster, and I struggled with the urge to use again. I'm so sorry. I can never go back and undo it, but, God, . . . I wish I could. I. Am. So. Sorry." William completely broke down before me.

I wasn't sure what to feel. *How much longer do I have to live with what happened? Haven't we all paid enough?*

Drew and I, and even William, had all suffered so much from that one night so long ago. But William's torment began long before that. His struggle, his fight. I was overcome with emotion. I knew what he needed from me, but I wasn't sure that I could give it to him. I wasn't sure that I could forgive him for all the years of torment, all the pain that he had caused. The way that he had purposely destroyed my friendship with Drew. The ripple effect from his gruesome attack was far too devastating to absolve him.

I pulled out of Logan's arms and stood in front of William, looking down at him where he knelt at my feet—bloody, beaten, and broken.

"I'm sorry too," I whispered and walked toward Logan's truck. And I was sorry. I was sorry that William was so fucked up; I was sorry for what he had suffered, for what had changed him back then, for what had unleashed the monster that he must see when he looked in the mirror. I was sorry for the way he suffered now, but mostly I was sorry for the time that I could have had with Drew. Now it was too late, and William's apology could never bring Drew back. It could never return to me the time that I had lost.

I heard Logan say to William in a strained voice, "This isn't over," as I opened the heavy door to his truck and hoisted myself up into the seat, closing the door with a weighted breath. Tears made their way down my cheeks as sobs shook my body. Logan opened the driver's side door and climbed in next to me, starting the loud engine before slowly driving away from the church, away from what was left of Drew, away from William kneeling in the dirt begging for forgiveness that I couldn't give.

Thirty-Four

Not able to face Drew's family, primarily William, especially
after his confrontation, we had gone to Logan's house. The
drive was met with silence as I watched Logan's anger
slowly recede, my own despair hovering on the brink, as I
tried to put it all behind me the farther we got from the
church. I had texted my mother to let her know where I was.
She didn't deserve to worry about me more than she already
had, and I didn't want her to wait up for me. It had been a
long day for both of us. We had planned to stay at our cabin
for the night, and I knew that she would be okay alone, with
all our neighbors close by.

Logan and I sat on his couch in his small house that rested on the property behind Sal's Garage, just talking. We were both still shaken up by the altercation with William.

"Gemma, you should've told me," Logan said, rubbing his hand over his face.

I took a sip of my water, staring straight ahead, lost in thought. I was taken back to that night when Logan had found me in the woods, crying. I had told him as little as possible, downplaying the incident by vaguely telling him that I had let things go a little too far with someone, that I felt taken advantage of, and that I was upset, unwilling to give Logan a name, despite his protests, or to recount the experience by admitting that I had been raped.

I could barely wrap my own head around what had happened, much less talk to Logan about it. I made him promise that he would never tell anyone, mainly Drew, and that we would never speak of it again. He had carried me to his truck and driven me back to my cabin, after asking me nearly ten times if I was okay. And that had been the last time that I had seen him until the other night. I shook the memory from my mind as my thoughts drifted back to Drew.

"What was he like in the end, Logan? What did you guys talk about?" I asked, still staring into space, clutching my water glass tightly in my hand.

"Well, he seemed fine at first. A little angry and on edge. We went out drinking a lot. He told me that he was taking a break from life for a while, and I believed him, knowing what an asshole his father was to work for. His behavior made sense. I didn't know that he was sick. He never told me."

Drew's words "taking a break from life" echoed inside my heart. His words from my dream, exactly the same.

"And then strange things started to happen. Like he would get sudden headaches that nearly brought him to his knees, and, a few times, I swear he couldn't see—like he was

246

suddenly blinded by the pain. He would wave it off, always making an excuse when I would start to get worried. And then one day I found him unconscious in his bedroom. We had planned to go fishing, and I had walked in just like I always do, but he wasn't answering when I called out to him. I had to call an ambulance. I was scared shitless. When I got to the hospital, they told me about his condition. At first I was pissed that he didn't tell me. But I get it. He didn't want to be treated differently.

"Anyway, he spent a few days in the hospital, and then he demanded to go back to the Manor. That's when he painted your cabin. He wouldn't let me help him, even though I knew it was taking every ounce of strength he had to finish it." Logan shook his head and took a swig of his beer. "So damn stubborn.

"And then I found him again. He was conscious but barely, and he couldn't get out of bed. I drove him to the damn hospital myself, called his dad and Will. They arrived just before he lost consciousness for the last time. His dad couldn't take it, left shortly after. Will stayed by his side for weeks. I was there as often as I could be. The doctors said that his brain was pretty much gone, but his body was still fighting."

He wiped away a tear from his eye with his palm and downed the rest of his beer.

"The thing is, I kept thinking he was going to wake up, that he was going to beat it. Sometimes when I was sitting alone at his side in the quiet, I would hear him make noises—the doctor said this was normal—but I swear a few times I heard him mumble your name. Of course they told me that I was crazy, that he couldn't possibly have any cognitive thoughts. But I know what I heard. So I thought for sure they were wrong, that he was going to be okay." He leaned forward and set his empty bottle on the table.

A chill swept over me then, and I set my glass on the table next to Logan's empty beer bottles and crossed my arms over my chest tightly, fighting against it. I reached up and wiped a tear from my eye when Logan suddenly gripped my wrist in his hand, startling me.

He pulled my hand closer to his face, twisting my arm gently until the small tattoo on the inside of my wrist was exposed. I felt his thumb trace the figure eight slowly as my breath came in steady, heavy pulls.

"What is this?" he asked.

Although the three of us had been close, some things were kept sacred between just Drew and me, like our tattoo designs and our promises. When I remained quiet with my eyes focused on the black outline etched in my skin, Logan dropped my hand. I slowly traced the tattoo with my own thumb.

"Drew had the same thing, but different and bigger, right here," he said as he pointed at an area of skin on his forearm. "Not a coincidence, is it?" he asked, knowing that he had missed out on whatever this meant to Drew, to me.

I shook my head to confirm his suspicions. "You guys were so close. I could never penetrate that bond between the two of you."

He shook his head, remembering. "And when we got older, this thick tension built between Drew and me whenever you were around. Like he wanted to keep you all to himself. He loved you, you know? That last summer, it was so obvious. At least to everyone but you."

He chuckled to himself as my mind drifted back to Drew's words the last time I saw him, all those years ago. *I'm in love with you. I'm so in love with you . . .*

"Anyway I knew his tattoo must have something to do with you, especially when he told me what it meant. He said it was to remind him that—"

248

"Nothing lasts forever," I whispered the words at the same time as Logan as we both looked at each other, my eyes wide with shock. My love for Drew slammed into me all at once, old feelings mixed in with the new emotions that had flourished inside me and filled me to the point that I thought I might burst.

That hope brought forth once again the idea that what Drew and I had shared was real, that it wasn't just in my head. Too many coincidences, far too tangible to be anything but real. I shivered against that familiar chill that invaded me, as I weighed the consequences of telling Logan everything in that moment. Unable to stay quiet with all the possibilities whirling around in my head, I finally spoke. "Logan, you know about my accident right?"

"Yeah, of course," he said, as he twisted a cap off another bottle of beer.

"Don't you think it's weird that Drew and I were both unconscious at the same time, in the same hospital? I mean, what are the chances?" I asked.

"Pretty bizarre," he agreed as he picked at the label of his beer with his thumbnail.

And then I launched into the whole story about my dream, every sordid detail, as Logan listened intently.

"Shit, Gem. That's crazy," he said when I had shared the complete story.

"Crazy, like I'm insane? Or crazy, like, crazy that happened?" I asked.

He tilted his head to the side and gave me a look. "Of course I don't think you're crazy. I mean, you're right. What are the chances? The whole tattoo thing and your pregnancy, makes you wonder, what if?" He shrugged.

"I don't care what anyone thinks, Logan. It was so real, I can't deny all the coincidences."

"So what are you gonna do now?" he asked.

I looked down at my hands, carefully considering his question. "I have to let Drew go. He's gone, and there's nothing that I can do. I have to move on." I rubbed my hand over my belly. "I have to think about this little one."

"What about your husband?" Logan asked, before setting his empty beer bottle on the table next to the others.

"I don't know, but, honestly after the day I've had, . . . what he did doesn't seem so unforgivable now. I still love him, and we're having a baby. I guess I need to focus on that." I turned to look at Logan again. "This whole thing has changed me though, Logan. I feel so different. The accident, the dream . . . It all changed me somehow."

Logan reached out and cupped my cheek in his hand. "You'll figure it out, Gem." He leaned in and kissed me on the forehead, before standing up to grab another beer from the fridge. "And you'll always have me. Anytime you need to talk," he threw out before walking back to sit down on the couch again.

"Thanks, Logan. What's your story anyway?"

"I don't really have one. You know me. I'm not one to be tied down. I tried the married thing, but it didn't work out."

"Still breaking hearts?" I asked.

He just shrugged. "What can I say?"

I shook my head as a smile spread across my face while Logan kept talking.

"It's funny. Drew told me that he always envied me. He said that I did what I did, loved who I loved, . . . that I was free to just be me. I never realized how unhappy he was until the end. It kind of makes me sad to think about it. I had always envied him because he had money. I thought that it gave him the freedom to do what he wanted, to be who he wanted to be, to really go places, ya know?" Logan looked at me with his lips drawn in, sadness woven through his expression. "But he fought against the chains that held him just as much as I did, maybe more."

We both let out a quiet sigh at the same time, thinking of Drew no doubt. We were all bound by invisible chains, holding us in place as if we were afraid to move on, afraid to let go. I found it unsettling that Drew never found his happiness. I sensed it in his letter, the regret, heartache—that he was never able to move on. *Let go of your regrets.* I could almost hear the pain laced in his words. Words that came from someone who wished they could go back and do it all over again. Someone who knew that second chances were rare and life was too short. Someone who was far too young to know the sum of their own life, to know that none of it added up to enough.

I knew what I owed him, that I couldn't afford to make the same mistakes. That I owed him at least that much. That maybe I was being given that rare second chance, a chance to make it right, to let go of my regrets, and to find *my* happiness.

I felt Logan's arm around my shoulders, pulling me against him. "Come here, you," he said, almost a whisper. I leaned my cheek against his chest, inhaling the scent that was all Logan. The outdoors, cigarettes, and peppermint. Still the same. We sat in silence, lost in our grief, mourning our best friend—remembering our past.

He wasn't Drew, but Logan was the closest thing I had to Drew. Logan was my friend and knew Drew better than anyone. In the moment, I was thankful for that. And I knew that Drew's memory would live on in our hearts as long as we had each other.

***

When Logan dropped me off at the cabin later that night, Ryan's car was parked out front. As I walked to the porch, a wave of emotion washed over me. I pulled open the door to the cabin and found Ryan sitting on the sofa, in silence, waiting. I glanced at my mother's closed bedroom door, knowing that she had already turned in for the night, leaving Ryan and me alone. He rose to his feet as I closed the door behind me.

We just stood looking at each other, in awkward silence for a moment, until I walked to him and crushed myself against him. Tears were streaming down my face. I had never been so happy to see him. He was like the light at the end of this dark day. And it wasn't until this moment that I realized how much I loved him and how much I needed him. I felt the comfort of Ryan's arms as they wrapped around me. He kissed my head, my ear, my neck, as I buried my face into his chest and cried.

"I'm so glad you're here," I mumbled against his chest.

"I'm sorry about your friend," he whispered into my ear. "You should have told me."

"I had a lot of stuff to sort out. I still do," I said in explanation.

"I love you, Gemma. I'll be here, waiting, while you figure it all out. I'm not going anywhere."

I wiped my face on his T-shirt and looked up into his warm brown eyes. I saw so much love in the way he looked at me now. I raised up on my tippy toes, bringing my lips closer to him. He leaned down into me until our lips met. A gentle connection at first, a simple brush of our lips. But seconds later our mouths crashed against each other, urgently —intensely—as all the hurt and anguish and disappointment flowed between us until there was only love and longing. We stayed like this for what seemed like forever. One thought repeatedly passed through my mind. *He chooses me.*

When we finally pulled apart, breathless, Ryan brought his hands to my belly, where a small bump was finally starting to form. I looked into his eyes, full of love, and watched them fill with moisture.

"I can't believe that we're finally going to have a baby," he said with a smile stretched across his beautiful face. I smiled back, and a small laugh escaped me as a rush of happiness filled me at the thought of my baby. Tears of joy spilled down my cheeks, and I reached up and brushed them away. It was crazy to think that after everything we had been through, we were finally being given this chance at happiness. What we did with this chance, and how we embraced it, was up to us.

Thirty-Five

I sat on the edge of the dock, my favorite spot, and watched the sun rise over the mountain peaks in the distance. To say that I was exhausted was an understatement. Ryan and I had cuddled in the full-size bed and had talked into the late dark hours of the night. Trying to keep our voices down, so that we didn't wake my mother who was asleep down the hall, made me feel like a teenager again. Ryan and I were adults, and we were married, but, given the circumstances, it felt like we were sneaking around.

We hadn't had sex, but there was plenty of kissing and caressing. We both knew that we had a lot to work out before we could move on. Once Ryan was softly snoring beside me, I had lain awake thinking about William. I couldn't help but feel that somewhere inside I had already forgiven him. There wasn't a definitive line between forgiving and forgetting, and I felt that maybe I was confusing the two. Nothing was cut and dry—black and white. It was messy and confusing and emotional. I couldn't shake the realization that the William from the woods wasn't the William that I knew, who wasn't the William that I had seen kneeling in the dirt the day before.

I heard footsteps approaching on the dock, the slosh of water beneath the wood almost thunderous in the complete quiet of the early morning. I didn't turn to see who it was. It was most likely Ryan, coming to find me after discovering my side of the bed empty. But, for just a moment, I closed my eyes and remembered my dream and pictured Drew standing behind me. His voice singing on the breeze as it touched my heart.

The voice I heard was not Drew's though; it was similar but deeper, more gruff. I stilled.

"I thought you might like some coffee," I heard him say as a white porcelain mug filled to the brim with steaming-hot black coffee was placed beside me. I looked at the coffee mug through the corner of my eye but said nothing in return; I didn't move to acknowledge him.

At my lack of response, he began to walk away, his weight causing the dock to shift and rock, spilling the coffee over the edge of the cup.

I knew what I needed to do, what the right thing to do was.

I turned to see him heading back toward the beach, his back to me.

"Will," I called out.

He stopped and turned back to look at me. His face was contorted in pain—his jaw swollen and bruised, dark circles framed his red-rimmed eyes. It was obvious that his night had been far worse than mine.

I took a deep breath and gathered every shred of human decency that I had, pushing aside the images from that night. I thought of Will as the boy who I remembered growing up, the smile that had once lit up his eyes, the way that Drew had looked up to his big brother, and the way that Will had protected Drew. The bond that they had shared.

"I forgive you," I said clearly and precisely, loud enough so that he could hear me. Who knew that three little words could be so powerful? I watched tears spill down Will's cheeks as his next exhale of breath caused his broad shoulders to crumble. I turned back to the lake, my own tears burning through the skin on my face. That was all I had the strength to say. I heard his footsteps as they drifted farther and farther away, until there was only silence. Even my heart was silent, for once.

***

I stayed on the dock until the sun had completely cleared the mountains, sipping the coffee that Will had brought me. I knew that it wasn't good for the baby, so I only drank a small portion, just enough to warm me on the inside.

When I finally walked back to the cabin, I found my mom sitting on the porch swing drinking her own cup of coffee.

She smiled at me and patted the space beside her. I lowered my tired body into the wooden swing and closed my eyes briefly as we rocked gently back and forth.

"I forgot how beautiful it is here," she said softly, as I opened my eyes again. "You used to sit out here for hours with your father, every morning. Do you remember that?" she asked.

"Yeah, we used to sit out here and plan our day," I said, remembering my dad from all those years ago. *What are the possibilities for today, Gemma?* And then a thought occurred to me. "Mom, I don't want to sell the cabin," I said before I could think better of it.

"You don't?"

I shook my head.

"I want to spend summers here with this baby. I want my family to know what I know."

"And what is that?" she asked with a small smile pursed on her lips.

"That this place is magical," I said, smiling. Remembering my father's words that he used in response to nearly every impossible question that I asked. He always said, "It's magic, Gem. Don't overthink it."

And I believed him now. Sitting on the porch swing with Drew's presence all around me, my baby growing inside me, and my heart full of love for my husband who slept soundly inside—I believed my father. There was something magical about this place, and I didn't want to let it go. I needed to hold on to it as if I was holding on to Drew.

"There *is* something special about this place, isn't there?" my mom agreed. She gently patted my hand where it rested on my lap. "So we keep it. If that's what you want, we'll keep the cabin."

I breathed out a sigh of relief. It felt good to make a solid decision. I was so unsure of everything in my life at the moment, but I found comfort in the idea of keeping the cabin. Its very foundation gave me a sense of stability and ease. I couldn't control most things that I had to let go of, but this . . . this I could control. I couldn't sell the cabin. I couldn't let go of the memories or the girl who had once lived inside its walls.

I heard the front door creak open and looked to see Ryan standing in the doorway in a thin rumpled T-shirt and a pair of gray sweatpants. His hair was sticking up everywhere, his eyes lazy with sleep. He yawned while running his hand through his hair, the other hand holding a mug of coffee. He looked completely adorable, and I felt a knot form in my chest, as I was reminded of why I loved this man so much. I smiled up at him, and he smiled back with a knowing look in his eyes.

"What are you two beautiful ladies talking about out here?" he asked as I scooted closer to my mother to make room for him on the swing. He kissed me on the cheek before squeezing in beside me.

"We're keeping the cabin," I said matter-of-factly.

"Oh, really?" he asked with a slight tease in his voice.

"Yep. I want to spend time here, in the summers, like I did growing up. What do you think?" I asked, considering his feelings for the first time.

"I think that's a great idea," he said. He brought his arm around my shoulders and pulled me closer to him, kissing me on the head.

I tucked a short, loose strand of hair behind my ear and nuzzled in closer to him.

"Your hair's growing back," he mumbled against the side of my face.

"Thank God." I sighed.

And we all laughed lightly before silence fell over us as we swayed back and forth, lost in the view.

Later that day I walked my mother out to her car while Ryan put her suitcase in the trunk. She hugged me fiercely while she whispered in my ear, "You're doing the right thing. He loves you." She stepped back and handed me the keys to the cabin. "These belong to you now," she said, as I clutched them tightly in my hand.

"Thanks, Mom. I love you," I said.

Ryan walked around the car to join us and gave my mother a gentle hug, kissing her on the cheek.

When she pulled away, she gave Ryan a stern look and said, "Take care of my baby, Ryan." Her warning was not lost on either of us.

Ryan stood behind me with his arms wrapped around my middle as we waved good-bye and watched my mother drive slowly down the dirt lane, leaving behind a small cloud of dust.

When her car was no longer visible, I glanced across the road to the Monroes' driveway. Will was loading luggage into the back of a black suburban. When he closed the back hatch, his gaze found mine. He hesitated, unsure of the appropriate acknowledgment, before he lifted his hand in a subtle wave.

I just smiled back, not wanting to draw Ryan's attention to Will in that moment. I would tell Ryan everything eventually, but not until we were home and away from here. I didn't think that Will's face could take much more pummeling. Ryan knew my past and how much I had suffered. I didn't think he could handle facing the cause of it all.

Will lifted his mouth on one side in an attempt to smile back, but I could see the pain in his eyes. He would live in his own prison probably for the rest of his life, but I had done my part. I had confronted him and forgiven him, and now maybe I could move on and finally heal. Whatever demons he still faced were his own doing, and there was nothing I could do to help him.

I felt Ryan grip my hand and slowly tug me in his direction. I turned, breaking eye contact with Will, and followed Ryan into the cabin.

Ryan pulled me into his arms once we were behind the closed door. "What now?" he asked, with his chin resting on the top of my head.

"Let's go home," I said, closing my eyes for a moment in the comfort of his arms. "Tomorrow. First, I just want to sleep. I'm so tired."

Ryan dipped down and pulled my feet off the ground, cradling me in his arms. "Come on. Let's get you to bed," he said as he walked down the short hallway to the bedroom we had slept in the night before. He laid me down and crawled in next to me, pulling the covers over the both of us. I felt him wrap his arms around me and bury his face in my hair. "Sleep," he mumbled moments before I drifted away, finally surrendering to the darkness.

***

Somewhere between the night and the dawn, I woke to find Ryan watching me intently.

"Hey," I whispered into the dark. He was lying on his side propped up on one elbow, his face resting in his hand. His expression was so intense, it took my breath away.

"I love you," he said, trailing his finger along the curve of my jaw to my lips. "The thought of losing you . . ." His voice trailed off as he began to choke up.

"Shh, I'm right here," I assured him.

He kissed my cheek, and I felt his wet tears on my skin.

"The thought of losing you was almost as unbearable as knowing that I had hurt you. You're it for me, Gemma, and I've known it since the first time I met you." He held my face in his warm hands and kissed me with the same intensity that he held in his eyes.

I opened up for him, and he wet my lips with his tongue before entering my mouth. It brought me back to that rainy day in his car, when we had shared our first kiss. When I knew that this boy owned my heart and I was lost to him in every way. After everything that we had been through, he could still make me weak in the knees, still render me speechless. I could feel it now as my emotions swelled under his touch—at his words.

My thoughts shifted to Drew for a moment and what I had felt for him, even if only in my mind. Drew was my soul mate. He had embedded himself into my very existence from the time I had learned to walk; he was everything to me. My family, my best friend, my first love. And he would always be there, branded on my soul forever. But Ryan was my heart. And I knew that I couldn't live without my heart.

My mind drifted back to Ryan as I longed to feel all of him, wondering how we had ever let this passion escape us. It had always been like this, until recent years had changed everything.

His hands left my face and trailed down behind me, pulling me closer to him. I reached over and tugged his T-shirt over his head. And he reciprocated by slowly peeling my shirt up and over my head. I felt his warm skin against mine, his heart beating strong in his chest, and I kissed him hard as my hands found the waistband of his pants. I began to pull them down, but, taking my lead, Ryan finished the job for me. He took his time with me, trailing his lips over every area of my body, slowly undressing me. Loving me, worshipping me, as if it was the first and last time he would be this close to me.

As he touched me, it was as if each kiss was healing, each caress mending what was broken, as we found each other again in the darkness. I called out his name as I felt him enter me, slow at first but each thrust became more powerful until he possessed me completely. I fell over the edge, hard, and was overcome with emotion as Ryan held me tight and buried himself deeper inside me, as if that were possible, spilling into me as he had done so many times before. But there was no ulterior motive, no regimented purpose to our connection. Just raw need and longing, feelings of hope and fear of what was to come, a true sense of renewal.

"I love you," I whispered when I had caught my breath.

Ryan squeezed me tight, burying his face in my bare chest. "God, I love you too, baby," he whispered before we both fell back asleep, clinging to each other as if our life depended on it.

***

When I stepped outside in the fresh morning air, I noticed an envelope taped to the front door with my name written across the front. I opened it slowly as I looked around to see if anyone was nearby, wondering who had left it for me.

> *There is something that you need to see with*
> *your own eyes. I left the key under the flowerpot.*
> *Check out the sunporch–*
> *Will*

That was it. Just a short note from Will. I could hardly contain my curiosity as I stepped back inside and slid my bare feet into my sandals. I heard Ryan start the shower before I slipped outside, closing the door behind me. I started to walk toward Monroe Manor, but, when the anxiety began to set in, my feet started to move with more vigor. I lifted the heavy flowerpot and found the single key that hid beneath it, fitting it into the lock. I turned the knob and stepped inside.

"Hello," I called out. Will's family had packed up and left, but I wanted to be sure that the cabin was empty. There was no response.

I took a deep breath as I walked slowly through the great room housed by windows that opened up to the lake. Sorrow held my heart tightly as I fought against my memories of Drew and the scenes from my dream. It was as if I was just here days ago, and yet I was never really here at all. I focused on the stairs, taking one at a time as I ascended to the second floor, proceeding down the hallway that led to the sunporch. The door was slightly ajar, and I pushed it open slowly.

I was blinded immediately by the morning sunlight that filtered in through the windows. As my eyes adjusted to the light, I gasped at what I found. I was surrounded by paintings, paintings of me. Me as a young girl sitting on the edge of the dock, me as a teenager jumping off Indian Rock with an amazing sunset cast across the sky, me standing on the shore smiling as if someone had just said the funniest thing that I had ever heard. Me standing on the dock with the mountains behind me lit up by the rising sun, completely broken with tears on my cheeks. The empty, pleading depths of my eyes taking my breath away.

It was as if Drew had finally seen *me* and how broken I was that day. Each of these paintings came from Drew's memories—through his eyes—the way he saw me back then. And there were so many more—dozens of them—hanging from a wire that stretched across two walls, stacked along the floor, propped up against the wall. They were beautiful, and I was in complete awe of his talent. The vividness and the profundity that each one expressed brought tears to my eyes. And I found myself, once again, feeling the unfairness of it all. That Drew's life had been cut too short, that we were both robbed of the time that we deserved. He was so young and talented—his whole life stretched out before him—and now he was gone. It was so unfair. If only we had had more time.

I wiped the gushing tears from my face as I continued to take in each painting, one by one. My emotions were thick, consuming me as so many thoughts whirled around in my head, until it all stopped on a breath. Time seemed to stand still. My eyes, my feet, my breath all paused as I stared down at one painting. Bare skin bathed in moonlight, eyes full of lust—conveying everything that I felt in that moment—so familiar that it brought me to my knees. It was the painting that Drew had done that night in this very room, the night from my dream. Every detail the same. I knew right then, in that moment, that Drew and I had shared something real, that we had loved and touched and healed. That there wasn't any other explanation.

My heart swelled and ached as I was filled with relief and grief all in the same moment. None of it made any sense, and the idea of it alone was crazy, and yet there was something so real and beautiful in the truth of the matter. There were so many mysteries in life and even more in death, things that cannot be explained. I didn't need an explanation, I just needed a sign. A sign that I wasn't crazy, that what I had felt was real. And it was as if Drew was giving me that sign that I was so desperate to find. I couldn't deny what I felt any more than I could deny the existence of this painting.

"Thank you," I whispered into the empty room from where I knelt on the rug, feeling grateful for this moment. The moment when I knew that I could finally let go.

Thirty-Six

One Year Later . . .

I stand in the lake cabin at the doorway of his room, the pale blue paint, white trim, and tiny sailboat border having its usual calming effect. I find myself mesmerized by the sight of him sleeping, feeling like I will never tire of watching him in this peaceful state, at the mercy of his dreams—whatever they may be. His small chest rises and falls as the sound of his tiny breaths fill the room, trumped only by the "Twinkle, Twinkle Little Star" lullaby that plays from the mobile overhead—a collection of tiny silver stars that dance in the soft glow of nursery light.

I have not taken for granted a single moment of motherhood since the instant he was placed in my arms, nearly six months ago. That moment is always present in my mind—the exhaustion from a long and brutal labor mixed with the euphoria of knowing that I had done it, that it was over, and that my little man was healthy and in my arms. Life seemed to really begin from that point on, as if nothing had existed before he did.

My heart is so full of love and joy that I feel the need to stand here, to make sure that he is real and safe and mine. I resist the urge to go to him and to cradle him against my chest, knowing that he needs his sleep and that a little separation is healthy.

Ryan is arriving today to spend the week with us. It has only been seven days since I last saw him, yet I soon began to miss him. We have fallen in love all over again after having fallen head-over-heels in love with our son. Knowing that we both created this amazing little guy, together, and that he is ours, forever, can have that effect on a person. What can I say? It took us a while to get here, but, with the help of our sessions with Jude, plus Ryan's patience with my jealous and untrusting tirades, I have been able to let the past stay in the past and move on.

The accident changed me in many ways. I never went back to my firm. My career felt so unimportant, meaningless, and small in the grand scheme of things. I resigned for good, and focused on my recovery and my health, preparing for my baby to arrive. Should I ever decide to go back to work, I have an urge to change the type of law I practice, maybe something that would make more of a difference in the lives of others. For now I am happy with my role as a mother.

Ryan and I sold our condo in the city—I couldn't really sleep in our bedroom without it conjuring up bad memories. We bought a modest house on the east side. Clyde Hill offered a more family-friendly neighborhood, great schools, and an expansive yard that we imagined filling with a swing set and various sports equipment one day. Our new home boasts four thousand square feet of warmth and charm with a slight view of Lake Washington from all three of the second-level bedrooms, but, even more, it represents our fresh start, our new beginning. I spent hours decorating one of the bedrooms in pale blues and greens, filling it with beautiful furniture and plush teddy bears from my favorite baby boutique, and marveling at how blessed I was to be preparing for the arrival of my baby—finally.

Ryan and I spent long weekends through the spring here at the lake cabin, repainting walls and making small updates, without changing too many details. We painted the sailboat room that I look at now, knowing that I would spend the summers here with our son while Ryan commuted back and forth as much as possible. It is a compromise of sorts, my need to be here greater than ever before. Ryan is supportive and enjoys his relaxing weekends that he shares here with us, free of his work obligations—yet, much to his dismay, I refuse to install Wi-Fi at the cabin.

I withdraw from my spot where I have been spying on my son, leaving him until he wakes on his own. I use these quiet moments leading up to dawn to savor a hot cup of coffee before my day of breast-feeding, diaper changing, and sweet cuddling begins.

I look around the cabin, taking in the things that remain untouched. The river-rock fireplace, the rustic furniture, the round table still surrounded by mismatched chairs. A new addition is my favorite painting from Drew's private collection that now hangs on the far wall. A whimsical piece of a girl and a boy jumping off the end of the dock, hands locked together, their feet suspended in the air as the sun sets behind the mountains in front of them, casting a fiery glow across the sky and the calm waters of the lake. I can almost feel the joy and exhilaration that they do right before they take the plunge into the cold blue depths. After all, it is a real-life memory captured on canvas, and sometimes I remember it like it was yesterday. This painting is a reminder of the simple joys in life, but, most important, it reminds me to live. And it keeps Drew close to my heart, bringing a new warmth to the cabin.

Since the accident, I have thrown out life's labels and definitive titles in reference to these crucial moments we experience, realizing that life is just one big puzzle. It's as if we were born with all the pieces and everything has its place in the end—when all is said and done, when the picture is complete. But—the length of time that it takes us to get there, the number of tries placing the pieces before we realize that they don't fit after all, the order at which we choose to put them together—that is all part of life, our own individual journey. We can finally make sense of it once every piece is in place and we can see the big picture.

I never believed in fate or destiny. Hell, I barely believed in God. But after what I have been through, I can't deny the presence of something else. Beyond what we can see and touch. And sometimes there is no logical explanation, no sense to be made—sometimes it just *is*.

As I finish the last warm sip of my coffee, I hear a gentle cry from the room down the hall. *Just in time*, I think, as I forgo my coffee cup and follow my heart, which leads me to my son, a smile stretching across my face.

I approach his crib and watch his tear-filled features turn to gold as he sees my face above him.

"Hey, little man," I coo.

He responds in giggles, tiny bubbles erupting from his mouth.

I drink him in, his soft chubby cheeks, tiny pink lips, and large round chocolate-colored eyes, just like his daddy's. My heart swells at the sight of my son, and I pick him up and snuggle him close to me, inhaling his sweet baby scent. I wrap his favorite blue cashmere blanket around him and make my way to the porch to enjoy our morning ritual just as dawn kisses the clear dark sky.

It is in these quiet moments at the lake that I sense *him*. I hear him in the gentle ebb and flow of the water against the shore, the steady stream of the copper creek that flows behind the cabin. I feel him in the wind that sways through the evergreens, carrying their scent in the air like a gentle caress. He is everywhere, in everything that I see, feel, and hear, and yet he is nowhere. But mostly he is within me, filling my heart and soul. Reminding me that, indeed, nothing lasts forever and that I should embrace each day for what it is and hold on fiercely to those I love, to not let the trivial things in life obscure the simplicity of love itself.

I sit on the porch swing, swaying gently back and forth, as the sun rises slowly over the distant mountains, shedding light on the trees, the lake, and everything else in its wake, while a new day unfolds before my very eyes. I hold my infant son tightly in my arms, quietly thanking God, the universe—fate—for this gift. I still can't believe that my son is real, that he is mine and here in my arms. At times I wonder if he is somehow a gift from Drew or that my baby's life is possible because of Drew's death. A life for a life. It is an odd thought to have and even stranger that I would find any comfort in it. Still I can't help but wonder. I silently thank Drew as well, feeling almost certain that he is sharing this moment with me, watching me, smiling down at us. I smile back and take a deep breath, enjoying the beauty of the morning and the peace that fills me when I am here, at the lake.

I look down into my son's big brown eyes, full of silent wonder, staring back at me, and whisper, "What are the possibilities for today, Andrew Jacob Walsh?"

I relish in the knowledge that the possibilities for this day, this moment—this life—are endless.

Acknowledgments

What a wild ride it has been. After the release of *Ripple*, I have been wrapped up in this crazy but cozy world of self-published Indie Authors and bloggers, feeling so much love and support. To my readers: Thank you for taking a chance on me, you make it all worth it. And please, consider leaving a review on Amazon. It makes a world of difference!

I have to start by thanking my husband and my two wonderful children for all their love, support, and acceptance! You three are by far my biggest fans, and I love you to the moon and back!

To my family: Mom, Dad, Christy, Alan . . . Thanks for always believing in me and for loving me unconditionally. To Scott Hille, Mitch Hille, Nancy Hille, Mary Reilly, RaeAnn Telecky, . . . summers wouldn't have been the same without you. Sailboats, firecrackers, sand castles, beer-bottle pipe organs. Love you all! And to Cassie "Valdez"—how could I forget your part in it all!

A special thanks to the Carper family: Robin, Sherri, Krista, Cory, Chad. . . . Thank you for all the years of memories at the lake. You opened your arms and welcomed me like family then and even now, years later. I can't thank you enough.

To my beta-readers: Colleen McCarthy, Kristin Gentry, Debbie Bayley, Maria Rafael, and Chauna Carlson. Thank you for taking the time to read this story, for loving it despite the work it still needed, and for giving me the feedback that was necessary to perfect it!

To my amazing friends and community, old and new: Thank you for the support and wonderful messages. You truly inspire me to keep writing, and validate my choice to write and share my words with the world.

Thank you to all the bloggers out there for the endless support! Indie Authors wouldn't be heard without all of you, so THANK YOU, THANK YOU! Special thanks to Ena Burnette with Swoon Worthy Books and Enticing Journey Book Promotions. You are amazing. Thank you for believing in *Ripple* and helping me to get it out there!

Thank you to Gary, Caroline, and Denise at BubbleCow. Your advice, expertise, and comments were essential in making this story shine. And I appreciate the fact that you can be critical without deflating my ego too much!

And finally a thank-you to Priest Lake for the inspiration. You will always be that special place in my heart, where the memories will live on and on. . . .

Contact the Author

L.D. Cedergreen loves to hear from her readers! She can be reached on Facebook at:
www.facebook.com/AuthorL.D.Cedergreen
or Twitter at: twitter.com/LDCedergreen
Kindly leave a review on amazon.com or Goodreads. Your review will help lead others to this story!

Printed in Great Britain
by Amazon

15825731R00164